THE
VIRTUE
SEASON

THE VIRTUE SEASON

L. M. NATHAN

■SCHOLASTIC

Please note that this book contains themes of eugenics,
discrimination, sexual control, suicide and enslavement.

Published in the UK by Scholastic, 2024
1 London Bridge, London, SE1 9BG
Scholastic Ireland, 89E Lagan Road, Dublin Industrial Estate,
Glasnevin, Dublin, D11 HP5F

SCHOLASTIC and associated logos are trademarks and/or
registered trademarks of Scholastic Inc.

ISBN 978 0702 33092 6

A CIP catalogue record for this book
is available from the British Library.

Printed and bound in Great Britain by Clays Ltd, Elcograf S.p.A
Paper made from wood grown in sustainable forests
and other controlled sources.

MIX
Paper | Supporting
responsible forestry
FSC® C018072

1 3 5 7 9 10 8 6 4 2

This is a work of fiction. Names, characters, places, incidents
and dialogues are products of the author's imagination or are used
fictitiously. Any resemblance to actual people, living or dead,
events or locales is entirely coincidental.

www.scholastic.co.uk

For Dad, from whom I learned to tell tall tales, and Mum, who taught me to fight for the right to tell them.

The Virtue Season

"Eighty-four full moons and it will be our turn," Agatha tells me as her breath fogs the latticed glass window of Penn House.

"Must you count?" I ask, a darkness creeping through me that seems to reach out from the night.

Agatha sighs in delight at the scene inside the ballroom, her hands clawing at the window ledge, her toes pointed like a dancer's on top of the rock she is perched on.

"You'll be the envy of them all," she tells me, grabbing my arm and trying to yank me up beside her. "Come and see."

"I'll keep watch," I reply, pushing her off and crouching beneath the window, my back to the wall. The night echoes with music, but my heart beats a quicker, shallow rhythm. "Ag, if we're caught, we'll be punished, and I—"

"Oh, look! The Madams are here!" She gasps, eyes sparkling. Until tonight, I have only heard tales of the councillors' wives from girls at school with older siblings; how elegant and grand they are. How decorative.

"What do they look like?" I ask, curious despite myself.

"Oh, they're stunning," she sighs. "Their hair is as intricate as lace – their dresses are scooped down to here." She gestures to her own neckline. "See for yourself!"

Unable to resist, I scramble up the boulder to catch a glimpse of these mythical creatures, if only to have the satisfaction of being disappointed. It is their husbands and fathers who rule after all. They have no power other than to inspire awe. The rock is too small for us both and I slip, catching Agatha's waist to steady myself, which makes her giggle.

"So much for Manon Pawlak having the strongest legs in Penn Vale," she guffaws.

"Shh," I scold, trying to stabilize us both, though I laugh too. "What's all the fuss about? *They're just dresses.*"

But they are not. Not at all. The picture is refracted by the bullseye panes: intense and unworldly, the light of the candelabra dazzling. In the grand ballroom, the older girls are no longer girls at all but have been transformed. They are *debutants*, a word that is dark and sparkling, seductive and lyrical. It feels like bait. The Madams are seated at long tables from which they watch the debs, their councillor husbands standing behind them.

"The Madams' gowns are *brocade*," Agatha tells me, her lips kissing the word.

"How do they make the colours so rich?"

Agatha shrugs. "I've never been able to figure it out. But I will," she promises, and I think of the concoctions she makes in her kitchen, every plant stripped of its colour and stored in a glass vial like an experiment.

"What are *those*?" I ask, my mouth agape as I watch the Madams. Each of them wears a fine crown made of twisted garlands of silver and gold that trail into leaves or vines and are decorated with gemstones of different colours: iridescent white; deep crimson; green that is as deep and dark as fern; blue that is neither sky nor sea nor the very centre of a flame but all of these pressed together – so blue it is almost black.

"Lost-World treasure," Agatha answers, her words glimmering as brightly as the stones.

"Where did they get them?"

"Where do you think?"

My stomach answers, lurching the way it always does when I think of the councillors. *They took them from the people of Calde Valley, the way they take everything else.*

I don't fully understand the dread the councillors provoke in me, only that it is somehow part of me, that not trusting them is as much who I am as my arms or legs, like fear has become another limb.

"The Penn Vale Madams wear red stones. That's why the Penn debs wear red."

The Penn debs do wear red, though it is only a taste of the colour, their dresses dyed with crab-apple bark, which means they are more of a suffused pink; the darker hues are reserved for those who can afford the cochineal dyes. The other debs match their Madams too. The Stone girls in white; Foxfields in green; Waddow in blue.

We watch, silent and awed, balancing as best we can as girls are led by the hand from one world into another, nervous and giddy and hopeful. But these boys are not the mud-stained work mules we recognize. They are scrubbed and refined, like a quartz stone polished new. Their doublets are starched and formal, so tight they stand as upright as ripe cornstalks. And their eyes are ripe too, ready.

"They're so impractical," I chide, looking down at my own dress, which is cut from boiled wool and ends at the calf, allowing me to clamber, unladylike, across the hills of the valley and dig in Father's fields.

"They are beautiful," Agatha chimes in.

"You couldn't plough the fields in them," I scoff, and she laughs. She gives me a shove and I shove her back, harder than I had intended, which makes her topple. She just catches the window ledge and steadies herself, but her hand raps the glass, which rattles in its frame.

There is a still second where nothing moves. And then I see a councillor's eyes turned towards us, fierce as an unsheathed blade. He is standing behind his Madam, his hand on her shoulder as if he fears she might flee. He

4

leaves her side when he hears the noise and Agatha and I tumble beneath the window, holding our breaths and each other.

My chest hurts. I ache to breathe.

And then I hear footsteps approach on the other side of the wall, and I know he is above us, looking out, searching. I think of our fingers pressed to the glass, the marks left behind. Agatha and I try to make ourselves smaller, hold our breaths tighter.

"Chief Torrent? Are you…?"

"I thought I saw something. What is it?"

"Sorry, sir. Hope is unwell. She is asking to go home."

"Then why have you not brought the carriage? Bring it. Quick, man."

There is a scuff of footsteps, and we are safe. But we dare not speak. We sit as if we are inside a bubble, afraid to break it, unable to run home, unable to move, just listening to the music rising and dying, each song a lifetime of its own.

"You know, Mother has a quartz necklace," I tell Agatha when my voice comes back to me. She has been winded, though her face is resolute, brave. "I suppose I'll be the next to wear it … in eighty-seven full moons—"

"Eighty-four," she says, eyeing me with suspicion, her eyes piqued.

"Eighty-four, then. It looks like a sugar lump," I tell her, shrugging with indifference. "I might not want to wear it anyway." She slaps my shoulder in reproach, forgetting the fear that trapped us here.

"You will wear it. And you will look beautiful. I will make you so," she promises, folding her arms. We laugh, the sound its own salve.

"It's strange," I say, "to think there's a boy in the world already who will one day be mine, that he could be anyone. Someone I know. Like a seed, buried in the ground."

"It's not strange. It is magical," Agatha beams, her eyes wide and staring, as if she looks into her own boy's eyes already. And I know what she is thinking, and whose eyes she imagines. "Eighty-four full moons," she breathes, the sound an incantation.

"I'm so scared I will not know him," I whisper, more to myself than her.

Agatha's future is clear, the way footprints can be left in the sand. Only hers are not behind but ahead, waiting for her to tread in them. She cannot wait to wear the soft pink of the Penn girls, to dance at the balls, state her preference and unite. Pink is the colour of her heart. And, with the start of our season, the colour of her love will only deepen, until it is blood red. But for me, there is no certainty, no one set of eyes that hold my gaze.

I watch the debs with the beating wings of fear in my chest. For I know I cannot live without love. I know that a loveless match will break me. And I know too that here, love is never a guarantee.

PART ONE

"We see beautiful adaptations
everywhere and in every part
of the organic world."

Charles Darwin,
On the Origin of the Species

CHAPTER ONE

Beware the Eyes
of the Wolf

The world didn't end all at once but drip by drip: land slowly sinking under a new tide. When the rain began to beat harder and longer, at first it was easy to ignore, to stick out your tongue and taste not death, but life in the cold beads that landed there.

Until the sun became too hot, the storms too cold and the space between each too small.

Crops failed. Famine spread. The population dwindled to almost nothing. Great cities went dark and silver birds no longer flew. The cables that connected the world at high speed were ripped into worthless tentacles, grasping at the surface of the water as if begging for life.

And then the last deluge came: the great rolling walls of water.

Survivors called them the Sephtis Floods. The waves that came too fast, too sudden, devouring buildings, tearing up forests, and sweeping whole cities away in one deafening explosion of sound: a swirling drift of brick and mortar, spitting metal carriages into the sky. One long tide of terror.

And when the seas calmed, the world was smaller.

It went on. But divisions remained. Wars raged across new borders.

The county now known as Penn Vale envied Foxfields its salt pans, Waddow its blacksmiths, Castle Hill its isolation, Stone Hamlet its books. And all eyed the thriving fields of Penn with gnawing hunger. Fights to the death over bread and seed became the biggest threat to life. So the Calde Valley Council was born. They built border walls, restricted movement and trade. The survival of the species became all that mattered.

But the counties were small, the gene pools shallow. Children died young, unable to fend off even the slightest cold. The chilled hand of extinction reached out again, and fear grew, the new world built on whispers of the old, half-memories turned into stubborn truths.

Only the healthy must be allowed to breed. Not for love, not out of free will, but purely to cleanse the world of defects.

No one remembers a time before the decommissionings, or when the borders were opened for the first Virtue Season. They only know the part they play within it.

))

"Beware the eyes of the wolf."

"Fear the sound of his song."

The tick-tock way the girls speak back to Miss Warne in the schoolhouse is familiar, if not comforting. The room is neatly organized with debs standing to attention before Chief Councillor Torrent. He stands with the air of a man who needs no introduction, confident his uniform alone inspires awe. Which it does. If it stood on the stage without him in it, we would fear it: grey hooded cloak, long boots, a mace at the waist. His hood is down, and his skin is pink, scrubbed and raw as if he's taken a sea sponge to it and rubbed too hard. His eyes dart, fast and fleeting, searching for defects, which he seems to see everywhere.

I smooth down my dress, scrape the dry mud on the hem, which itches under my nails. I spent the morning digging ditches with Father to tempt the rains away from his crops and I am as hot and sticky as the storm.

Torrent lifts his hand to quiet the already silent debs, raises the piece of paper and reads, without needing to look at it. "Debutants, now that you are in your eighteenth year, each of you will participate in the Virtue Season. At its culmination, you will be united with a suitable partner, one who is likely to produce healthy offspring and ensure the successful proliferation of our kind."

The letter closed in my fist matches the one in his. I don't need to read it either. I grip it lightly, as if it's made of glass. Every deb in the school does the same, watched by wide-eyed girls in lower years whose turn is yet to come, but my hand itches – I want to screw up the paper, rip it into a thousand pieces, but I fold it calmly, put it in my pocket. I'll burn it later, scrape the ashes to nothing.

I've always known this letter would come, the precise wording even. I have heard debs speak these words season after season, numb to the sound. I didn't know it would feel like this. Even this morning, the hawthorn on the lanes to school appeared the same as always – thorns no sharper today than any that have preceded it. The spring sky wrapped me in dense cloud as it always has; water cloaking us on all sides, just the same. So, the desperation catches me off guard, fear frothing in my throat, bitter and bubbling.

"Over the course of the next year, you will give yourselves to this process freely and, in return for your obedience, each county will be afforded the privilege of hosting a ball."

Agatha is here, her hand a lightning rod in mine: velvet and steel. She and I have taken the same winding route together every day since we were seven – friends communing daydreams through linked hands; dandelions plucked from overgrown paths; ignorant of the watchers in green cloaks that blend with the hillsides; innocent of the rules of Calde Valley. And despite knowing our paths will soon be hewn, her fate and mine have always seemed as one. Until today. And yet she holds my hand as if my fate is worse than hers.

"If you conduct yourselves morally, within the guidance and sight of the council, you will be able to state a preference. If you form no preference – or your preference is not sanctioned by the council – a mate will be chosen for you."

"As long as you're not flawed," Agatha says in a breathless whisper as Chief Councillor Torrent reads aloud. I kick her as subtly as I can but don't completely manage to smother my smirk, don't completely try.

"The Chastity Rule must be observed. Infringements will invoke the death penalty."

Chastity. Death. These words hover around the hall like seagulls on a wave, travel the long lengths of the floorboards like footsteps. I shiver. We all do. The sting between my thighs is raw, hot with the memory of cold surgical steel. Our first chastity checks were this morning.

"Decommissions will attend the balls in thanks for their sacrifice and as a reminder of its purpose."

"So generous." Agatha seethes, the weeping wound beneath her eye glistening sorely as her salt-grey eyes roll. Her sarcasm stretches as thin as the skin that tries to seal itself over the brand of a freshly made decom.

Torrent is a stone sculpture, stiff and proud on the stage, a metallic glimmer in his eyes. His emblem flowers writhe on his chest as if caught in the breeze as he heaves with the thrill of power. Miss Warne sweats beside him, lathered in his heat. She is not an old woman. Her eyes sparkle with youth, neat brown hair shows no sign of grey, but her spine arcs as if she has aged prematurely and tugs her shoulders forward. Her eyes are lined with pain, though she sets her mouth against it. She wears black, like Agatha. She turns her head from Torrent as if he smells bad, though the smell of meadowsweet is almost toxic, rolling off him even from this far away. He rests his thumb in his belt loop, cradles the mace that hangs there and flexes his fingers.

"Debutants, stand with me and remember," he commands.

We know the response and our fragile assembly inhales and speaks as one: "In the name of our ancestors, and the Lost Cities, we must make this land fruitful, strive for virtue. Now and always."

Our voices fuse together, rise and echo back, the sound forming living tendrils.

"I'm going to faint," I whisper to Agatha – my voice dry.

"No – you're going to get through it," she says too loudly. Always just a little too loud. She squeezes my hand, jolts me into the hot space beside her.

"He's coming," she says as I struggle to stay in the room, my mind soaring over the green and blue, out beyond the Drift to an unknown world the council says doesn't exist.

And yet my heart burns to find it.

Torrent makes his way down the line, girls speaking

the same words one after the other. One by one, they fail to meet his eye as he brings his face close to theirs, inspecting the resolve of each one. They shrivel, wilting flowers.

"Manon Pawlak. It is an honour to dedicate yourself to the Virtue Season. What is your pledge?" he says, looking down at his list where I imagine my name flaming in fiery letters. His clean, pock-marked skin is taut over the muscles of his face. He doesn't blink. Do I?

"What is your pledge?" he asks again, harsh and unfeeling.

"I pledge my body and soul willingly, Councillor," I answer – the words taught to us by Miss Warne, rehearsed over and over until they are meaningless exhalations. He doesn't seem to notice how my body is rigid; my soul suffocated. My voice, thankfully, is steady, though I must be gritting my teeth because my jaw aches.

He nods lightly and moves along the line, concealing a yawn, I think.

Bastard.

Agatha gives her consent too, despite that seeping red crescent that half-circles her left eye. The slightest tightening of her grip gives her away as she speaks and I know what's about to happen, hope I can get her to safety before it does.

Defects are the end of our civilization, the council says. And even though every fibre, every sinew in my body aches to fight what I know is wrong, I give my consent. Because it is only the illusion of choice they offer, and I know it. What choice can there be when every attempt at rebellion ends in death?

Torrent ends the ceremony and shuffles Miss Warne away — slowed by her curved spine and tapping cane but no less beautiful for it. The debs filter into the yard, uncertain and slow.

We are at the furthest edge of Penn, the Boot, where the world slips off a cliff just beyond the schoolhouse door. The hot wind whirs around us and will soon rupture into fevered rain. Again.

Agatha walks heavy, hanging on my arm.

Not yet, Ag. Please.

We follow the line of the huge metal fence that severs us from the boys, and I feel the familiar fight to look away. Someone is always watching. One of the watchers will see. Brack is in his tower, sharp-eyed as always.

Beware the eyes of the wolf.

It is forbidden to speak to the boys until the first ball, and even looking at the fence feels criminal. But the blond-haired boy pulls my eye. I try not to think of his name, though I know it and it sits on my lips unspoken.

Tomie.

And then it happens.

"Not yet," I say pleadingly, as if I can delay her seizure by wanting it so, but her eyes are hazy, her body stiffening. Before she falls, I take hold of her and lay her down as carefully as I can, as I have done many times before. She's

16

still for a moment, and then the twitches take her. Her hair, the colour of cracked wheat, splays across her face and her back arches, somehow elegant, even now.

Some of the debs snigger and huddle, staring as if they haven't seen it before. Brack – a dirty hateful man whom everyone in Penn despises, leans out from his tower, laughter ruffling his broad shoulders.

Like me, Agatha will go to the balls, but she will not be allowed to choose a mate because the council say her blood is flawed. Because they have ripped her motherhood from her flesh and branded her face with a crescent scar to show her failing.

"Leave her be," I cry, pushing at Tabithe who is heading up the crowd as always. She steadies herself, her neck long, her chin pointed, as fierce as the mythic swans in Miss Warne's stories. Her eyes shimmer with the threat of a fight as she edges towards me, her full lips pressed into the cold sneer that I'm sure will soon set there for ever. But she won't take me on whilst the councillors are here.

"Come on," she mutters to her hatchlings, "we need to get home before curfew anyway." And they waddle after her in a line.

I crouch beside Ag, who's still now but not alert, and cradle her head in my lap. Her cheek is grazed and pooling with spots of red where her skin has rubbed against the hard floor as she's seized. I wipe the abrasion clean with my thumb, but the red pools again.

The seizures began last year but no one knew. She told no one. Until she had to. I still find it hard to believe. Her parents' bloodlines were pure, sanctioned by the council.

When it happened at school, Miss Warne was bound by law to report it, the scar below her own eye lending no allegiance to her favourite student.

"Agatha!"

His scream is sudden, splits the air. And I know the mouth that makes the sound belongs to Alsis: dusty hair and moon-shaped eyes that have followed her always.

"Agatha!" he shouts again. I lay her head on the floor as gently as I can, run to the fence before she's fully alert, the beat of my heart propelling me. I've never been this close to the fence before, nor spoken to a boy as openly as this. The metal wire seems to hum.

"She's fine. Be quiet. It'll be over soon," I hiss, shaking the fence as if to shake him off it, the fear in my gut solid.

"Come away," Tomie says, pulling at Alsis but looking at me with eyes that see more than I want them to. I blink in thanks – can do no more with the thrill of his scent hanging in the air. Carved wood, cedar, and oak – the carpenter's son – who so many girls prefer because they will never go hungry in his house. He tries to yank Alsis up, but he is a dead weight and stockier than Tomie.

"Torrent's still inside. *Think*," I seethe. But Alsis isn't thinking. He shakes the metal fence, screams into its metallic sound. His body shakes, as if Agatha's spasms have travelled to him by some hidden channel between her heart and his. It has never happened in front of him before. And seeing it is like a puzzle you cannot solve. How do you fight something that's so out of your control, beyond your understanding?

"Come on," Tomie begs. I try not to notice the way his arms harden with the effort.

But it's too late. Torrent emerges from the schoolhouse, Miss Warne lagging behind. Her hair is dishevelled, her cheeks flooded red. Her black cloak is gone, and her skirt is askew, her eyes smeared sore. There's a circlet of tiny red pressure wounds on her cheek that look a lot like the spikes on the end of Torrent's mace. And he is angry, fiddling with his grey cloak, refastening the loops and buttons at the neck.

"What is going on here?" he demands, a little relish staining his temper. He steps around Agatha with barely a look and heads straight for us. I step away, ashamed.

"Explain yourself, boy," he commands. Alsis still clings to the fence, silently gritting his teeth in a way that carves a hollow into his cheek, dusty fringe framing his eyes.

Another Councillor – Reade, I think – stalks up behind Alsis on the other side of the fence, his eyes wide but controlled. He walks steadily, measuring the scene, flanked by a couple of watchers, including Brack. Reade must have taken the boys' pledges whilst Torrent took ours. Brack's crooked teeth gape in a smile.

Shit.

I open my mouth to speak – but my voice hitches, sharp in my throat.

"Reade," Torrent barks, his mouth slanting into a smirk. "I believe we have an infringement here. This boy has formed an unsanctioned preference, I'd say. Who for, boy? Not that hideous decom, surely?" He glances at Agatha, something unreadable softening the hard lines of his eyes, as if seeing something else, or *someone* else. He stares at her, bewildered, his head tilted to one side.

Agatha is sitting now, a girl in our year kneeling next to her. I try to remember to be nicer to Bertie.

Torrent shakes himself free of the image that has tamed him, and makes a show of disgust, coils his lip around his practised revulsion of decoms.

Hypocrite.

"Sir," I say, my voice catching. If I was as strong as everyone says, I'd spit in his face.

And be hanged from the nearest skeleton tree.

"There's no preference. That's just... That's how people react sometimes, the first time they see a seizure like that. A lot of people are ... disgusted." My throat clasps tight around the word, angry at the feel of it, at the lie and the twisted truth inside it. I look down at Alsis to censure him for a crime he couldn't even begin to fathom. He has always loved Agatha.

Torrent tuts, his hand tickles his mace. I wonder, when he was doing what he was doing to Miss Warne, how did he manage with one hand always on his mace?

The councillors treat decoms that way – safe in the knowledge there'll be no damaged spawn. The decoms don't fight it. Not after a while. It is just another part of their world.

"Reade," Torrent orders, "take this boy inside. Remind him of our rules. The council will rule on the penalty for this disobedience at the hearings."

Reade – a small man neatly packed with muscle – looks unwilling, and I notice his mace looks unused, the grip still perfectly varnished where Torrent's is worn to the bare wood. It is not him but the watchers who yank Alsis away, Brack lugging his fighting body like a rag doll.

"As for *you*," Torrent snorts, stepping closer to me. I feel around me for the blond-haired boy, for Agatha, for their strength to aid mine. But I feel only the glare of Torrent, who seems to grow into the space around me, making my heart flare and burn until I think I might strike him.

"Councillor?" Miss Warne interrupts, shuffling towards us as quickly as she can manage, her cane tapping the floor with a click-clack sound. "Won't you accompany me back to my office?" she asks, as she hooks her arm through his and tries to pull his bulk away. He is still at first, looks down at her with that same practised horror he looked at Agatha with. But it soon turns to a thinly veiled desire.

"Of course," he says, giving in to the strongest pull.

"You were showing me examples of the students' work." They walk away, not quite in step as she struggles to match his pace, and it is the wind that speaks his words. "The girl's family will donate *double* to the claims this season," it says, carrying the sound.

Bile twists my stomach, the threat of hunger burying the deep gratitude I feel to Miss Warne.

This is how my season begins.

CHAPTER TWO

A Howling Cry

Mother and I are sitting on the porch outside Wild Fell. The rain is petering out now, the air cleansed. Father is inside, mending a scuffle hoe that's come apart, and the sweetness of his whistling song strikes soft against the metallic clangs of his work.

Looking out over the night-black water, it's hard to imagine the death beneath its depths, but not far below its stillness, the Lost Cities lie. Clint is in his watchtower, his silhouette framed by the night.

Most of the houses on the hills around the flooded valley are made from metal scavenged from the water, but Wild Fell is a survivor from before, made of yellow stone, all neatly cut and pieced together in a pretty patchwork. Only the roof is scrap tin – flattened out cans reclaimed from the sea, chiming when it rains. When I was little, I thought the rain was singing me a lullaby.

"I've already taken in the seams," Mother tells me. She has the family unity dress on her lap and is weighing the cloth between her fingers, surveying the damage since she wore it at her own union ceremony.

"Why are you sewing it now? The unity ceremonies are months away," I say. The sight of the dress makes my skin crawl as if I'm already wearing it.

"It needs doing is all. I've patched up the hole on the sleeve. Practically invisible," she says, holding it up to the moonlight that is enough to see by, though not enough to stop her squinting. "There's only the embroidery left to do now."

Her voice is lifeless: no pride or joy, fear or sadness carry in it. She squints over her work, red hair falling limp around her face, tamer than mine. I wonder it doesn't irritate her. Her coat is too thick for the warm evening, envelops her like a great bear. It must have been made for a woman three times her size, and she shifts its weight around her shoulders as if balancing uneven loads.

"I'll take your coat," I say, holding out my hand.

"I'm cold," she answers, without looking up.

"But it's so warm—"

"Leave me be, child," she snaps, and I sit back down, dejected.

"I can sew a bit for you," I suggest, taking up a spool of white thread and a needle, which seems to have firmly closed its eye on me. I poke and prod without success and Mother sighs.

"Give it here. Anemones are purple anyway. You'd never see white against the linen," she says, scowling and snatching the thread from me. The needle pricks her thumb and a bead of red puddles, but she doesn't yelp or scold, only sucks the blood away.

I feel the fight brewing in my stomach, heating to a boil.

She threads her needle with purple and I think of last summer: steeping the skeins in cabbage water, pomegranate, cornflower blooms – a rainbow of looping strands hung to dry across the kitchen.

"Father's anemones?"

"Aye. Who else's would they be? You only have one father."

I bite my lip, hold my tongue.

Her hands are beautiful when she sews. The thread seems to grow right out of her soul, weaving it into the cloth. But, as she adds Father's emblem flower, her fingers are less fluid. The stitches seem to need tugging like surly children, yanked at their mother's command. The silken thread glistens and jars in the moonlight.

"What was your unity ceremony like?" I ask, goading her. I can hear Father chiding me: *she's in her black fog. Leave her be*, he'd say.

"Were you nervous?" I ask, pushing again. "Were you scared?"

"Of course, Manon," she spits. "Everyone's nervous at their ceremony … but I found the strength and so will

25

you. There's no sense recounting it all. It does no good to dwell."

Like you do.

"Did you know Father would state a preference for you?"

"No."

"Did *you* state a preference for him?"

"Stop! No more."

Her face is pulled so tight, it makes me think of the fruit press we use to squeeze berries in summer. I think she'll lash out, but then, as quickly as it's fuelled, her fire dies.

"We need to get on," she says, her face blank.

"I suppose," I reply, wounded and angry, almost wanting to feel the keen slap that didn't come, simply to feel something between us.

She leans into the dress, away from the nuisance of me.

The emblem flowers represent the male line and bloom in a cacophony of colour all down the dress's back. The council say the male line is strong, so it is that which they track. If there is a mutation, it is the female blood that is at fault. But there are more decommissionings now than ever, and an ever-increasing list of flaws.

"Didn't you ever find it difficult, though?" I say, trying to borrow some of Father's gentleness but failing. "To unite with someone you didn't know?"

She winces as if she's pricked her finger, but it's me who has stung her, not the needle this time.

"I did my duty. What more can you ask? It's unrealistic to imagine anything else can be possible. Aye, it was difficult, but the council doesn't care." She looks around in panic, but no watchers are wandering the shore just now. Clint is visible in his watch tower, but he cannot hear from his platform. His face is in shadow as he leans against the fence panels, lamplight flickering from the shadow-black hut that juts into the sky.

"What about crossing the county lines? Coming to Penn?"

A sound catches in her throat, and she closes her eyes, for the briefest of moments.

"You aren't a child of Penn, Manon, nor I a child of Foxfields, and you mustn't believe yourself to be. We are all children of Calde Valley; you belong nowhere but where the council tells you. And if you're chosen to cross the borders, you need to be ready to fight for your place there. They won't accept you willingly. The boy's family will be suspicious—"

"Was it like that for you?" I ask, a desperate tone filling my voice.

"No. Your father's kin were already gone. But I felt I didn't belong."

"And you missed Grandfather and Grandmother? Your friends from Foxfields?"

"Listen," she says, looking straight at me, her eyes wild, "there is no one you cannot leave behind, no one who matters more than your own survival. Your union is secondary to that. Affection, love – all that, it's got no place in our world. All we can do is follow instruction, do as we're bid. If we are clean, virtuous, we survive. I won't relive it. It's over."

Not for me, it's not.

"If you could have chosen, would you have chosen Father? Did you get to prefer him in the end?"

"Stop it. Preferences are for children. There's no choice for any of us, and even those who get their preference – who's to say they really know what they want? At the balls you'll dance, laugh and be joyful. You'll forget. But you won't ever truly know a boy until you unite with him."

Mother's familiar refrain fills the air between us – between my need and what she is able to give. And it's there again: the current that sparks on both sides. Even in silence, its hum is tangible.

"Can I try?" I ask again, desperate to please her. I try to take some purple thread, but she holds on to the other end.

"I'm nearly finished," she says.

So I sit staring out at the fishermen's boats whilst she broods into her sewing, shoulders turned away. There are still two little black silhouettes bobbing gently on the flood plains, Castle Hill a black smudge beyond. I've never given much thought to leaving Penn, but now I feel the way it's pinioned between the other counties – as if the borders are closing in. The walls seem to grow even taller.

"White," Mother demands briskly and thrusts out her hand without looking at me. I fumble with the basket and find what she needs.

"Careful as you split the threads. Don't let them tangle." They do tangle and she rescues them abruptly from my hands.

She is sewing a whole bouquet of Father's anemones, clustered with vines and buttercups. Above them, Grandfather's asters grow in a grand wreath. Grandmother's work. Mother wouldn't have been scolded for twisting the threads.

And below all those grand flowers, there's a mass of white space where one day, in an unknown future, I might sit with my own daughter, desperately trying to weave her father's flower into that abyss. I can't imagine what colour or shape it will take. Maybe the flower of a boy from Penn – someone I already know, although I find it hard to think of uniting with any of the boys from school, from behind the fence. Wrong somehow.

Cedar and oak.

A tremble runs through me, and I have to look away, back to the fishing boats I've seen every day of my life, adrift on the blackness beyond the bank.

"Hand me that red floss," Mother says without looking up. She rearranges the dress, so the bare fabric is hidden beneath the anemones. Did she do that for me, I wonder?

I hope.

"The anemones are pretty," I say.

"I've always loved anemones," she says with a sigh – her mood mended a little but still precarious. "They used to grow in our garden at Foxfields, all bunched up like they

29

thought they'd be safer in a huddle." Her eyes crease at the memory. "Your grandmother used to make me gather them for her. She'd always be excited when spring came. Every morning, she'd look out to check if they'd broken through." Her eyes flicker with the picture behind them and I try to follow her gaze into her imagination. "Your grandmother always said they grew there to protect us."

"I wish I'd known her," I say. Grandmother died before I was two and Grandfather shortly after. Not that it would have mattered, not with them in Foxfields.

Mother's face darkens.

"Anemones at springtime. They were bright and pure. But that was before. They meant something different then." A worm of discomfort wriggles across my skin. She means before anemones came to represent Father. It makes me sad for him, and angry at her. He has always been my hope for myself. He has an open heart and gives it freely. But Mother has always been my fear. Her heart hides in the darkness – in the black fog – and even though I know that same darkness is in me too, I blame her. It feels deliberate … Agatha calls it *drifting*. It sounds trite on her lips, but I've always sensed its danger and feared that something in me is broken, that my mind works differently. I drift because I am unhappy. It is my way of surviving the world. I drift and dream and lose myself, and Agatha knows as well as I do that I could succumb to the same fog, the same flaw as my mother. And sometimes, I'd rather *not* come back. I imagine giving way to it and *want* to. It is not a dark thing yet, but its shadow creeps towards me. Agatha doesn't see it as a flaw. But *they* will. The council.

Even if it never comes for me the way it did for Mother, it will not matter. If Mother's flaw is discovered, I will be tainted too. It is dangerous, hereditary. *They* will come for me instead, a worse kind of darkness.

A shadow of a memory seeps back to me, watery and indistinct. Mother crying and Father grasping her arm, pleading. They were standing at the edge of the flood plains, just beyond where Mother and I sit now. She was barefoot, her feet wet.

"Drewis, think of what will happen to Manon if you do this. You'd be reported." And then Mother slumped to the floor, whispering, *"I'm sorry."*

It's a painted picture of a memory; I can't tell how much of it is true, whether it happened at all – or maybe it happened more than once.

Mother bites the embroidery floss and tidies the ends under the back of the stitching. The dress is finished. Her long sigh fills the air.

"The courtship balls are a difficult time. Much more than the unions. There's hope, longing. And hope is no use to you."

She has tears in her eyes, but the picture doesn't clear in them. "Sow the seeds of virtue; reap the flowers of hope," she says at last, the fog enveloping her again.

That's all she has to offer me. Not her words. No words

of comfort but the hollow platitudes of the council. Words that echo empty.

My stomach tosses with disappointment. She could have told me she would choose Father today and tomorrow, even if she hadn't back then. That – even if I don't form a preference – I can still be happy. That it will all be OK in the end. I would have believed it from her. I need to believe it.

My eyes sting and I look away.

"Take this inside," she says, offering me both the neatly folded dress and a chance to escape with my tears unshed. I can't cry in front of her. "It's going to rain again," she says, "we don't want to spoil all that stitching."

I don't speak as I leave.

☽

I'm putting the dress in its casket when I hear it: a howling cry that rips through the house, a common call when you live so near to the water, but one that is always terrifying. It is the call of the fishermen for help, a call to all nearby boats.

My legs won't carry me fast enough as I run back – I know instantly it's her. *She* is the reason for that shrill call on the water, the piercing cry for help. I think of the two lonely boats I'd seen earlier. There is not much help on the water tonight.

It seems to take an age to tear through our tiny house, down the stairs and out of the door to the porch where Mother's chair rocks, empty. My bare feet are sucked into the sodden ground as I scramble towards the shore.

I stumble and sink, my chest compacting. The shadow memory comes again: Mother crying; Father grasping her arm. Mother barefoot, her feet wet. I cannot go on, and have to catch my breath on all fours, the chill air cooling my neck, which has bloomed with sweat.

When I get to the shore, she's already out. A young fisherman is working hard on her chest, trying to pound a life back to her that's simply not there. It's in the drenched ground, quickening to the water where it has always wanted to be.

I *know* this boy. His boat skirts our shoreline every day – sometimes he nods a greeting, but I never nod back.

He falls back on his heels, panting and soaking wet.

"I'm sorry – I tried—"

"He's down from his tower, son," an older man says from inside his boat. I look up at Clint's tower. He's right; Clint is gone, the orange of his light taken with him, the tower abandoned to the dark.

The older man holds the boy's boat by a rope. There's no mooring at this end of the plains and the barren boat will drift out if they aren't tied together. I wish I had a similar tether to hold on to Mother's spirit. Later, I might notice they look a little alike, these men: their shoulders similarly square; hair a semi-tame wilderness of black. But now I cannot see beyond the fear and panic.

Mother's hair is slicked across her face in blackened red wisps, like my own when it's wet. Her green eyes are gorged. She's still wearing the ridiculous coat.

"She's gone," the boy whispers.

A sound erupts from my chest, feels like lava, burning as it explodes.

"What have you done? How could you?"

"You have to be quiet, Manon," the boy pleads. "Clint is coming." He's quiet but severe, gritting his teeth, pulling me off Mother, but I don't want to give in.

Where's Father?

Then something happens I can't understand. The boy tries to take her coat, shrugging it from her lifeless shoulders. I grasp at it – grasping at the life that's gone from her – but it's inexplicably heavy and I can't free it from him.

"You can't," I scream, pulling with all my might. "It isn't yours."

"Please. We *have* to take it. Clint can't see it, Manon."

Why does my name sound so familiar on his tongue?

She's ebbing away and he's taking another piece. But it's so heavy. And he's so strong.

When the seams give way, rocks tumble from the lining.

Did she sew them in?

A little cluster of flowers has been sewn into the lining. They're not Father's anemones or Grandfather's asters. They're red with delicate fronds in the middle and a sharp halo of petals around the edge.

I look at Mother as if she can give an explanation, but the puddle of flesh is not her. I gather the rocks as if I'm gathering pieces of her, but the boy is there again, tugging my arm so swiftly it hurts – it will be bruised tomorrow.

"They'll decom you if they see."

Something in his voice or expression – or just the word "decom" – makes me let go and he takes the coat, the leftover rocks, the puzzle of the flowers, and tosses it to the older man still floating on the shoreline.

He's already in his boat, pushing off with one leg, mouthing something forcefully, but I can't quite make it out. He nods in a familiar way, sends his hair into a dancing frenzy.

Don't leave me. Hold on to me. Come back.

The earth is turning to water, my feet dissolving into the cold liquid pain.

And then Clint arrives, murmuring questions but my body swims, my mind is submerged. Fragments of sound come to me. All formed in questions.

"Did she jump?"

And then I understand.

The female blood is at fault.

Ailments of the soul are a flaw, and if the council thinks Mother has an ailment of the soul, if she jumped of her own free will, she is flawed. Damned. And she will damn me with her. *I* will be decommissioned.

"She fell in," I say, hollow – the boy's mouthed words coming through me.

It is then that Mother spits water from her lungs, forced fitfully back into a life she doesn't want.

CHAPTER THREE

Wolf in a Trap

"You can go in front of me if you like," Bertie says, her smile as precarious as cracked glass. She is the youngest in our year – only just old enough to be a deb. If she'd been born a week later, she'd be in the year below. Her small round face and full pink cheeks are childlike, and the green flecks in her eyes sparkle with tears as she speaks. I step into line ahead of her, remembering her kindness to Agatha at the fence, though I am as nervous as she is, and feel lopsided without Agatha. She doesn't have to attend the chastity checks.

We are outside the little white schoolhouse on the edge of the Boot. It is conspicuous in its perfection. Even its roof has proper tiles. It sinks into the lush green, lonely against the blue edge of the world. Behind us is Wild Fell. If I turn and look down the hill, surely it will have burned to ashes, bleeding black smoke. My heart aches. But I can't let myself dwell on the image that's stuck behind my eyes. Mother's face, slicked with wet hair, flashing across the place where my eyelids distort reality with memory.

Just focus on now.

A tidy queue of girls is already waiting ahead of Bertie and me. They stretch out in a line, a caterpillar bucking and stretching as each girl takes her turn.

"Don't worry. It'll be quick," I offer.

"Last time I was so sore – and I bled," she mumbles, pinching her bottom lip between her thumb and forefinger. Blood fills the fleshy mound she's made and turns it red. "I had to sit in a bath of cold water," she says, her pink cheeks flaming brighter.

"Cold flannel," I say sideways. A mutter goes down the length of the caterpillar: salt water, lemon juice, turmeric. Almost everyone has a cure for the sting and even Bertie laughs. She lets go of her bottom lip, takes the edge of her dress in her fingers instead, and twists it into a spiral.

"We have to *cleanse the bloodlines* – don't we?" I say sarcastically, mimicking Torrent's voice very quietly. Brack stands straight as a spire about ten girls ahead of us, ticking each of them off a list as they pass. He fills up the entrance with his body, so each girl is forced to slide against him, trapped for a moment, their faces twisting away from his.

"Virtue or death!" I whisper to Bertie, drawing my finger across my throat.

"Guard your virtue," Bertie answers, her face a storm, humour caught in the stronger wind of fear.

"Saviours of the species," we say together, choking sniggers. It tastes good.

The line shuffles on until I'm standing directly in front of Brack. He could be another of Penn's swollen hills, a beast of a man. Watchers' cloaks are green to make them invisible. You start to think they're there even when they're not. It's part of the trick.

"Name?"

"Manon Pawlak."

His breath rattles through his chest as if snagging on something inside. He checks my name off and draws his pencil across my lip, which sends a shudder through me – not from fear but anger. I try to swallow it and pass by him to the examination room without exploding. He doesn't move aside and his hip grazes mine, which makes him smirk, his twisted teeth sparkling grimly.

"Guard your virtue," he says, flicking his tongue across his grin. Bertie doesn't laugh behind me this time.

"Saviours of the species," I answer, dipping politely into a shallow curtsey as the constricted space inside my chest shrinks smaller, squeezing.

It's not really a room at all, just a curtained-off partition in Miss Warne's classroom with a hard metal gurney wheeled in. The window is open, the air as salty as the sea, and the curtain swishes in the breeze so I see the girl ahead of me shuffle her dress down before she leaves.

It is my turn to sit awkwardly on the edge of the gurney, lay back with my cheeks on fire.

"Manon, love? Try to relax."

Mrs Byrd is the mother of a girl in my year, Tabithe. Tabithe was ahead in the queue somewhere and I try to think it could be worse. The checks could be being done by my own mother. But I hate Tabithe because Agatha does. And I can't feel sorry for her. Mrs Byrd is a robust-looking woman, known for the swing of her hips, and the tut of her tongue. But she is always kind to the girls.

My virtue is intact. *Obviously.* But I'm nervous anyway. *What if they make a mistake? How do they actually know?*

It feels cold and red. If red is a feeling. Like my bones are expanding. I panic, my breaths coming shorter and I think I might break with the force. I inhale and hold, brace even though she said to relax. And then the slip and slide as it's over. The cold red metal is gone, and everything convulses back to its smaller form – but pulsating and sore.

"Thank you," I say politely, though the rough anger is rolling to a boil as I try to stand modestly and arrange my skirts.

"Bertie, love? OK, try to relax."

☽

Agatha's house is one of a row that dips into the sea. The ground floor is completely submerged, leaving only the upstairs rooms inhabitable. A flight of steps is the only way up to the deck that's been built round it.

"Wild Fell is the other way," Clint says, as I round the corner and almost bump into him. The memory of the night on the water is fresh between us.

"I have a script," I say, scrabbling for the paper in my basket. It's not a lie – I applied for it from Miss Warne but couldn't bear to ask Brack to sign it off and scribbled his signature myself. I hope Clint can't tell the difference. He is shorter than me and I stare at the tip of his long nose as he analyses the fake signature.

"How's your mother?" he asks, cheeks bulging with mirth, dropping the script in the mud. "Not the best swimmer, is she?" I feel the top of my lip tense but don't speak or bend for the script, can't give him the satisfaction. When I don't answer, he mutters, "One hour. I'll be back to check," and strolls off, stepping on the script as he passes. I pick it up, wipe it on my dress and stash it back in the basket.

At the door, I'm afraid to knock. Since the pledges, things are different. Agatha and I are no longer equals. I am a deb and she is a decom. She pretends the world is unchanged, but it has to. We have to.

I wonder if she has heard about Mother and my heart stops inside my chest. If she has, will she finally see the flaw inside me? Will she do me the favour of hiding it?

"Are you coming in?" Wren asks from behind me. She marches up the stairs to her home with a pitcher of water she has fetched from the well, and is careful to balance the weight so the precious drops don't swill over the side.

I've always loved Agatha's younger sister. Her bright face is clear of the decom's scar for now, but she already wears the black gown that marks her as different. Agatha's flaw belongs to them all, and the council dictate they show it, though it has remained only Agatha who has seizures. It seems so unfair. She walks past me and lifts the latch of the door with her elbow, pushes it open with her backside and waits for me to pass before closing it.

Inside, the Curlews' kitchen is overflowing with the instruments of Agatha's remedies and Agatha stands with her back to me, lost in her work. Chamomile flowers grow on the windowsill and bloom, yellow and white, like sunshine spilling into the sink. There are pots laden with chicken bones for broth on the open pantry shelves. Endless rows of labelled jars fill the walls like jewels.

But not everything is pretty. The smell takes my breath: sweet angelica and cinnamon battle the pungent tang of goat's piss.

"They for us?" Wren asks, taking the basket of eggs from me without ceremony and breaking Agatha's concentration. She turns and takes me in, looks at the basket that Wren has set on the table.

"Eggy bread then, Wren?" Agatha asks, her voice the same calm song as always, but her saltwater eyes not quite as sharp today.

Wren is already cracking the eggs into a bowl in a fever, giddy with the promise of a treat.

"I was about to throw this out," she croons, rolling a

41

piece of hard bread out of a length of linen, which clatters as it hits the wooden counter.

I sit at the table and Agatha continues to work. She is boiling potions in pans, which clink as she stirs them. There's a musicality to it that reminds me of Father playing the schoolhouse piano, or the rhythm of Mother's sewing. A layer of scum has risen to the surface of one, dancing pretty and iridescent in the afternoon light. Agatha dips a spoon under it, lifts it away.

"How'd you manage to get a script?" she asks, and I gesture at the basket, Agatha's leather-bound schoolbook tucked inside, a posy of liquorice and marshmallow roots wrapped in paper that she asked for days ago. She ignores the book but inspects the tubers.

"There's an outbreak of scarlet throat," she tells me, plunging the roots in fresh water and patting them dry.

"Will those help?"

I grow all sorts of things for Agatha in the hot house at Wild Fell. I can get anything to grow from seed, and use many of them to cook with, but I have never learned their medicinal purposes, not like Agatha to whom it's another language. It was her mother who taught her.

"Liquorice root soothes a sore throat if you steep it, and marshmallow tincture will calm the fever. Wren will take them when they're ready."

Children don't need a script to wander the valley. Her legs must tire with Agatha's errands.

"I thought scarlet throat was rare."

42

"Not any more..." She sighs, patting the roots dry with a cloth and tying them with string to hang. "Hoop cough, measles, flu. It's like the children aren't strong enough to fight them off."

"How many cases?"

"A handful at Radley Scar, but it's spreading like drought fire at Wanderer's Ditch."

I don't ask if any have died. It's written all over her face as she glances at Wren, the robust girl she will send with the medicines. The watchers won't give Agatha a script even to nurse sick children. It is a medic's job, though Agatha knows far more about medicinal remedies than Mrs Byrd.

It makes me think of the skeleton trees. One at a time each ash tree succumbed to dieback, their leaves becoming crisp as the disease soaked to the root, and now, only bones are left of them, though they were native to the valley once.

"Miss Warne has set you some exercises so you don't fall behind," I tell her, to change the subject.

She nods, wipes her hand, and lifts the book from the basket, thumbing through it as if through time, from back to front when everything was different.

"It doesn't really matter, does it?" she says, tossing the book across the room on to the table.

I wish I could say it did.

"I heard about Alsis," is what I say instead. It was all people could talk about at school – the result of the hearings, which are read out in assembly every morning.

"I heard about your mother. Wren heard it up at the Summit," she says, going back to her stirring instead of acknowledging what will happen to Alsis. I don't say the word, fearing she might shatter. But it is sharp and strident in the small room. *Cleansing. Cleansing. Cleansing.* Her hands move in circles – slow and soothing. "Is she all right?"

"Aye. A little tired is all, but she's busying about the house as if nothing's happened – happy as a bird in flight. I feel sad for her," I add, trying to make it true. It feels wrong to seek comfort in Agatha. I can hide my flaw. She could not. She must feel the injustice.

"No, you feel sad for *you*," Agatha says, turning and folding her arms in her usual, matter-of-fact way. She's the "good in an emergency" type and hides her feelings well, though I know they must be there, and I can guess what they must be. "And so you should." She rubs the scar on her cheek. "I could have told 'em years ago you were a drifter."

She laughs, a bittersweet sound. She has always called me a drifter. And I have always known it was code, a pretty way of naming what I have inherited from Mother, a balm for my worst fear. Others do not see the darkness in it. Agatha pretends not to. But I cannot. Even so, I pick up the towel that's been left on the table and throw it at her; it lands square in her face and slides to the floor with a slap.

"Ow! I'm just telling the truth ... there's no need for

violence," she says, laughing and tossing the towel back, but I catch it before it lands, and we both laugh that healing laugh you fear will turn to a cry.

"Drifter," she says again.

"Well, I'm not drifting today," I say, pinching my nose. We're standing right next to the bucket of piss.

"The debs still need hair dye," she says, shoving the bucket into a corner with her foot. A little of it sloshes to the floor.

"What's that?" I choke out, pointing to her hands, which are stained autumnally orange. She is grinding some mystery flower into a pulp at the table now.

"Safflower." She drops refined wheat water into the mixture, stirs and scrapes it into a glass vial. Wren scribbles a label and pastes it to the front. Every eighteen-year-old deb will want to trade with Agatha at the markets. Even with that fresh scar, people envy her beauty – her swathes of wheat-blonde hair, sandstone skin.

She smears my face with a little of the ground safflower paste.

"Cover those freckles. We can make you almost presentable, I reckon – even with this nest," she says, tugging my hair. Her laugh infects me, but the laughter lets in the smell of the goat's piss and my head starts to whir.

The paste is sticky and cold as she pushes it into the folds of my face. I close my eyes and feel the drift begin, a queasy lightness. The harsh lines of Calde Valley dissolve, and I lose myself in a world that no one else sees, real and beautiful. I am free and happy and able to choose. The tightness in my chest lifts. I soar. I wish I could stay. Never come home. Never emerge.

"Maybe someone will even form a preference for you," she says, and I snort, drenching myself in that smell again.

"Pigs in the sky!" I laugh through choked breaths. A mist of cold sweat licks the back of my neck, and the vomit hits the floor before I have time to run. Laughing in Agatha's kitchen is dangerous.

"Although … you'll have to learn some manners!" She sniggers. She wipes my forehead of its slick sheen with the towel she had draped on her shoulder, and gestures silently to Wren who picks up a mop with the merest shrug.

"Manners have never been my strong point … but I reckon I could whip him in a race no matter who he is."

"Aye, nobody can wade through mud like Manon Pawlak!" She laughs, eyeing my permanently mud-soaked boots and a tell-tale streak of green that starts at the hem of my dress and continues down my knee, turning into a scrape of red scratches.

She opens the window and plonks me down in a chair near to its breeze. I take greedy gulps of freshness. It's almost as it was before, as if we've forgotten again. Almost. If there wasn't a perfectly framed view of Castle

Hill – the tower a flat black square against the sky, its cut-out windows lit by the trailing sun.

They'll decom you if they see.

When the iron melted the skin along Agatha Curlew's cheekbone, she never made a sound. When my turn comes, I'll howl like a wolf in a trap. Not in pain but fury.

Agatha wipes my forehead with a cold flannel.

"Nobody will be able to tell," she says, following my eye to the hill where she was branded, "they have no proof – how can they prove an ailment of the soul? They're much better with the flaws you can see." She tips her head, eyes steely and soft at the same time. For the millionth time I wish things were different.

"They're watching me now though, aren't they? Every step. Maybe if it wasn't my season I could handle it better – but I'm on show and they'll be watching. Any sign and—"

"And you'll end up like me," she says flatly.

I wish I could skim the pain from her eyes the same way she'd carefully lifted the scum from the top of her potions.

"But you have Alsis," I say. "I don't think I'll ever have that. The best I can hope is to be like Mother."

Her face wrinkles at the temples, her eyes shrinking to a question.

"Alsis will survive the cleansing, Ag."

"Sure as swallows," she says, tasting the words as if they're nourishing. "But we're saying goodbye no matter

47

what. When the balls are done, and the unions made … and I ascend to duty."

The terror of her fate becoming mine balloons in my chest again.

"He'll always love *you*, Ag. No matter who he unites with."

"Maybe. But he'll survive me like he'll survive the cleansing. And when there's children … I'll just be a dull ache. Right now, he's mine – nobody has a claim on him but me, and that'll never be true again, will it?"

Her pain spreads into my own.

And then the door explodes open, Agatha's father carried on the flow of the warm wind.

"Is Manon here?" Barrett asks, his voice frantic. He stands stoic but his eyes search, restless and frightened.

"Open your eyes!" Agatha chuckles, pointing at me where I sit by the window.

"You have to go home. *Now*," he spits, eyes wide and unblinking. "*Go*," he cries, pulling me up and shoving me towards the door. "Clint's made a report – it was read at tonight's hearings."

I'm already sliding down the steps, missing the bottom few and setting off into a run across the half a mile track towards home.

Nobody can wade through mud like Manon Pawlak.

☽

When I arrive home at Wild Fell, Father stands sentinel at the empty hearth, guarding Mother who is so still and silent, it seems as though her spirit has left her body. Her fist is clenched around the note – the only muscles in her body that seem to work. I prise it from her grip and her fingers give way.

Clint has listed the accident as suspicious, thinks she jumped. Possible ailment of the soul. Appeal for witnesses. That's it. No more. Clipped and brutal.

"What will we say?" I turn to Father, my chest constricting.

"That she *fell*. The truth is all," he says calmly, firmly.

"But that's not… We have to be ready. We have to prepare what to say."

"The *truth*," he repeats, biting at his words, and at me. "If—"

"Enough, Manon. Please think of your mother and do as you're bid."

His expression is so firm, so empty, not Father at all. He snatches the note, throws it in the fire. "Leave us be."

I sprint from the house, daylight fading but a while before curfew. And there he is, the boy who pulled Mother from the water, black hair tangling in the wind, standing by the elm tree. He looks marooned, unsure of what to do with his legs on dry land, and I almost laugh but there's no laugh in me. *Who are you?* His face contorts with an awkward smile as if reading my mind, the last of the sunlight splitting behind him.

"Wick," he says, his name a lost memory that unfurls somewhere out of reach. "I brought you this." He offers me Mother's coat and the heaviness of it makes his arms tense, testing the seams of his doublet – a hand-me-down from his father maybe, a little too small. His eyes are unreadable, a mixture of hope and fear and something else. I don't take the coat, fearing some sort of trick.

"The claims are coming," he says. "I heard you've been asked to give double. Maybe you could use it to supplement your offering," he adds quietly, blinking too much, his dark eyes fluttering with something like shame.

"Maybe," I say, wondering anew what we'll give – our furniture? Whinny, the mare? We have little else. "Or you want rid of the evidence?" I spit, momentarily redirecting the course of my anger at Torrent and the council towards this boy.

"That's not it," he says, his eyes ruffling, but I'm too lost in the storm to fathom what he's thinking, or to care. "Clint will pass on his patrol soon. I need to get back to Walker Clough. Take it, will you?"

When I don't take it, he steps forward, drapes it over my shoulders, soft and strong – insistent. I sway with its weight, notice someone's mended the broken seam, and pull it around me as if it's Mother's reluctant arms.

"Where's your boat?" I ask, and it sounds like a taunt, but I don't want him to leave. Arguing with him is better than dealing with everything else.

"I walked," he says with a flash of a smile – looking

down at his legs as if he's surprised to find he has any. "There's no mooring and I didn't want Clint to see me here." He looks around, expectant, but there's only us and the wind that whistles through the elm's barren branches.

"They're going to investigate," I say senselessly. He already knows. That's why he's here.

"Aye. A messenger came to tell us we're to be interviewed." He stands mute, looking at me – through me – in a way that makes me shiver. "I won't say anything."

"They'll make you."

"What can they do? I swear, Manon – you're safe. We won't harm you. We're not scared of Clint."

"Everyone protects their own. Why wouldn't you tell?"

"Why would I? What could I possibly gain?"

"A share in the claims maybe?"

He looks at me as if I'm missing the obvious, rakes his hands through his feral hair, walks away then back again on a hot breath.

"We don't need it. We have all the fish we can eat. Isn't that obvious?" Again, that look inside me as he stills in front of me. "You won't owe me anything."

"Until one day I will."

"Never," he says, his dark eyebrows a knot. I try to stalk by him, but he grabs my arm, pulls me back. The curl of his fingers thrills along my skin. Something pulses between us, something dark and the moment distorts, time stuttering between one path and another. Before it decides, I run.

Agatha, Sixteen

Agatha stood on the deck at The Dell in the dawn light, watching a torch blink in the Clines' barn. The light moved quickly, illuminating the wide-open blackness of the door, then retreating inside again, orange fading to black, the doorway a candle in the wind.

It was lambing time and that soft, shifting light heralded the birth of the Clines' new flock as it moved from one ewe to another, helping each mother in turn. The sweet bleating sound of newborns taking their first breaths multiplied into the night, an echoing song. Agatha hadn't fully understood the feeling that squalled inside her at the sound of those first cries, only that her stomach roiled into her heart somehow, unlatched and roving.

She was sixteen; old enough to understand the future as more than an abstract puzzle. The words of the debs had crystallized solidly inside her, only waiting for her to say them herself. She watched them make their pledges with fresh wonder as each new season began, inexorably moving towards one fate. One boy. In every mind-drawn picture of her life to come, she sketched Alsis Cline, over and over until the marks made by her imaginary pencil were so deeply scored they were a permanent longing pain.

With the slow beat of time and tide, knots had looped in her stomach as she watched, dreadful and lovely at the same time. Waiting for him was always this way, a delicious ache. Clint had passed on patrol twice, but he wouldn't skirt back for a while, and she willed Alsis to come out of the barn before then.

And then he had. Almost as if he had heard her silently asking, he stepped out of the barn, stretched into the morning, shook the night's labour from his back. He wiped his hands with a rag pulled from round his neck, and leaned against the door frame of the barn, his whole body seeming to yawn. She thought he would stay like that, sleeping whilst awake, but then he saw her, and his tired stretch burst. He came to life, leaped over the small stone wall with one hand propelling him, an arrow through the sky.

The deck was wet, and she slid her feet around as she waited, holding on to the rail as if she were dancing with him. It made her think of Miss Warne's tall tales of a world frosted with ice, children skating on its frozen surface, and she laughed at the ridiculousness of it, a world so cold it froze. Calde Valley was always warm, even in the wet months.

She stopped when Alsis was close, so that she could watch him come to her. He ran through the dewy grass, then scaled the steps two at a time so that he reached her at such a pace his momentum had nowhere to go, and his stop was too sudden, his need too violent. There was a moment when they should have embraced, when they should have melted into each other. They both felt it, as they had both felt how wrong it was to ignore. But they had ignored it nonetheless. Because those were the rules, and the need had ricocheted around them, tangible.

"I thought I saw you," he said, smiling, that smile untying the knots in her stomach one loop at a time.

"I couldn't sleep," she answered, which was true. She had seen his light glowing from her window and it had brought her out to the deck.

For now, the world was theirs, but day was beginning to break, the pink threads finally overpowering the night, and folding themselves into the dark sky. They did not have long before others awoke and the valley was populated once more.

"You're tired," she said, noting the yawn he tried to suppress but which travelled through his face and shoulders.

"Never too tired for you."

So many loops unfastened themselves as he spoke, she felt a looseness inside herself, a wonderful lightness that made her feel like she was swimming.

A ewe mewled from the barn and Alsis looked reflexively back, his jaw tense, as if checking on his own young. He was still wringing his hands with the cloth, rubbing it over each finger one at a time as if polishing them, and Agatha couldn't help but look at those life-giving hands, gentle and knowing. Hands that had touched hers ever-so fleetingly, only to trade a sack of cheese, or cotton. She imagined a world where the barn below was theirs, full of their newborn lambs, where they would work together to pull them free, and where those hands belonged only to her.

"You have new lambs?"

"Five born tonight. And a few more due. Enough to pay our share of the claims and still have plenty to trade," he said, green eyes full and thankful, "if they all survive, that is. One lost its mother, but I've managed to attach it to another ewe for now."

It caught her off-guard, the peril that held these newborn creatures in its clutches – death and life so tremulous, and her insides churned again with some threat she didn't understand. She clenched her lip in her teeth to stop the tears from rising, and let the strange, bewildering grief out on a sigh.

She leaned forward on the railings, perched her elbows there, and looked out at the coming of day. Along the crawling coastline, Clint was a growing shadow. She counted in her head the footsteps that would bring him close. A few minutes was all they had. It was all they ever had: a series of tiny moments to be cherished until the next one.

"Look," she said, and Alsis followed her gaze, his

midnight eyes waking bright and verdant at the sight of Clint coming. He looked at her intently, the weight of his want balancing heavy on top of her own. A word she barely knew the meaning of lanced through her.

Desire.

"He's almost here." He sighed, leaning on the railing next to her, his arms stretching in front of him, mirroring hers. Their elbows touched, and then their forearms. The soft hairs of his arm tickled hers, her own stood on end, and she stretched more, to feel the length of his arm more fully against hers, longing for Clint's footsteps to stall so she could know, finally, how that feeling ended.

"There's never enough time," Alsis breathed, his eyelids sweeping slowly closed and open again in one beautiful butterfly movement.

He was right. They were out of time. Again. They were always out of time.

"We have time," she said, breathing so quickly she could see her chest rise and fall beneath her. Alsis was an absolute certainty to her; he always had been, but telling him this truth out loud was still a hot agony of doubt.

"Aye," he said so simply, so easily, it took her breath. He turned towards her and took one of her hands in both of his, and stroked each of her fingers in turn until she did not know which were his and which were hers. I like *this* knot, she thought. This one can stay tied.

"I state my preference," he said with a smile, standing up straight, his eyes eager.

"And I mine." She let a smile spread through her cheeks.

Her edges were blurring the way they seemed to do so often of late. She wasn't sure whether it was the touch of his hand and the thrill of his words that dizzied her, or this new thing, the sensation she had felt more and more frequently, losing herself, as if she slept and woke in the blink of an eye. The sweep of his fringe and the warmth of his smile were no longer clear but a smear of themselves, a smattering of him. She knew he was there, but his concreteness was fading.

She struggled against it, tried to hold on to time, but the shape of his face was dimming, the world was no longer real. His voice floated as if from far away, and she could almost see the letters disparate and flying like they had slipped off Miss Warne's blackboard.

A

    ga

th

      a

It was only a second or two, but she was gone, she knew not where and, when she returned, a thickness clouded her, her limbs felt heavy.

"Where did you go?" he asked, alert, closer than he had been before, his arm around her back to steady her, though she had not seen him move, and did not remember him catching her. What she had registered was the way he tried to conceal his concern in a smile, and how the lying smile had revealed it anyway, so different from any of the smiles she had memorized. He stroked her cheek with his thumb as if waking her, his eyes sad and questioning.

"I don't know." She blinked, shaking her head, her hair caught by the breeze. "I lose myself sometimes." She shrugged and tried to shake the feeling back into her limbs by pulsing her hands and flexing her toes.

Alsis caught the long lengths of her hair to stop the wind flicking them in her face and gathered them into one piece. He curled it round his hand and brought it to rest at her neck, letting it fall on her shoulder, smoothing it down with the palm of his hand.

"But I'm back now." She smiled, and turned her eyes to his, still slightly smoked with dizziness, but asking, pleading.

His mouth parted as if he was about to speak, but instead he held his breath and moved towards her and this time she stayed in the world with him. He pulled her close, gentle at first as if she might break, then pulled her arms around him as if he wanted to tie himself up in her. He took her face in both hands and ran his thumb along her lips. The numbness left behind by the leaving dissolved at his touch. She felt herself surging back to life, that life blazing a trail down her spine, and she watched the delicious slowness of his skin creeping towards hers, held on to every beat of her heart as they kissed, memorizing this moment as the moment her forever began.

I don't care, she thought, almost hearing Clint's footsteps as they edged ever closer. *Let him come. Let the world end here.*

It was Alsis who detached himself from her with that same robust care she imagined him using on the lambs. It made her smile. Or it would have if she hadn't been so angry.

"Until forever," he promised.

"Until then, my love."

As she closed the kitchen door, and slid the bolt safely across her for ever, both her head and heart were throbbing, and the leaving came again. But she heard Clint bid Alsis good morning. And she heard Alsis's ringing, singing voice in reply, full of the secret joy only she understood.

Lo
    vel
y
morn
    ing

CHAPTER FOUR

Shackled by the Neck

When we were little, Agatha and I would come to Nag's Bay to collect stones polished smooth by the tide, and make prizes of them, fill our pockets, and trade them with the other girls at school. This one for its shape; that for its distinct red sheen; this for its concentric grooves like a spiralling skeleton. I would stack them in my room at Wild Fell, a teetering tower of wonder, then knock them down and watch them tumble.

The bay is inaccessible when the tide is in, like a secret garden hidden beneath the sea, but when the water is out, you can clamber down the short, steep cliff to the beach below – as we do now, hands clasped tight as we edge towards the shore, our families one long string that unravels downwards. Father is at the front, then Mother and me, with Agatha, Wren and Barrett behind.

The cloudless sky sings of summer, a breathless moment between the storms and the dry heat.

Though it is the same shore we trod then, as children, still lined with rocks that tempt my hand to reach for them, the world is different now. I do not pick them up, do not feel the joy I did then. There seemed possibilities in the line of that horizon but those possibilities, once endless, have shrunk to nothing. None of us wants to be here but attendance at cleansings is compulsory.

I lick the salt from my lips, remember the taste of the crab we cooked and ate from its shell, seasoned by the sea. Back then we had everything we needed, and never doubted happiness would be ours. Now Mother's hand in mine is only a reminder of the flaw the council will say we share, how it must pass through her to me, from her hand to mine and on for ever. The stones speak of her coat, too heavy, seams splitting apart.

I remember the first cleansing I saw. It was a grieving mother who had been caught trying to scale the wall between Penn and Waddow to be at her daughter's graveside. She didn't survive the cleansing, but I doubt she wanted to. The council did her a favour, reunited her with her lost child.

Skimmed stones don't ripple across the water today because, if they did, they'd be met with the fierce, flat shape of the dipping stool that rises from the water when the tide is low. Cleansings are a common punishment, a favourite of the council. But they never lose their horror.

You never get used to the way the skin turns grey and the eyes roll back. Today, it is Alsis's turn to be cleansed. And because it is Alsis, it is also Agatha.

I want to ask her what it's like to love someone that way, so much the fear has made a new shape of her. But I can't. Friends as we are, I cannot show how I envy her his love because she has nothing, and I have everything. For now.

"Almost there," I say instead, and she nods, pulling her hair back from her face and tying it in a bun at the nape of her neck with a swift movement of her hands, long fingers moving deftly.

"So he will see my eyes," she says.

Blue as the winter rain.

The whole village is gathered on the shore, waiting and whispering – tossing the story of Alsis and Agatha to and fro. They are forced to witness, but some enjoy it entirely too much, I think, and linger over the details with too much delight. But there is something else, something new, in the way their voices rise and fall. It's in the way they become still and quiet as I pass, the way they eye Mother and me with suspicion, only to begin chattering again as we go by. I move through them stiff and stout, brushing shoulders as I pass, but each body that recoils feels like a blow.

"Pay no heed," Agatha whispers as we edge towards the front of the crowd. She returns their gaze coolly, astringent and poised. But there's something in her eyes too when she looks at me, a chink in the armour of our friendship. As though she is wondering if I'll escape what she could not. And I can't tell whether she wants me to.

Mother looks down, shuffles slowly, and Father herds her through the throng as if he can surround her with himself.

I am face to face with the fishing boy, Wick, before I realize he is there, his fresh, salty smell filling the space around me, sweet and sour. I am pinned between him and the rest of the crowd, caught by his knowing eyes, as variegated as a hawk's wing, a threat behind a smile.

"Can't run from me this time," he says, catching the fullness of his lip in his teeth and holding his breath as the crowd pushes him.

"No," I answer, equally constricted, waiting for the crowds to part and free me, which they do. For a moment, I stand as if I'm still held there, gawp at him not knowing what to say or do. The breath in my throat is loud. He opens his mouth to speak, which forces my feet on. His words have a way of making me feel like I'm burning, and his eyes make me uneasy. There's something in them I don't understand. If it's suspicion, it looks different to the way it looks in others.

"Where is he?" Agatha asks when we get to the water's edge, her cool eyes settling on the stool, which looks like a sea creature's arm, reaching from the depths. For a second, there is nothing but its monstrous grasping hand and the sick feeling in my stomach and then...

"There – see?" I answer, pointing to the water, where a black shape drifts towards us, bobbing on the sparkling sea. The boat seems not to make progress at all at first, and then it emerges from its black blur: crisp edges, tall sails, the bow scooping the waves, up and down. They are bringing Alsis from Castle Hill, where he has been kept in chains since the day of the pledges and his infraction whilst the hearings were held, and judgment was made. Until this day.

Castle Hill. Where a report about Mother and me sits on a desk waiting to be read.

"What is it, Mama?" a boy asks, standing on tiptoes to see over a huddle of taller siblings who are deliberately obscuring his view. He is perhaps three or four, with a furrowed brow and sensible eyes. He looks at the dipping stool, not with terror but wonder, not sure whether to fear the beast that lurches from the sea or to beckon and try to tame it.

"Let's build a house," his mother answers, kneeling and beginning to shift stones in to piles.

"Nonsense, they must see," her husband insists, pulling her up to standing. She looks as if she'd like to close her eyes but doesn't. "It is penance for the unclean, Nathan," he says to his son. "For those who take the wrong path."

"What path, Father?"

"The path of destruction that leads us to extinction. What do we say, boy?"

"Sow the seeds that hurt you, rake the flower of—"

"No, boy," the father seethes, crouching to correct him. His lips are close to his son's, whose face is all terror now.

Sow the seeds of virtue. Reap the flowers of hope.

When the boy gets it right, the father claps his hands together, and sweeps him on to his shoulders for a better view of the sea monster, and this time the boy gasps, as if the world has crystallized before him. It is to be feared then, not tamed after all.

And then the boat moors, the faces coming sharply into focus. Alsis. Torrent, and Brack. Of course it would be him. I can almost see him volunteering, his hand hoisted like a child in school. Alsis is shackled by the neck, the chain held by Brack, and he holds it taut, never allowing it to slacken off. Alsis doesn't wince but the skin around his eyes is tight.

"He'll be OK," I say, grasping Ag's hand.

"Aye," she answers, her voice withered. Anger broils in her eyes again: envy, blame, injustice. She lets my hand drop from hers, balls her hands to fists at her sides.

"His *eye*," she whispers, looking at the ground, swallowing tears. For the first time, I think she might crumble. Alsis's eye is blue-black and swollen shut. One side of his mouth tilts upward like a fish released from a hook. He searches the crowds with one good eye.

"Look," I say, nudging her. She looks up in time to catch the moment he finds her in the crowd, his face more swollen with love than pain. And she doesn't crumble. She doesn't smile either, but her eyes change, her shoulders lift, body braces. I can't breathe.

Alsis does a little bow for the crowd and is instantly yanked backwards by Brack, which makes him stumble, and he ends up lying on the floor on his back. Brack straddles him, bending down to squeeze his face, and pulls him up to stand as if he were no more than a toy. He pushes Alsis up the long arm of the dipping stool, straps him in the seat at the end, then makes his way back down. At the bottom, he grasps the lever, his knuckles tense against the wood, one hand controlling the crowd who bray at his command as if he has a second lever attached to them.

"This deb is unclean," Torrent announces to the crowd, who hush as one at the first exploding sound of his voice. "He is a threat to our species. But his blood is pure and the people of Calde Valley need his seed. It is his duty – and ours – to cleanse our species and rid ourselves of the defects that would end us if we let them."

Something inside me readies itself, like a cornered animal. Perhaps that is the defective part of me.

"Join with me as we ask for him to be purified."

The crowd unites, voices surging – reverberating on the open sky.

"*In the name of our ancestors, and the Lost Cities, we must make this land fruitful, strive for virtue. Now and always.*"

Alsis laughs from his seat at the edge of the monster's arm, his head lilting from side to side, waving his hand as if conducting us. But I don't laugh with the rest of the circus. Every word adds coal to a growing fire in the pit of my stomach, as if every repetition of the Dedication Prayer has stacked up inside me, one tumour growing on top of another until they threaten to burst and weep.

"Cleanse him," Torrent cries when the prayer ends – his hand striking the order as if he himself pulls the lever. But it is Brack who plunges Alsis down. There's a sound like bark cracking – and Alsis is propelled beneath the water with a great *whoosh* as the arm breaks the surface. The circus of an audience whoops. Somewhere swilling inside the shrieks of fervour is the quieter, more deafening sound of terror.

I hold my breath, feel Agatha do the same. *How long will he stay under? How hard will his lungs have to fight?* She is fighting too – every second. And I am choking, tumours bursting.

Sixty-three. Sixty-four. Sixty-five.

"Bring him up!" I scream, feeling as though I'm drowning with him, his fight and mine somehow the same. "Enough. Bring him up! Have mercy!"

Others call too, and when I take Agatha's hand, she doesn't let go this time but laces her fingers through mine.

There's a huge gushing swoop of water as Brack pulls the lever back with both hands, forcing the arm that grips Alsis up into the air. His chest spasms in desperate breaths but then he's pushed down again. And again. Over and over.

When he's limp, they send Mrs Byrd along the shaft of the great arm to check he's alive. She struggles to balance herself, teeters as if she might fall and the circus jeers. She smooths his hair back from his face as gently as if he were her own child, bends her ear to his mouth. Alsis's mother is a few feet away, holding her breath, her face twisting with the kind of pain I've only imagined in nightmares – something too sharp to be felt in real life and survive. Mrs Byrd nods, mother to mother, and the woman lets out an animal sound.

"He's breathing. But he needs to come down," she warns, her voice pleading. "He can't stand much more."

Alsis's arms and legs hang down from either side of the frame, soaked and dripping. He's no more than a wet cloth on a line, wrung out and flopping lifeless.

"Is he conscious?" Torrent asks.

"Barely—"

Torrent silences her, holding out his gloved hand for her to step down from the frame and she takes his fingertips gingerly – the way you'd hold something dirty.

"Then the test must continue. Brack?" The hulk of a man stares at Torrent, eager. "Again," Torrent hisses. "If he survives, he is clean. If not, he is beyond salvation. Let *us* learn his lesson instead."

Brack cracks his knuckles – or is that just in my mind? *Seventy, eighty, ninety…*

When Alsis comes up this time, they unhitch him,

drag his limp body down and lay him on the stone beach. A trail of water streaks behind him.

"Not on the stones," Agatha says, her breathing as ragged as the surface of the beach.

"They're smooth remember. Come on," I urge, tugging her forward, but she is stuck, her legs won't move. It's the sound of *his* voice that frees her – just a splutter that seems to reverberate within her. I try not to think of the sound Mother made, how similar it is. How grief is a thick slab starting to crack inside me.

We stand close enough to see the way the water has soaked through the boy we know from the other side of the fence. It hasn't just soaked into his clothes, it's soaked into him, made him heavy with its weight.

"Stand," Torrent says as if Alsis is no more than a lazy field hand, but he can't, though he tries. His legs are no more solid than the water and he flops back to the ground. Brack holds him up, careful not to get himself wet.

"Alsis … Cline," Torrent says, searching for the insignificant name in a pile of other insignificant names in his mind. "By the might of the Calde Valley Council, you have been cleansed," he announces with a flashing smile. "Now, you must take your place in the Virtue Season with all your heart. It is your honour to do so. Do your duty." He looks at the crowd and they chant: "*Sow the seeds of virtue.*" Their arms are raised, fists clenched. Torrent takes Alsis's chin in his hand, strokes it with his thumb. "Find a *suitable* mate and your preference may stand," he says, all compassion and grace. He looks out to the crowd as if to receive his praise – the Merciful Councillor – and they roar with applause and forced gratitude.

"Reap the flowers of hope."

"My preference *will* stand," Alsis echoes, his voice a breathless bark, his chest sucking hungrily at the air. Torrent smiles in victory, claps his hands together mutely, taking Alsis's words as obedience. But I know, and I hope Agatha does too, that they are anything but: they are a promise of unending devotion, despite everything. He will love her until the end.

That's when I catch that pair of stormy eyes again – Wick's eyes – stirring with something I don't understand. I only know that it frightens me, that something of me recoils from it, a feeling as dark as the eyes themselves. I have to look away.

CHAPTER FIVE

Flesh, Blood, Bones

"At least we've still got Whinny," Father says as we watch Brack and Clint roll away in a cart full to the brim with our lives. The cart's wheels groan with the weight of grain sacks, furniture and farm tools. But it is the rooster hanging by its neck from Brack's hand that really sears my heart. It'll feed his family for a day, but we would have bred from him all year. Chicks are always our best trade at the markets. Now all we have is root vegetables – if they grow in time. No one wants to trade for those.

"We'll manage," Father says. He puts his arm around me, pulls me into his side and smiles, but it's a smile scorched with fear. "We'll always have eggs," he says defiantly. I think of the surly hen who lays an egg a day if we're lucky.

"Maybe the Clines will need help," I suggest, feeling guilty that I could think of turning Alsis' misfortune in our favour. He is too weak to work; they will be short at the dairy. "Perhaps I can trade labour for food."

Something glints on the water, silver against the blue, a little white boat drifting, oarlocks twinkling as they bounce into the sun's rays and out again. It is Wick's boat. He stands in the hull, stirring the current, treading water. Watching. We haven't heard about Clint's report. No one has been to interview us, and I feel like that boat, drifting but not moving, waiting for the wave that crashes too high over me.

"Come," Father says. "It's time to get dressed for the Commencement Ball."

It is not a wave but a squall, a storm of hope against reason, of fear and dread and desire. Like climbing, and the acid burn, the single-minded will to reach the peak, and the freedom of the place where green meets blue. That is where this ends. Where earth meets sky. Where sea meets land. Where two waves crash into one.

☽

Penn House has a huge arched window, split up by lots of little latticed panes that remind me of the pastry tarts I make from Grandma Pawlak's recipe book. I've seen the ballroom before, but only from the other side of that window, gaping at the grandeur through its bullseye panes. It is where the councillors have their offices, so even when lit by candlelight, it retains its sinister façade.

I wind the rose quartz necklace round my finger, a worry that began long ago.

"Welcome debutants!"

We are greeted by Clint who guards the door, wearing a smile that suits the occasion but not him. Father and I stand in line, waiting as, one by one, the names are called.

"Hilda Asquith … Jaqueline Barnett … Alice Carter."

I can see the ballroom in snapshots, and the picture is just as dazzling as it was through the warped glass window. Everything sparkles and splits in the candlelight like a dream. It is like being inside a glass cloche, the kind that Father uses to protect tubers in winter.

Violets droop green and purple all around the grand ballroom, so many their scent fills the air. I breathe it in, but it is not sweet, it is bitter. This abundance has come from the claims. The feasting table, laden with poached fish, fruit, wine and cheese, are meant to be symbolic offerings from the people of Penn to the visitors from other counties. But it serves to fuel the falsehoods spouted by the council, and the dislike between the counties that keeps us from joining together against their rule. The people of Foxfields, Waddow and Stone think this is how we live, that we exclude them from it, but I have never seen such plenty.

"Leonie Clarke."

Every familiar thing is tempered with strangeness. The walls are hung with gold framed pictures from long ago, tables laid with silver cutlery, the ceiling dripping with crystal candelabra that shouldn't exist in our world of need.

The hosting village always heads the parade: boys first

then girls. The boys have taken their turn already, faces smudged in candlelight, silver buttons like winking stars as the doors open and close. I'm surprised to find, beneath all the curdling fear, excitement spikes. Mother was right. You forget. You want.

At least the first ball is here. Home. Agatha is far behind, the thread that binds us stretching thin. It was her who dressed my bonfire hair, pinned a posy of purplish crocuses on one side, though they've done little to tame the wildness of me. Some of Mother's carmine dress has been dipped in mud from a climb before the ball. The pretty cotton hangs limp against my bones, like one of her hugs. Agatha never did figure out how to simulate the rich dye extracted from the pricey cochineal insect that plagues the farmers of Penn. Though, in the end, it did not matter.

"Don't stoop. Stand tall. Dance with the Briddick boy from Waddow," Rosie Docke's mother begs, fiddling with the lace neck of her dress. Rosie recoils.

"I don't want to leave Penn," she protests.

"I grew up in Waddow. His family has a forge. *Dance* with him." Rosie slaps her hand away, but nods. They are one of the poorest families in Penn, with no real trade. With Rosie's father gone and her mother too old to reunite, they rely mostly on charity and foraging.

"Rosie Docke…"

It's almost my turn. Only the pressure of Father's hand halts the beating fear. When I take my place amongst the debs, it's real. There's a boy in this room who I'll unite with.

One step. Then another.

"Emmeline Law … Manon Pawlak."

I take my place, hemmed in amongst the closed buds fighting for space to open. Father is lost to the crowd, swept away.

And then the decoms scuttle in unannounced, heads bowed. Only Agatha's head is disobedient, held high. She catches my eye, winks, and I shoehorn a sudden sob into a smile. There are eleven decoms from across the counties who should have been debs this year. I count them. It's their scars I notice first but am ashamed and force myself to memorize the colour of their eyes, the turn of their noses, see beyond the scar as if each one was Agatha, as if each one was *me*.

"The Calde Valley Council and the villagers of Penn Vale welcome you to the Commencement Ball." Torrent says from the stage, a brace of councillors seated in a row at a feasting table behind him, watchers guarding on all sides. Of course the Madams are there too. The child I once was remembers them just as they are, as if they've never moved from this ballroom: crowns sparkling, dresses rustling as they shift in their seats, whispering to each other and pointing at the debs that strike them as pretty or interesting, imagining they have influence over their husbands, which they almost certainly do not.

"The beginning of the Virtue Season is a time of joy.

Let us celebrate the success of our community – share our wealth as we share our children," Torrent announces.

The councillors applaud and the crowd follows. Their share of *our* wealth is brimming from a grand table of food, overflowing, and my stomach growls. The councillors are only half listening, too busy tasting the fruits of our labour, but they feign interest in Torrent, knowing too well the taste of his temper.

"Let us remember, it is also a time of reflection and *duty*. Let us not forget the past. We must cleanse our flesh and rid ourselves of pestilence and plague."

I search for the pestilence and plague he speaks of, find only fresh faces, wide eyes sparkling. Bertie, fidgeting and nervous but pretty and alive, her dress as pink as her cheeks, a chain of daisies in her hair. Tabithe – who looks at the boys like they're mouldy meat – a tiny crimp at the edge of her mouth. Agatha, statuesque in black. And me. Desperate with hunger.

"Now, as is tradition, the first-born male will commence the dance with the female of his choice." He rustles his notes, finds the name. "Wick Flint, please make your selection."

My breath catches as I see Mother's reaction in the crowd. Her chin trembles, and she bites her lip. She knows about the boy who rescued her from the water. *This* boy.

Torrent glowers as Wick fails to appear. The councillor's eyes roll towards the crowd, and I'm afraid his glance will fall on Mother. He would only see a woman watching the ball, nothing more. Yet it feels as though he could see right through her.

"Wick Flint," he repeats, "make your selection."

The swarm of boys parts and Wick emerges. Torrent looks at Wick as though he were an insect, but Wick walks past him calmly. His gaze ripples across the debs, a hand slides across the dark hair that does not match the slick finish of his clothes. His slowness is galling.

Three more steps.

How can he be so calm when I feel like my insides are working their way out?

Two more steps.

His faded red doublet is missing a button near his neck, and it flaps open, skin stained by the heat of the spring sun.

One more step.

He is here, a stone wall, blinking – swallowing a breath that feels as though he's swallowing me. I put out my hand reflexively, but he chooses a girl next to me, takes her by the wrist, all but drags her to the centre of the dance floor. I don't know if I'm angry or ashamed. Or something else.

Breathe.

The piano begins, Father's fingers moving deftly, wrapping me in his familiar song. How many times has he played at school assemblies?

Just another assembly.

Wick and his partner – who is not a girl from Penn Vale but dressed in the blue of Waddow – hold each other awkwardly, as if their skin is hot to the touch. The girl is wearing a pair of blue earrings, a tribute to the artisans of Waddow who use their forges to make blue glass. The cobalt chips glitter, tiny but precious.

The watchers study the emblem books, tracing the purity of the lines, whilst the councillors drip our food down their chins.

Time beats as slow as the song. And then it is time for others to join. Couples trail on to the dance floor, awkward at first.

"Dance with me?" a boy asks, blue eyes bathed in ember-soft candlelight. I don't see whose eyes they are at first, but then I catch the scent. *Cedar and oak.*

"Aye," I say, offering my hand, heart thrumming. Tomie leads me on to the dance floor and the music blurs. My feet are numb.

"I'm Tomie," he says, taking my right hand in his and setting his other on my waist. The warmth of his hand trails down the line of my hip. I can't tell if my steps are right.

"Manon," I say in reply, and he smirks because he already knows. Just as I already knew. I've watched him, trailed him on the lane home, trying not to notice the way his long blonde hair catches the breeze, or the way his long legs scoop the ground in a race with each other. This is awkward, like trying to dance with the fence between us.

"I like your dress," he says, and I fumble for something to say back.

"It was my mother's."

"It suits you," he says, smiling.

"I prefer my day dress."

He strokes the line of lace that trims the scooping neckline, all the way down to the hollow between my breasts, and back up to my shoulder, so that a tingle shivers across my skin and my head spins. "No. This one is definitely better," he says. "Your family has a farm?" he adds, as if the world hasn't pivoted.

"Wild Fell – though it is smaller now than it was, so we don't grow as much. Grandfather Pawlak had to give much of it to the claims when the crops failed. The land was divided. But we have chickens." *Or we did.* "Your family are carpenters?"

"Aye. I've almost finished my training," he says, pride tugging both ends of his mouth into a smile. His palms are smooth, no trace of the callouses that will come – the mark of a Calde Valley Man. But I like the softness of them. I like the feel of them on me. "The trade has been in our family for five generations," he says, and I can tell he's thinking about the next one, which fills me with a strange sort of terror. I understand Mother a little better, how dangerous hope will be to me now the season has begun.

"Do you like it?"

"Aye. It's steady, although we're short of wood just

now. Most of it was claimed for the building work at Castle Hill and with the drought fires last year—"

"What are they building?" I ask, too keen, a little rude.

"Not sure, but the blacksmith has given much of his steel supply too. His forge is close to the carpentry and we work with him often. Our decom was redeployed there, others too – so it must be important. Father thinks a hospital maybe."

"The council always provides," I say flatly.

What need is there of a hospital on Castle Hill when each county has their own medics?

My stomach rumbles so hard I think he must feel it. All I ate before the ball was a bowl of weak potato broth, eked out with the last of the bread and I feel dizzy with the smell of the food so close by. There is a small table laid out for the debs and their families, though it is not so grand as the councillors'.

"I've never seen so much food," Tomie says, following my gaze and I smile guiltily.

"Me either."

"I fancy a piece of ruby pie," he says, almost salivating. "Donated by the Feys." I can't stop myself looking and he laughs as the music stops.

"I'm glad we got to dance," he says, a tinge of sadness in his voice as he bows, his hair softly framing his face as he looks up. "I was hoping we would."

I smile in answer, pushing at the fence between us.

It bends but snaps back, and I curtsey awkwardly, unable to say what I know he wants to hear. We part, the shiver of his touch lingering.

"I'll see you on market day," he calls.

Fences. So many fences.

The food is already disappearing when I make it to the table, many of the debs having seized the opportunity to fill their bellies between dances. I tear a full leg off the dismembered remains of a chicken, fill my cheeks with the familiar taste, knowing it will be the last time I taste it now that we have no rooster to breed from. I pile a plate for Agatha too, though I'm sure she'll have little appetite. She is sitting on a bench by the band, a row of black gowns all seated together. She hasn't danced, even though the decoms were invited to by Councillor Torrent. The others do, some able to forget just as I have done. But not Agatha. Nor Alsis. He is sitting at the opposite edge of the dance floor, refusing to tap so much as a foot, glaring at the councillors when he thinks no one is looking, or intent on Agatha. He hasn't recovered from the cleansing, so at least he has an excuse to sit this out. Insolence won't be tolerated but injury will.

I'm about to join Agatha when "The Iris Path" begins. Father knows it's my favourite and I catch his eye, smiling at the memory of him twirling me around the kitchen as a child, dancing on his toes as he sang out of tune. "Do you remember the steps?" he'd said, laughing this afternoon, though his laughter had been forced this time.

"My father plays guitar. See?" Wick says, pointing from behind me, and catching me by surprise, his face too close to my cheek. I notice his father for the first time, playing in harmony with mine. The man from the water. He and Father bounce along to the rhythm of their hearts, drawn out through their music, a safe harbour. I can't help but smile.

"Shall we?" Wick asks, putting out his hand formally. I almost refuse but Brack is close, watching. I'm supposed to accept every offer. It is for them to deny the match. Not me. That is why they have the emblem books.

I abandon the plates and take his hand, coarse with the scars of ropes and net. It sends a cold thrill through me but is warmed by something else inside it. Like a hot shiver. Panic. It must be. It turns to a watery sickness, acid burning, charged by each note of Father's song.

What does he want?

He sweeps me up too vigorously – as if he's misjudged my weight and our bodies meet in an uncomfortable clash. Brack is quick to part us, snatching my hand from Wick's, snatching away some other feeling too, before it had a chance to take hold.

"Not too close," Brack hisses.

"Sorry," Wick whispers as he pulls me into the throng, away from Brack, more careful to preserve the space between us. I can't tell if he's amused or embarrassed because his face doesn't change. Maybe he's even scared. But he's as wooden as the hull of his boat. Until he dances. And then it's like he's dipped his oars into the flow, graceful and smooth. Other couples surround us, dancing at odd angles, fearful of each other. But not Wick. He's comfortable, relaxed, holds me firm and steers me without effort. Like gliding.

"You didn't have to dance with me," I say, not sure how to begin. I don't understand this boy, or what he wants from me. He tightens his grip around my waist.

"No. Maybe not. There's plenty of fish in the sea, Father says."

"So why did you?"

"Because—"

"Of Mother? Because you felt *sorry* for me?"

"No."

"Why then? To check on Clint's report?"

"Maybe. It would be nice to know my family is safe." I hear the warm way his voice folds around the words *my family* as if he is wrapping his arms around them. I ignore the way it softens my insides.

"Well I haven't heard anything, so now you know you're off the hook," I snarl. But he doesn't let me go.

"They're watching," he chides, tipping his chin towards the watchers and councillors who crowd us. Torrent is close, braced for infringements. He almost salivates with wanting it. I try to make more effort to match Wick's steps, though my feet feel heavy and slow. "Can your mother be trusted not to talk?" he asks.

I glance her way. She's standing with Father at the

piano, tapping her foot slightly out of rhythm with him, small and vulnerable.

"I think so."

"That's good. And no news is good news. Maybe they've given up. There's not much evidence," he says.

"Why were you never at school?" I ask – a meek attempt to change the subject.

"I was when we were little," he answers, a smirk in his eyes. "Nice to know you remember me."

The councillors flick the pages of the emblem books, spill raspberry wine from over-filled cups, send watchers to part couples they don't consider to be suitable matches. They don't part Wick and I, though I will them too. I feel too hot, like I'm being crushed.

"I never saw the point. Doesn't matter whether I can read, write or do a backflip off the school roof, I would always have ended a fisherman. Anyway, Father needed help to set more nets. It takes a lot of fish to feed a family as big as ours – *and* satisfy the claims. The waters aren't as full as they used to be. I *can* read and write though, don't worry," he adds.

"But you *knew* me. That night on the water, you said my name. How—"

He laughs and his eyes narrow, entertained at my apparent foolishness. He looks at me fully for the first time and I see his eyes, as raging as the sea he loves.

"I've been on the *water*, not on the *moon*!" He laughs again, and turns me in time with the music without missing a beat. "All the boys our age know *all* the girls. Surely you know that. It's all anyone ever talks about. *Who would you unite with? Who do you prefer?* You're not telling me you don't do the same?"

I blush. Of course we do. I try not to look at Tomie or think of all the times I've pretended to unite with him in the school yard, Agatha or Bertie standing in for him, though I never confessed his name – even in the game.

"It's common sense to know your enemy," he says, flicking his eyebrows into an arch, his mouth twisting with a smile – I want to take his lip and twist it harder.

"So, what did you learn?" I ask, one eye on Brack who's still watching the crowd, ears pricked.

"Let's see. Manon Pawlak," Wick says, rolling his eyes as if he's checking the pages of an invisible book. "Best friend to Agatha. Fastest girl in the school, obviously. Dreamer."

He looks up, pleased with his assessment. My heart breaks to hear myself so neatly summed up; all my strengths footnoted by the one thing he knows I most want to hide. Dreamer. Drifter. Ailment of the soul. They all amount to the same thing: a flaw. And it feels like he's mocking me.

I try to pack him into so small a box. *Wick Flint: catches fish, saved my mother's life, kept my secret. Fuck.*

I feel like my whole body – flesh, blood, bones – is nothing but a portrait of this flaw and I want to scrub it

86

from my skin. Or dig my nails into his, slice the words from his tongue with his own gutting knife.

"You planning on forming a preference for the girl with the biggest boat?" I say, too snide, too angry. He answers through a forced smile, aware of Brack watching the crowd, but he doesn't manage to smother his surprise.

"I don't think it works like that," he says "You don't *form* a preference, Manon. I think preference just *grows* … whether you want it to or not."

"Like weeds?" I hiss as the dance ends.

"No—"

"We don't let weeds grow at Wild Fell. We wrench them out before they poison everything," I say, bowing.

I turn and leave. He says something behind me, but I let the words fall, unheard.

Agatha sits on a bench with her hands in her lap, watching the debs dance. She looks tired too, a little grey, like the black of her gown is spreading through her.

"Preference formed? Story over?" she asks, only a mime of laughter in her. Everyone is forcing a smile for me today.

"For a fisherman who never even finished school?" I spit.

"Bet he doesn't smell as bad as the goat's piss," she says, a real smile warming her face, bringing her back to me a little, not enough.

"I wish he hadn't asked me to dance."

"He just did what any fisherman does," she says,

holding my chin in jest, "catch the *best* fish." She puckers her mouth into a fishy kiss, and I can't help but laugh, even though I feel like I'm lying on a slab, waiting for my scales to be sliced off, filleted into perfection.

CHAPTER SIX

Little Sheaf of Leaves

"What'll you take for the hen?" a woman asks, basket tucked into her hip. She's small – shrinking with age, the lilt of her voice different from any in Penn, a tone reserved for strangers. The borders have been opened for market day and everyone has their wares spread across tables, pitched on blankets, even those with little to trade. Even us. Our table is almost empty. The hen is the best we have so I need a good price for her. But Penn folk are suspicious of other counties and they of us.

"What have you got?" I ask and she unwraps a slab of beef skirt that makes my insides groan. It's greying around the edges but could be trimmed for a stew. A little salt if I can get some, and some of our dwarf vegetables and it might even feed us twice.

"She'll give eggs for years. That's only one meal," I barter, picking up the hen defensively. She hasn't laid for weeks. We'd have had her for a meal if we didn't think we could get more for her today. The woman rolls her eyes, considers.

"I have some kindling. You could maybe have half," she adds, gesturing at a sack she's pulling by a string. It won't feed us, but it'll save us chopping any more of the stair's spindles. Without fire, we can't cook and there's only so many raw vegetables you can eat.

"All of it," I say, the hen tucked under my arm, legs pinned in my hands. Her eyes narrow but she agrees, and we make the trade.

"It better lay," she says, stalking off, the hen clucking wildly.

I hope so too. I hate to think of the woman going hungry, spiteful as she is.

This market is different from the everyday trades of the Summit where there's only the same wares of the Penn folk. Here there's mined quartz, woven coats, clay pots, foraged mushrooms – an array of wonders from across the counties.

The ground is still slop. Even though the rain has slowed, the sun is not yet hot enough to bake it, and Father's cart has sunk into the mud already. We'll have to dig it out later. Our stall is meagre: spinach, cabbage and kale – bundles of dwarfed root vegetables, not quite ready to be pulled, but pulled all the same.

Agatha leaps over the enormous puddle that surrounds our stall. Her's is up the hill from ours, but I can see the debs clustering and clawing at every glass vial from here whilst Wren tries to fend them off, slapping their hands away until they show their trade.

"Good view," she says, pointing, and I look east to the end of her gaze where the black spirals of Wick's hair bob in a frenzy as people grab fish from his hands. He smiles coolly at each, passes the time of day, despite their grasping hunger.

I ignore her and she laughs, just as Chief Councillor Filley – a squat, slow-moving man with a horseshoe of hair at the back of his head – moves through the crowd like a plough horse. As he passes us, I smell the freshness of the fish he carries, a parcel big enough to hold a whole perch in his hand, though he gave nothing in trade.

"Unbelievable," I say, almost loud enough for him to hear.

"He has three children to feed," Agatha says, her voice soft and guilty.

"How can you sympathize with one of them?" I ask. *After what they did to you* is the part I don't say. *And what they might do to me.*

She shrugs, turns her eyes away. "His children are still children; you can't blame them."

As if on cue, a scrawny woman trails a line of children up the hill, each one tied to the other – and all tied round her own tiny stomach to keep them together. She clutches a small bag, as the children fight and tangle behind her.

"All she has is minnow. What about her children?"

I ask Agatha. She shakes her head sorrowfully but doesn't answer.

The woman stops to catch her breath. There are grey threads at her temples, a darned hole on her sleeve, sickly shadows under her eyes. The children's clothes have seam lines in odd places – across the chest, at angles – and I know she's made them from other garments, pulled apart and re-stitched time and again.

Before I can think, I've dropped the wrapped beef skirt into her basket. Agatha follows suit and drops a vial of marshmallow tincture for the children, to ward off scarlet throat, I think.

The woman feels the shift of weight and looks down, looks at us both, and ponders – suspicious of these girls from another county, one of whom is a decom – then squeezes my wrist, smiles at Agatha, and walks on without words. I try not to regret it as I watch our stew disappear, the water in my stomach stirring.

"Go and explore, I'll manage here for a while," Father says as he appears from behind Whinny, who he has tethered to a stake hammered into the ground. "Not busy today." He throws a pile of rocks around the bottom of the stake to stop it from slipping in the wet ground and wipes his hands on his trousers as he walks towards us. He hasn't noticed the hen is gone, nor asked what I took for her.

"We could walk along the harbour," I say to Agatha, but she shakes her head.

"I have to help Wren," Agatha says, tiptoeing over the puddles back to her stall. Each step feels like a step away from me, and from us. The distance that began to divide us on pledge day is growing every day.

I walk alone, not caring for the colourful stalls or the hawkers who thrust their goods in my face. I am locked away in that other place, a world of my own making. Until I see Tomie. He's helping a man carry a table down the hill, slipping and sliding as they go, their boots leaving muddy tracks in the grass. I watch his strained smile, flexed shoulders, until they're out of sight.

Tomie's stall is full of things I could never hope to own, a dressing table with elaborately turned legs; delicately carved trinket boxes; polished wooden toys. I try to pass by, but I can't resist running my fingers over the things his have touched, linger over the handle of a fine mirror, which has acorns and leaves carved into its frame. Next to it lies a matching comb, another little sheaf of leaves sprouting from it. I let myself imagine owning such a thing, wearing it at the next ball, threading it into my unruly flames of hair, but it's an idle daydream. If I trade for anything so frivolous, it will not be for me. I put it down and pick up the mirror, which feels heavier than it should be because it is not a trade I want to make. Debs are expected to give a union gift to their new mother-in-law. Something that shows sacrifice. If I show up empty-handed, I'll never get on. Especially if I'm united across the borders.

"Would you take these for the mirror?" I ask Mrs Samms, laying out some of Mother's linen — embroidered handkerchiefs and tablecloths — but keep the very best piece in my sack. Standard practice for all trades.

"It's fine work," she says, turning each piece over to look at the back, which is as neat as the front. Her eyes widen but she keeps her voice flat, flings the linen down. "It's not quite what we need just now — there's better things to trade for at this time of year."

"As you please," I say, folding the linen slowly. "But isn't Tomie uniting this year? They'd make a fine show for the binding supper."

She glances at my emblem patch. All debs have to wear their emblem flower on their upper arm so that watchers know who is who. The rules are different during the Virtue Season. Contact, within reason, is allowed. Her small eyes do the equation. A deb, like her son.

"I should like to give the mirror as a gift when I unite," I add, a slow unease crawling through me as the reality of Virtue Season unfurls. The words come out small, too potent to speak loudly. And somewhere too is the thought of uniting with Tomie that comes unbidden, flushing my cheeks.

"Aye — it does you credit. It's proper to give your mate's mother a gift. I'd expect a good Penn girl to know that."

It is proper. I know it, and I know the hardship that will fall on me if I do not follow this custom, if my mother-in-law believes me poor or discourteous. But it will not satisfy our stomachs in the coming months. My stomach growls in protest and I almost make a different choice and walk away. But then I see Clint at the next stall, which is full of sugar and cinnamon sticks that scent the air. He licks his finger and dips it in the vat of sugar, lets it melt on his tongue with his eyes closed. And when he opens his eyes, they fall straight on me, accusatory and wide. *I know your flaw*, they say. Your time is coming.

"Take it," Mrs Samms says, snatching the pieces of linen and folding them into a neat pile. I had almost forgotten her, but I take the mirror in a hurry and stow it in my sack, guilty it's not food. The snarl in my stomach is fierce.

I turn my back on Mrs Samms and Clint and hurry away, wishing I had a cloak and a hood I could pull tight around my face. I walk into the wind, and it slaps against my cheeks, biting and chiding.

"Manon?" Tomie's ragged voice says from behind me. He has his hands on his knees and draws shallow breaths, speaking through them. His clothes are caked in mud. He must have slipped after all. Crimson creeps up my cheeks.

"What happened?" I ask, handing him one of Mother's best handkerchiefs, the one Mrs Samms didn't take. He refuses it and I'm relieved it won't spoil.

"It's steep," he says, still breathing hard, gesturing down the hill with one hand, the other still bearing his weight on his knee.

"It looked heavy."

"You've been watching me then?" he asks, straightening himself and lifting his chin. I stammer but don't reply. "He gave us a lamb for it," he says, pointing to the animal tethered to his stall, "although I'm not sure what we'll eat it on – that was *our* kitchen table," he says, laughing and smoothing his hair back from his face.

Mud has tainted the strands of blond that frame his face. "Did you want to trade for something?" he asks, looking back at the stall and my heart skitters with embarrassment.

"No. Well, your mother already helped me," I stutter, unable to look at him.

"Scraped your bones clean, no doubt. What have you taken?"

I unlace my sack and show him the mirror, not sure why I feel so ashamed, except perhaps he has guessed my reason for wanting it. He raises an eyebrow in question – but doesn't ask.

"I made that," he says, cheeks plumping with a grin.

"It's very pretty," I answer, my cheeks hot. He takes the mirror out of my hands, turns it to face me and I watch the pink flush spread through my face, deeper and darker by the second.

"As pretty as this?" he asks.

My emblem patch has wriggled down my arm again, too big after so many weeks of broth and he shuffles it back up for me, turns the flower back to the outside with such gentleness, it feels intimate. His fingers linger, light and heavy at the same time. I scan for watchers. Even the emblem patch doesn't allow for this.

"Are you looking forward to Foxfields?" he asks.

Mrs Samms is watching, smirking. I feel like the whole valley is looking, making a sport of who will unite with who and I suddenly want to shake off his grasp and hide. It is then that I see Wick, away from his stall and carrying a box with holes in the side, holding it as if it is precious. He doesn't seem to see me though – he walks right by us and I'm relieved.

"I've never seen Foxfields," I manage, trying to steer away from danger, pulling my arm gently away from his hand, but it just falls further down, his hand on mine.

"Me either. Reckon it looks much like Penn though," he says, eyes cinched in a silent laugh. "You'll save a dance for me?"

"If you like."

His smile is so warm I can't keep my own from matching it.

"Until Foxfields then," he says, releasing my hand at last. I tip my head at him and walk away, trying desperately not to look back, but my neck aches with the effort.

"Wait!" he shouts, skidding down the hill and almost knocking me over. "That mirror," he says through a laugh, "I wish you'd asked me for it."

"It's not really for me," I say.

"Aye, I reckon I knew that already," he says, with a knowing look. "But… Well, it's part of a set, you see." He opens his hand and tucked inside is the comb, leaves almost alive in the light. He must have seen me looking at it. A fresh bloom of red singes my face. "Acorns are part of my emblem," he whispers, putting his lips so close to my ear it feels like a kiss. They brush my cheek as he pulls back from me. "See," he says as he taps the patch on his arm where a bouquet of leaves and acorns circles his bicep like a bracelet. Wearing the comb will be like sharing a secret with him.

"I can't take it. I have nothing to trade."

"I wouldn't take anything if you had. I want you to have it," he says, and when I don't take it, he slides it into my hair, gathering it up on one side. He lets his fingers tangle in my hair, trailing them down to the end. Each hair thrills to the root and, for a second, I allow that sensation to move through me. I think I even close my eyes.

"Wear it for me," he says, his fingers coming to rest on my collarbone. His eyes burn. "There's a place on the moor," he tells me, his voice quiet and needful, his lips close to mine. "We can be alone—"

But a watcher's cloak swishes, and he steps back, leaving me breathless.

"Until Foxfields," he says, walking backwards up the hill, smiling – a shimmering, reckless thing.

☽

Father is talking to a stocky man whose back is turned,

but I know the broad shoulders and steady stance, the greying curls. It is the older man from that night on the water, Wick's father. He chuckles and Father laughs in return, sharing a private joke.

"Thanks for the fish, Gillam," Father says, taking a parcel from the man who pats him on the back.

"Anytime, Trent."

What has he given for that?

"Plenty left today," Gillam says as he leaves, nodding as he passes me. I nod in reply, fearing the words that'll come if I speak. I want to tell him that we owe him nothing, to leave our family alone. But I let him pass without speaking.

Father hands me a spade and sets to a leg of the stall with a similar one. It's time to go home. I am strong, have a sure swing, but the ground is boggy, and my boots are swollen with mud. I'm becoming the mud – or it's becoming me.

"What did you give for the fish?"

"Nothing. He thought your mother might like some – make her strong."

"Another favour we can't return. They are determined to own us."

"Don't be so ridiculous. They're just being friendly. They are Penn folk, like us."

"Mother is from Foxfields," I remind him and regret it when I see the way his shoulders fold. "What were you laughing about?" I ask between swings.

"Just our season. Nothing criminal!"

"Why? Were the Flints in the same year as you?"

"No – they're older. They've had children unite already. Mrs Flint's another on the way, Gil says."

I hate the way he calls him "Gil" as if they're old friends.

"Just two old men reflecting on how the world turns, is all. Nothing changes."

My shovel clangs against a leg of the cart and a bit of wood splinters off, lodges in the thick of my thumb. I pull it out with my teeth, suck the bead of blood, swing again and stagger. My strength is no match for my hunger today. But I am determined.

"Mind out or we'll be digging *you* out," someone says, the sound new but familiar. Wick catches me, though there was no danger of me falling, and holds me steady like he's planting a tree. He tries to wipe the mud from my face, and I check my hair in a panic, relieved I put Tomie's comb in my pocket.

"Leave it. I'm fine," I say, wiping the mud out of my eyes with the back of my even muddier hand, the gritty wetness of it smearing down my face.

"Of course you are," he offers, the sound of his laughter lodging somewhere dark inside me. He takes the shovel out of my hands. "But you'll have your eye out if you carry on. Or worse still, mine."

He begins to swing the shovel, shoulders rolling under his light shirt, and has the leg free in seconds.

"I could've done it."

"I know," he says, and it sounds true in his mouth. He's barely out of breath, his words are crisp and even. I remind myself it's because he has a ready supply of food. "But it doesn't hurt to accept help either." He raises a hand to shield his eyes from the low sun. "There's no shame in it."

He holds the shovel out for me to take it back, and I snatch it from him then feel foolish.

"Thank you," I say reluctantly.

"You're welcome, Manon Pawlak, fastest girl in school." I can't tell if he's mocking me, it feels like a compliment and an insult all rolled up in one. "Make any good trades?" he asks, and I tuck the comb deeper inside my pocket, the tiny stabs of the tines laced with a secret shame.

"Salt," I lie.

"Nothing else?" he asks, and I wonder if he saw Tomie and I together. There's a question mark shaped in his eyes.

"We've not much need of anything else," I lie again. "You?"

"We've had a good day," he says. "Lots of fish to trade." He looks at a box he's stashed on the back of the cart that's punctured with holes. The one he carried down the hill whilst I was with Tomie. He doesn't tell me what's in it, but it's moving as if something is living inside. He rests his hand on it so it can't wriggle to the floor.

"Mother's getting ready for another babe," he says

affectionately, "found herself a crib." He smiles, and I imagine him holding a tiny brother or sister in his arms, throwing them up with glee when they're older, the laughter filling his house. It suits him. I always wished I'd had a sibling. And I envy him his security of home too. He will stay when he unites.

"Although we've been left with some things we can't make use of," he adds, gesturing at the box with a nod. "Someone left this on our hands."

He taps the top of the box and tips his head in farewell, leaving the box behind. He doesn't look back, though I watch him go, and I don't protest this time. I hope it's simply a gesture of friendship and not some bargain I don't understand.

When I open the box, there's an eruption of sweet sound, the faint tweets of a whole brood of chicks, just balls of yellow fur squatting inside, all bunched together and chirruping in harmony. A high trade.

"Not sure if they're any good to you," Wick yells over his shoulder, "but you're welcome to them." I'm glad he doesn't look back now because my chest explodes with relief and gratitude and hope, all rolled into a tiny yellow ball.

I check the chicks, trace the curve of their wings. Five hens and three roosters.

"Let's go," Father says as I put the lid back on. It's in the sound of his voice too.

"Home," I say, wanting Wild Fell to be my home for

ever, though I know my time in it is coming to an end. But when I am gone, they will have food. The means to trade. And it is all because of the boy on the water.

CHAPTER SEVEN

An Audible Ache

"Father is uniting again," Agatha says, her voice as dry as the air.

"What? Why?"

"There's a woman been widowed in Stone who's still viable. They're sending her here."

"How old is she?"

Agatha shrugs and says, "I don't know. I'm not going to meet her. I'll be gone before she arrives."

She means when she ascends to whatever duty she is assigned. The council call it *ascension* as if the decoms are reaching a higher plane. But it is the last acknowledgment that Agatha's first life is over and her new life as decom will truly have begun. We have been avoiding that truth for months, talking around the edges of it. I hope she ascends to be a scholar's assistant at Stone, or an aid to Mrs Byrd, Penn's medic. But it could just as easily be the molten heat of the scrappers, where they melt down salvaged metal and beat it into new shapes. Or worse.

I search for something to say but I am empty. There are no words to lift the weight of the world that pulls at her shoulders.

"She's a daughter coming with her. About Wren's age, I think."

The air feels charged, the sun hot. The other debs sit in the school yard, the last time we'll ever do it. When school finishes at the end of the day, we'll no longer be children. Not yet wives either. It is a strange in-between: fresh and stagnant at the same time. It amazes me, the way the other debs laugh lightly, excited and hopeful. The sun is unrelenting, baking and compressing every strand of feeling into something more. We're fraying away from each other.

"They'll be needing her house," I say bluntly. The world seems to be shrinking as the population grows, and every year, when debs unite, homes have to be found.

"Aye, for some new couple. After the unions," she says.

I should reach out to her, take her hand. But I don't. She is about to lose everything: Alsis, her family, me. I see it through her eyes, and I want to hold her. But I see me there too, the world she wants at my feet. The council unaware of my flaw. My inability to embrace it all and be happy. Some part of her blames me. So, I don't hold her, though I know it will bring me shame later.

Instead, I think of Wild Fell. It is already so much

smaller than it was, so many of its fields claimed and given away. The house could be taken too, once Mother and Father have no children at home, just as this woman's house is being taken, and if I am beyond Penn's walls, I won't even know what happens to them.

"At least your father will keep the house. Wren will have a home," I say brightly, taking a length of Agatha's hair and twiddling it between my fingers, the way we used to when we were young, the way the other debs do. But it feels silly now, like trying to calm a lion by stroking its mane.

"Until she ascends to duty," she says, "and then the Dell will be for his new family. It'll be like we were never even here."

Of course. How careless of me. When she is eighteen, after her season ends, Wren will be chattel for anyone who cares to have a field hand, or a nursemaid … or a councillor's maid. She will be no more than a commodity that anyone can apply to own. Even if the council recognize her as skilled, even if she is assigned a key role, like Miss Warne, she must live in a watcher's house, report there at the end of every shift.

Agatha's face is blanched, stone white, despite the dry heat of the day, but her eyes are wild and full. I don't know what to say, or do, so I just hold on to the strand of hair, as if I can hold on to *us*.

The other girls gossip about the ball, smiling at the sound of some boy's name on their lips, the whispered syllables of the boy they prefer. They braid and un-braid one another's hair, still in that place of joy and hope that Agatha and I have been forced to leave behind. There's a lightness to them that doesn't reach us on the little mound of grass that's always been ours, set apart from them.

It is our spot where we have sat almost every day of our lives, shaded by the boughs of an ash tree that guarded our secrets always. But it's a long time since the ash tree sheltered us in dappled shade. It is a skeleton tree, like all the other ash trees in the valley that slowly died and became extinct. Now, its boughs reach over us like bones, and don't deter the beating heat of summer.

It has always been Agatha and me versus the other girls. It was funny before. As if we were right and they were wrong. But today, I feel as though it was a mistake to make Agatha my world. I won't have her much longer. I won't have the others either. Before I'm ready, I realize that this is the moment our world ends. When school finishes, we'll no longer belong to each other.

Next year's debs have their eyes on our spot already – even this small piece of land is a battle.

I bring out Tomie's comb and hold it out for Agatha to see. I want to tell her everything – the way she told me about Alsis all those years ago. I think back to that day, the way we had argued, how fiercely I had reprimanded her, how defiant she had been. I didn't understand. I still don't. And I don't think she'll understand about Tomie either. But I have to tell her because shutting her out is the same as letting her go.

"Nice," she says, blinking the tears away before they fall. She rights her voice too, the sheared edges of the sound smooth again. It reminds me of the way you'd smooth out the wrinkles from your dress. "Where did you get it?" she asks, taking it from my hand. She handles it lightly, strokes the tines, presses her thumb against the sharp ends, which leave a dent in her skin.

"Tomie gave it to me."

She gapes at me. I'm not used to seeing shock in her eyes. Stubborn humour, fear and anger, but not this. It shakes the last of the wild weariness from her, which makes me smile through my awkwardness. I try to commit it to memory, commit her to memory.

"Has he told you he'll state a preference?"

"No…"

"But he *will*."

"I don't know. He hasn't said so. He's promised me nothing. Except a dance at Foxfields."

"Do you prefer him?" she asks, her eyebrows arching.

"I don't know… I've danced with him once and talked to him twice. How could I know?"

"You just know," she says, eyes turned inwards. "If it's really right, you'll know."

She rolls her thumb over the acorn, carved in relief. It seems so sensual — to caress the emblem of a boy like that. I stay silent.

She doesn't laugh or ridicule me, as I'd hoped she would, as she *normally* would. But she smirks a little when she asks, "What about Wick?"

"What about him?"

"He likes you."

I handle the words in my mind, turning them over and over as if to assess their authenticity. I shrug, admitting nothing, confessing nothing, and she lets it go, looks over my shoulder at the fence and the boys beyond it. Tomie will be there, and Alsis too.

"I'm not like you," I say, shame rolling through me because I cannot feel for Tomie the way she does about Alsis. I let the other thought fly before it tries to land, the one that's an echo of her words: what about Wick?

"Not *flawed*?" she says, a thickness in her voice that catches me by surprise.

"No – that's not what I meant." I scramble for the words that will make it right. "You know I don't think that." She smiles but there's still something jagged in it. "I just don't think I can love someone the way you do. Maybe it's not in me."

Her lips pucker as if she's sucking on something bitter, and she looks beyond me to the fence.

"Well, if you don't state a preference for Tomie, you're a fool," she says, her voice creeping with anger.

"Do you think I should?"

"I'd do it just for his forearms," she says, and I see a faint shimmer of her old self. "His family don't have any other children. Carpenters are an essential trade. You'll have a good life. You'll inherit the business and have food. Maybe that's better than love," she spits, cold, more distant, prodding the facts as if checking fruit for its ripeness. "Would you rather end up with someone you don't even know? Or across the border?"

"Do you think they really do match preferences?"

"Probably not, but it's worth a try. And it's better to have someone with a solid trade who can give you a future. They could pair you with a layman with no land or trade."

Trailing a line of children, each one tied to the other.

"You can choose, or the council can. Maybe you're right. Maybe you don't need love," she continues.

My stomach rolls. I didn't say I didn't need love, just that I don't know if I'm capable of it. It's one more rip of the threads between us, like she's tearing them deliberately now.

"I think it's what drove her to it. Mother."

"How so?"

"Living without love," I admit, even now wishing that loving Father could have kept her from the water. "What if I am like Mother? What if I can't be happy in my union?"

"Then you deserve to be unhappy," she says, shooting for mocking and spearing cruel. She'd have covered it better before the season began. She has always fought through pain – even before the seizures, and before

110

the decommissioning. It was her way. But now it's as though she's a cannister filling with liquid, about to overspill.

She's still holding the comb.

I snatch a look at the fence where Tomie is talking to a crowd of boys. His eyes meet mine and he smiles, sleeves rolled up, forearms browned, as carved as the wood he turns on his lathe.

"At least you get to unite with *someone*," she says at last, following my gaze, and there's a little relief in the words, as if the words have set her free. It's as if a breath of wind has crossed the path of the sun. "Maybe you should be thankful you get to run from *your* secret – it's not as easy to *see* an ailment of the soul."

It is the second time she's used this phrase. *An ailment of the soul.* She has always called me a drifter. I wish she would say it now. It feels like she's turning against me. "Not everyone's as lucky as you."

The size of her words fit the hole in my chest like a fist. She digs her fingers into her temples, fighting the storm in her head.

"Didn't Miss Warne say something about a teaching apprenticeship?" I ask desperately, trying to turn the rudder away from the squall.

"Aye. The elevens' teacher is being retired. I could be trained in time to take up post in autumn."

"You'd be *here*. If I state a preference for Tomie, I'd stay in Penn, and we'd be together."

It's the first time I've really imagined doing it, and it feels OK.

"But I'd be under Torrent's supervision, like Miss Warne."

I don't miss the fear in her eyes, though she's quick to smother it. I remember the bright red pin marks on Miss Warne's face.

"You'd have a decent share of the claims, live above the schoolhouse with Miss Warne—"

"Brack permanently watching?" she says. I don't look, but I feel him looming in his tower. How much worse must his shadow be over her?

"I don't want to lose you," I say, my voice a guilty whisper.

"How many decoms have you seen with united women, Manon? Do you think I'll get a script to visit you?"

I shake my head, look down at a patch of sun-soaked grass, brown and coarse. No, she wouldn't be given permission. We'd see each other in passing, that's all, a core of remembrance faded between us. Worse than separation.

"You could apply to *own* me," she says bitterly.

I consider it. I could unite with Tomie, ask for a decom to help around the house, do chores.

"You'll have a family. *Children*." She says the word as if its sharpness will cut her tongue. "You're going to get through this; unite – with Tomie or Wick or someone else, it doesn't matter – and then you'll forget. You'll all forget."

"No—"

"And the irony is, you don't even *want* it."

There's an audible ache in her voice that cuts me to shreds.

And then the anger comes, as fast and fierce as a stampede of horses over my chest.

"You think it's easier for me?" I ask, my voice quiet but bursting. The other girls don't look at us, Brack doesn't step down from his tower, because we are quiet and still. Our friendship doesn't explode, it implodes. "It's just a *different* sort of black," I say. "I might not wear the dress, but the shadow's the same. They're taking my life from me too."

There isn't a breath of wind. The heat throbs.

"I tried to protect you, Ag. I *tried*…"

"Don't," she says, eyes flashing feral.

"I know you've lost Alsis, your family, your future. But is my life any better?"

"It could be if you let it."

"You're wrong. I have no choice. I'll be united – but it might be with a boy I barely know. They might send me to another county with a boy I *hate*, to be hated by his family for ever."

"You can *choose* to be happy as long as you're safe."

"Safe? If I don't produce a healthy child within three years of uniting, I'll be decommissioned. Let's say I find a mate who makes me happy and have a healthy child. Clint's report could still ruin it all – it still hangs over me."

I look up at Brack in his tower, imagine him examining me from a distance. Yes, the threat is still there. I still feel it.

"You could tell them."

It doesn't dawn on me straight away what she means. Until I see it in her eyes.

"You could come with me," she murmurs, close to weeping, hugging her knees.

I could. I could go to Brack and confess, tell him of my inherited flaw – and we'd stay together, ascend together. Cheat the system. I *want* to…

"You don't prefer Tomie – or Wick. You don't want this, you never have."

She's right. I open my mouth to say "yes" – and then she says, "You *are* like your mother. There's no shame in it."

A bruise purples the edge of the idea. Agatha and I are together, but Mother's there too, *decommissioned* too. And there's Father's face, tattooed with everlasting pain. I can't do that to them.

She sees it in my face and her own collapses from hope to despair. Then spite.

"*I* could tell them," she says, her voice a desperate growl. "I could tell Brack right now – just march up to his tower, yell for Tomie to hear—"

"But you won't," I say, crawling nearer to her, grabbing at her hands that fight against me. "We *protect* each other. We always have," I plead.

Her eyes are vacant of everything but pain, a flood of it, dark and murky and stormy.

"You're wrong if you think I'll forget you, Ag. I *am* you – and you are me," I say.

She stands, and I blink into the sun, the watery sun that seems to bleed with tears.

"I'll forget *you*," she says through gritted teeth. "If it's the last thing I do, I'll forget you. I *swear*," she spits and throws Tomie's comb to the ground, splintering one of the tines.

"State your preference, Manon Pawlak," she commands, an echo of the preference ceremonies, and a chill slides into my bones that I know will never leave me.

Agatha, Thirteen

Agatha knew this boy. She saw him every day. He was her neighbour. Her father worked for his. But her heart was pounding at the sight of him so near. A boy. In her house. A place where a boy should never be. And not just any boy but The Boy. He was an idea that had been slowly forming inside her, bigger and bigger all the time. So big now, she could explode.

"Mother isn't here," she said. He looked around as if to check. "She's gone to the Summit to trade for flour and eggs."

The boy nodded. Smiled. They were alone, except for Wren who was only seven and was busily cleaning a jar of apricot preserve with her sticky fingers. His sandy hair hung over his eyes, tickling his nose. He flicked his head to shift it and dropped more of the fleece as he did.

She could hear her father's rough grunts from the window. He was shearing the sheep whose wool the boy had brought. Perhaps it would be all right then, to let the boy come in, if Father had sent him. She knew she should not be near boys. It was not just a threat from her parents. Boys were dangerous. Miss Warne had taught them so. But this was for Mother's work. And anyway, this boy was no wolf. He had come dressed as a sheep; his arms full of the cloudlike substance that Agatha's mother turned to wool.

She went to him, took an armful of fleece, and stashed it in the crate beside Mother's spinning wheel, next to the hearth. It was invitation enough and he knelt beside her, helping her fill the crate a handful of fluff at a time.

"Your name's Agatha," he said, but he sounded uncertain, and his forehead puckered as if he was wondering if he had misheard the name.

She was only thirteen, but she already felt the shame of her name in his mouth. He was a boy. He was not meant to speak it. And yet it sounded so musical.

Shame was what school was for, she thought. She had understood early that it was not letters or numbers that mattered, but obedience and guilt. It was to teach you how to behave, how to be virtuous at times like this. How to be scared. That was what the stories in the Mythic were for, all neatly bound in leather to keep the cautionary tales inside. But she could not resist the pretty sound of her own name on this boy's lips. It did not sound wrong. It sounded pure and whole, and made her shiver warmly. She wanted him to say it again.

"Aye," she said simply in return, and he smiled, made happy just by knowing the word that was hers. As if saying it out loud meant he owned it now too. She did not say his name, though she felt it on her tongue, and she did not take the piece of fleece from his hair – too afraid to risk touching him, although she did want to know what his hair felt like to touch, whether it felt as soft as the fleece or as coarse and scratchy as the jumpers Mother made from it.

"I'm Alsis," he said, offering his hand, and dropping it with a forlorn look when she did not dare to take it. The dashed hope in his eyes made her sad to her bones. But still, she did not dare.

"Have you ever been to Jaynie's Foss?" she asked instead, not really knowing why, but thinking how nice this boy would look amongst the moss and the rocks and pooling water that was so like his eyes, and thinking how nice it would be to go there with him, if only she could find some secret way to do it. She imagined the way the dappled light would make his dusty hair blond.

"We swim there in winter, though it's dry just now," he said.

"I hate the summer," she said.

"And winter too." He laughed. "It's hard to know which is worse: the endless rain or the baking drought."

"I prefer the endless rain. If there's firewood," she admitted, knowing there often is not.

"I'll bring some this winter."

Their eyes connected in a way that their hands might one day. There was nothing else to say. Unless she said the things she knew she should not.

"You'll bring more fleece?" she asked, staring at the crate instead of into his eyes. The crate was already crammed and overflowing with fleece. "Mother is making jumpers for the market," she added, her cheeks flaming.

"Of course. We have plenty," he said with an eager, ready smile. "Though Father is keeping some to trade with the Pawlaks for mulch and some for the claims."

She knew the word *claims*. She had heard her parents use it in whispered, desperate voices. It was one of the council's words, a word to be feared, like all their words. Though she did not fully understand what it was, not yet, not in the way she would come to later, when her parents could no longer shield her from the truth of the valley and it became synonymous with other words, like "hunger" and "injustice" and "horror" and "blame".

"I'll take the fleece to Manon," she offered, knowing she would be allowed a script for such a reason. Clint would allow her that. If not for a visit to the Foss.

She was full of the need to tell her friend about this boy and his quiet eyes, the way they saw inside her, the way they opened him up to her so that she could see inside him too. How it was terrifying and tender and glorious all at once. Manon would not approve. She did not yearn for their season the way Agatha had begun to.

Alsis turned to go, a smile spreading through his features that told her he would be back soon. She did not say goodbye. There was no need. Between the two of them, such a word would never exist.

"I prefer you already," he said through a grin, and she tried to place this word as one she knew too. Like the other, it was a council word but there was no pain or suffering or injustice in this one. She liked it. It sparkled. It made Alsis sparkle too. But best of all, it sparkled in her stomach, spinning and hopeful and brave.

CHAPTER EIGHT

Fire Angel

At the school gates, the debs are hugging and crying, saying goodbye for the last time, as if we aren't going to see each other again. As if we aren't neighbours. I try to feel the same pain, but all I feel is the desperate desire to run far away from them, and from Agatha who is still inside, saying goodbye to Miss Warne. I had hoped she would come out, and walk home with me like always – one last time – but she hasn't.

I almost wish the unions were today, and we really were leaving each other here at the gates; I even long to be united across the borders, where all this would be just a distant memory I could tidy away and bring out to shine up occasionally.

"It's the end of an era, isn't it?" Bertie says, her bright eyes shimmering, and I wonder if I'll ever see her without tears in her eyes. She seems to have a whole library of them, for all sorts of occasions, like books selected from a shelf. These ones gather in pools but don't fall.

"I'm sure I'll see you soon," I say, returning the hug she's inflicted on me as best I can. Her head comes up to my chin and her hair grazes my jaw. "The season has only just begun."

"Aye," she says. "Have you made a preference yet?"

I'll never understand how they discuss it so openly. I only shrug. I try to smile at the kind girl in front of me, but I've said my unwilling goodbye to Agatha – or she has said it to me at least – and I don't care to say it to anyone else, so an awkward silence settles on us, and she has to admit defeat.

"See you soon then."

I leave them all standing there and head for the gravel path that leads out on to the moor.

"Can I walk with you?" Tomie asks, catching up with me on the path outside the gate, the stones crunching under his feet. A cluster of boys titter, but he waves them off and they turn away, back to each other, gossiping as much as the girls. If Tomie hadn't stopped me, I'd have run all the way home – or climbed the rocks at Jaynie's Foss, let the lactic acid burn through me, through all this. But he's here, and part of me is happy.

"OK," I say, thinking about the comb stashed in my pocket, stroking its tines, the broken splinter spiking my thumb. And we walk on, our rhythms not quite matched, as though our legs understand the awkwardness between us.

We leap the stone wall at the end of the lane, on to the moor that winds up and arcs down again, back to Wild Fell. Tomie's gaze is heavy. Though I don't turn to see it, I feel it fall on me, as if he wants to ask me something, or he's trying to read something in me. It's as hot as the sun.

"It looked like you and Agatha were having an argument," he says, and I can tell it's not the words he wants to say, but the first footstep towards them. "Are you OK?"

He is so close beside me that his arm brushes mine.

"It must be hard for her," he says.

I nod. I'm still angry, but not with Agatha now. I hate the council for taking my only friend away, and I hate Alsis for letting her love him, even when he knew it would come to this. But mostly I hate myself.

Tomie and I head on to the open moor, to the kiss gates. The word hangs invisibly between us as I pass through. *Kiss gate.* Such a childish thought that flowers with something not childish at all. The second stalls and stretches.

I push through the metal gate, swinging it too hard, so that it clangs behind me and breaks the spell, and I am at the very top of the valley, nothing but open sky and rolling land as far as the eye can see. The hills meet each other like baking bread, rising into each other.

Tomie catches up to me and I hear the gate bang closed, and we stand for a second, looking out at the small world that seems so huge up here.

"I'm glad school is finished," he says. "No more boring lectures."

I laugh, a breathy, silent thing.

"What about you? Aren't you glad it's over? I never liked the look of Miss Warne – like a gnarly tree," he says, with a mock tremble. I stand more upright.

"She never liked me, but she always knew how to make things interesting," I say defensively. "Her stories were the best. She had a way of telling them – with her hands." I gesture with my hands, mimicking the way she used hers to tell the stories from the Mythic, and it brings a smile to my lips I hadn't expected. I feel sorry I hadn't lingered with the others, said our last goodbyes. "I used to think if you tied her hands up, she wouldn't be able to speak." He nods and I think I see an apology in his eyes.

"Well, thank your lucky stars you didn't have Mitton then. He was as dull as notchwort, stiff as a rod," he says, scraping a piece of notchwort from the moor and flinging it at me. It hits me on the chest, leaves a dusty stain that will pat off easily, dry as the earth is now. I pick up a piece and throw it at him, though a little mechanically, as if I'm playing a part I know is expected.

We walk on but he walks slower than me, even though I know his natural pace is a gallop. I've watched him race home a million times before, his long legs striding almost impossible lengths, imagining racing him up the hill and winning, though I never did try.

Mother wouldn't have liked it. So we walk at an amble that neither of us is used to.

"Your folks are well?" he asks, a polite question but it reminds me of Clint's report, and I wonder if he knows, search for it in his eyes, a tiny fleck of black somewhere in their metallic glint. If he knows, he doesn't show it.

"Aye. We've had a good crop this year," I answer, "we dug irrigation ditches, which seem to have saved the harvest."

"I'm glad," he says. "It's been a tough year, especially for you…"

So he does know. I think of the way he trembled at the thought of Miss Warne, and imagine him reacting that way towards Mother, and me. My chest tightens. The moor is getting steeper and as my legs tense into the climb, that familiar release comes. I can rely on it always. My pace quickens and the caustic burn swallows the other pain – the one I left at the school gates. Tomie gives a gentle pull on my hand, slows me to a stop, forces me to turn and face him. He is standing downhill from me but still stands over me, so I have to look up.

"Don't be in a hurry," he says, brows knitting, "we've a while until sun fall and this is it until Foxfields. It's our only chance to talk without anyone watching."

Something has steadied in his voice, a decision made, and he's already sitting on the grass, unbuttoning his doublet and spreading it out next to him for me to sit on. I'm caught between the relief the climb is beginning to bring and a different need I don't understand.

"Sit with me," he says, something in his voice pulling at me now, joining with his hand, invisible but strong.

We are completely alone, far ahead of the others who lingered at the gates. There are no watchers this far on to the moor – just the vast expanse of hills, blanched white by the sun. I sit, careful to leave space between us. Even here, even where no one sees, I need that space, like a friendly fence.

The moor is dry, strewn with bedstraw. I pluck the white fronds and twiddle them between my fingers whilst Tomie hums to himself, leans back on his elbows. The hills undulate, hide us in their curves, like we're the last two people on Earth. Stone is microscopic, far across the water and Castle Hill floats between it and us. I wonder if the councillors can see this far. It feels as if they could – as if their scopics are on us now. I know they can't see this far. Even through a scopic, we'd only be blobs on the moor, but it doesn't stop me feeling captured in their lens.

"I was hoping we'd get a chance to talk before Foxfields," Tomie says, "just us." He sits up and strips a purple heather down its shaft, flinging the buds on to the moor. "The season is going by so fast. Soon, all my chances will be gone, and the balls aren't good for talking."

"It feels like everything is speeding up," I say. "I'm afraid I'll blink, and it'll all be decided."

"Aye. The preference statements aren't far off. Maybe it's best to get a head start on decisions."

The end of his nose is turning pink in the sun's gaze but it's his words that catch fire in me, blaze red, and I hear my own breathing, loud and sharp, squeezed.

"I like you," he says simply, braiding the stems of the barren heather into twists.

I like you too.

I almost say it, despite myself. For the blond hair that shimmers gold as he concentrates on his twisted creation. He tosses it away, looking directly at me, eyes grey and shining, waiting. I want to take his face in my hands, say things I think I mean – but when I try to think beyond this moment, everything is black. I can't see it. And I can't make any promises to Tomie – or myself.

"I know," I say, heart beating. "But it all feels so rushed. And they're always *watching* – I don't know how to feel."

"I know it's hard. I do understand that – and I would never push you," he says. "There's still time. We have Foxfields and Stone and Castle Hill, but I want you to know I've decided, even if you haven't. I thought, if you knew that, you might start to think about it. That's all I'm asking." He sighs, staring at the flat heat of the moor, hazy and swirling. I feel like *I* am hazy and swirling.

He takes my hand, circles my palm with his finger. The slow touch burns the space where chastity checks have left me sore again. No one is watching. I check.

The sun has dipped and spread across the moor. I'm exhausted. I feel as though I've been shoving my shoulder up against the world for a long time. So I give in, lie back, one arm over my eyes to shield them from the winking sun and Tomie lays down too, our hands still linked, stretching into the open space between us. I imagine turning on to my side, silently asking for more. A touch – a kiss maybe. I want so badly to do it – to lose myself to this feeling. I can almost feel the flame of his lips on mine and know it will happen if I let it. Tomie will risk his life and mine. *I* will risk his life and mine.

The Chastity Rule must be observed. Infringements will invoke the death penalty.

It is not the thought of death that makes me move but the thought that giving into him is a promise I do not know if I can keep. I cannot make this promise. Not yet.

"I need to get home," I say, breaking my hand from his and standing abruptly. He sits up slowly, shakes himself out of the daze we'd got lost in together.

"Father will be ravenous. Mother's a terrible cook."

"Wait, I'll walk with you," he says.

"No," I say, veering off in the opposite direction of Wild Fell. "I have to go by Jaynie's Foss – pick some herbs."

He squints at me, confused.

"OK," he says. "At Foxfields then?"

"At Foxfields."

He is shielding his eyes and I'm suddenly aware of the burn of the sun on my back, the way it must burst out from behind me.

"You're the Fire Angel," he says. "You have wings."

The Fire Angel wraps you in borrowed sun to protect you from evil. Miss Warne told us that story too. She lends you its light, which burns around you always in life, until your death sends it back to the sky, back to the Fire Angel.

"It's just a children's story," I mutter.

He steps towards me, slow and quick all at once, and takes my hand in his, pulls me close into him until his lips are so close to mine they're almost touching. I think of the kiss gate again, the childish hope that seems to have ripened into fullness now. We breathe each other's breath, in and out, rhythmic and soft as he pushes one hand through my tangle of red hair.

"That's what I thought. But here you are. *My Fire Angel*."

PART TWO

"There must be, in every case,
a struggle for existence."

Charles Darwin, *On the
Origin of the Species*

CHAPTER NINE

Black Shadowy Horizon

Half of Penn's debs are knotted into Father's cart for the journey to Foxfields, which is half a day's ride away. It is early afternoon, but we are dressed in our Penn gowns, and ready for the evening's ball, sweat sopping them through, freshly pinned hair sliding down our faces already. I have a fan made of hen's feather but the effort of waving it seems to heat me more than it cools me so I stop and hope the speed of the cart will bring the sweet relief of a breeze.

"On we go then," Father shouts, lashing Whinny, who nickers and rears, the cart shaking until she finds a trot and it seesaws on. There are shrieks and laughs as we're all thrown skyward.

The road is rough; weeks of beating sun has split the ground with cracks and crevices, and we bounce wildly, cling to each other, or the sides of the cart, choking on the dust stirred up by its wheels. The faint smell of salt stains the heat, the air as dry as old bones.

"I wish I'd brought a cushion!" Bertie says, laughing with a closed mouth to avoid the dust. She's crushed between me and Rosie, and her limbs seem to have lost all sense of gravity as she jolts around, swinging first into me and then into Rosie. I smile back and feel the gritty mist of dust coat my teeth and prick the back of my throat with thirst. Wild Fell's well is almost dry now and filling a flask would have been a waste when there's water waiting at the ball.

Agatha is hemmed into a corner by Tabithe, the spiteful girl who bit her on the first day of school. Every time the cart lurches, Agatha clouts into Tabithe with a momentum that comes from her long-held fury, rather than the movement of the cart. I try to catch Agatha's eye, but she refuses to let me share the humour, looks everywhere but at me.

"Who are you going to dance with?" Bertie asks.

"I don't know," I lie.

"Didn't you dance with that fisherman at Penn? Will … Wilf?"

Agatha is pretending not to listen, but I can almost see her ears flex.

"Wick. Aye, I danced with him once."

"Maybe he'll ask you again."

My stomach leaps as if the cart has heaved, but the ground here is flat. I smooth an imaginary crumple on my lap, rearrange the dress, the colour of ripe rhubarb.

"I doubt it."

"And that blonde boy from school – the tall one…"

"Tomie," I say, unable to resist the taste of his name. I haven't made a decision, I tell myself.

"He's lovely."

I see – or feel – Agatha's gaze flick away from us, though she'd been intently listening until now. She's fiddling with the bracelet on her arm, the way I've seen her do so many times when she's about to cry and is trying not to. The black of her dress is so severe next to ours, all dressed in the brightest red-hued dyes we can afford.

I look at Bertie as levelly as I can manage.

"Lovely," I agree, breathless with the thought of Tomie's lips, so close to mine on the moor. And just then, Father rolls the cart over a stone, and we all bounce so that Bertie doesn't notice the way the grin spreads through my face.

"I hope Matthie asks me again. He's from *Stone*," she warbles, her eyes widening at the dazzling mythology of the faraway place. It dazzles me too for a second. Until I remember how the people of Stone hate us for having land when all they have is books. And how I hate them for taking our food.

"I'm sure he will," I say, although I see Tabithe huff and shake her head as if she knows better. She danced with Matthie at the Penn ball too – and, whilst her mother's rounded hips have become matronly, Tabithe's still sing with the promise of something sensual. Poor Bertie.

"I wonder what it's like in Stone," Bertie says, and I wonder if she's really considered what life will be like away from home. "I suppose I'll have to dance with Joelle again. I hate him but he's determined. He's going to state a preference; he said so." She crosses her arms, sulking. "Mother wants us to unite – to keep me in Penn. And our lines are pure, so it makes sense, she reckons."

It makes me look at Father, driving the cart with Mother beside him.

"Slow down!" Mother cries, her voice echoing across the valley, dying against the hills, but Father lashes Whinny, and Mother laughs, the unfamiliar sound whirling into the sky. I send a wish with it, for this new seed of peace to grow.

☾

The sun is setting on the folding velvet hills when Foxfields appears in a dip ahead. The sky darkens quickly, and we're swallowed into the depths of the valley, the blackness distilled. The only light comes from the aestival moon and from the stars and the fire of lanterns in the distance, where Tomie flickers brightly too.

"All out," Father says, flipping the iron step into place at the side of the cart, which clangs as it lands against the wood. The debs file down, careful of their best leather shoes on the dusty road. Agatha jumps down too, her dress so dark, she fades into the night. She thanks

Father with a kiss and hurries off, disappearing into the blackness.

Foxfields is smaller than Penn, the houses all linked to each other in a maze of linear patterns. You can smell the salt pans: fresh and elemental, but the sky seems smaller, the buildings crowd us, and there are no green fields, only the green chlorite rocks of Longridge Peninsula that peter out into the sea where the houses end, the land thinning into a scaly tail. The colour of those rocks is why the Foxfields debs wear green.

Father takes my hand, raises an eye at the field boots I'm still wearing.

"What happened to the leather pumps? I traded a bag of seeds for them at the Summit," he says, and I pull them guiltily from behind my back where I'd lashed them to my belt.

"You'd better put them on," he chides. "You can't dance in boots!" He gently readjusts the comb in my hair. "Where's this from?"

"It belonged to Ag's mother," I lie, blushing invisibly in the night's shadow. Lying about Agatha's mother feels shameful and only reminds me of the many times I've listened as Agatha has sobbed for her, the many times she's begged the skies to know where she might be, what duty she ascended to.

"I'll give it back," I say when Father starts to protest at the borrowing of such a precious object.

Mother jumps down from the front of the cart and

runs ahead, grasping a woman she seems to recognize, and I remember she has come home tonight, wonder if that's why she's so merry.

Councillor Reade is standing close by and nods awkwardly to Mother as she passes. I recognize him from the fence, a small, neat man.

"He was in our year," Father says in explanation, and we walk on, hand our invitation to one of Foxfield's watchers: a man almost as square as the door he guards.

"Trent Pawlak, along with his daughter Manon," he reads suspiciously, inspecting the paper as if it might be fake. He licks his finger and tries to smudge the ink.

"You never know what families will do for a good union," he says, feeling my emblem patch with his finger and thumb, as if he'd like to smudge me the way he did the ink. "There are always some that want to force a union for the sake of *preference* or *greed*." He says both words as if they are equally ugly. "*Forge* an invite before their season so as to be united well."

"Unthinkable," Father answers, no trace of sarcasm in his voice. But no trace of fear either.

"I've even seen decoms disguised as debs," he growls, flicking his nose with his thumb. "Trying to escape ascension."

"What happened to them?" I ask.

"Hanged from a skeleton tree," he grunts. He takes the invite and gestures us in, but I hear him telling the next family more stories.

"It's not only *your* idea of love that counts," Father says, taking me by surprise when we've taken a few steps inside. My heart swallows. "You don't have to form a preference to find *real* love — sometimes love is much quieter, grows with time, and it's no less real. Preferences change, anyway. I've seen it happen."

"What if I can't change this thing in me? What if it grows into Mother's fog?"

Confessing is like throwing up. The words come out involuntarily. "You know I'm like her. I'd rather be outside this world than in it. You call it dreaming or drifting as if it's harmless but what if it's not? What if I lose myself the way she did—"

"It is not a sickness, Manon," he says quietly, gripping my arm. "What made your Mother sick was *them*, this system. It's armour to be able to dream. To see hope where there is none. It will lift you up, if you let it. *Never* be scared of who you are. But you need to know how to fight, which dreams to follow."

"But she gave up. She tried to end it."

"She had a moment of weakness in a lifetime of strength."

My throat thickens.

"I'm scared," I whisper. "I want to find happiness. I want to be strong. But it's like I have a hook pulling at my chest, a rope anchored somewhere in the darkness, and to ignore it would be to tear a hole in my chest."

"And what if the council choose wrong?"

I nod, tears springing.

"I think it's the way everyone feels at the start of their season, as though there is one person they are already attached to, someone they must find, that their heart cannot be forced, But you have a choice, Manon. You have a way to fight. Choose acceptance instead of resistance. Drift towards something rather than always away. Anchor yourself with the mate that is given you. *That* is how you win in their world."

I want to weep for him – for the rope that swims loose from his heart with no anchor. And, maybe for the first time, I want to wrap my arms around Mother too, melt her pain and mine into one. But most of all, I want to believe he's right. I think of Tomie, try to make him my anchor, but all I feel is the rush of open water.

☽

The Foxfields ballroom is smaller than ours, which makes the eyes of the council seem multiplied. Watchers line the walls and councillors peer from tables dripping with food. It is not the food of Penn. The fish is brined to preserve it and it is sliced so thin it is almost translucent. It is scarce and too salty or too smoky and doesn't taste how I know it should. The pottage is thickened with wheat kernels that stick in your teeth and the crowberry wine Mother has crooned about drinking again is bitter but somehow tasteless too.

The watchers search for infringements as if they want to find them, and the walls press in. It's so hot that most of the ball will take place outside. The debs have drifted out, dancing under a sail-like canopy that would billow in a breeze if there were one. It is the height of summer now, and it lays flat and undisturbed.

I find the water trough and drain my cup three times, then take the flask from my belt as discreetly as I can and fill it so that I can take some home, then search for Agatha or Bertie. But they are nowhere. I am alone.

I lean against a stone wall and watch the smiling partners swirl. It is a pretty scene, the way the coloured dresses of each county curl around each other, like a rainbow being stirred. County lines are blurring now; caution abandoned.

Some of the Madams dance too – if their Councillors will oblige. And their jewels glitter almost as brightly as the stars. Even Torrent dances, though his partner wears a veil. They say the woman beneath it is his decom, passed off as a Madam.

There is a sense of freedom. Preferences are blossoming under the cloudless sky. I feel it too. I want to give way to the longing and believe there is a happy ending for me, but there is still a stone wall of fear I cannot seem to shake.

I lift my face to the open sky and wonder at its oneness. No borders split the stars. No star is thought better than its neighbour, its beauty less complete. They all just belong, together in the same sky.

"I see you've had a wash," Wick says, his voice full of

mirth. Talking to him is like climbing: pain and relief as one.

"And you're just as rude as ever," I stab back, only half serious. He snorts, satisfied, leans against the stone wall next to me and we stand silently, comfortable in our discomfort somehow.

Clint's report is in the past, or maybe the future, but it is not here, not now.

Wick taps his foot to the music, missing the beat even though I know he grew up with his father playing guitar and dances as if the music swirls in his veins. I laugh.

"Something funny?" he asks, one eyebrow curling at an impossible angle that makes me laugh even more.

"During the Virtue Season? No. Absolutely nothing at all," I say, and it's so true it makes him laugh too.

"Might as well dance then?" he says, looking right at me in that unapologetic way he has. I remember that first dance – the cool coarseness of his hand in mine, the way he seemed to feel inside my flesh with it and understand me in ways I don't understand myself.

"Later," I say, looking at the floor so I don't have to see his disappointment. When I look up, he is smiling but it is a small, sad smile and I wish I had said yes.

"Later," he echoes but chews his lip, thinking. "Will you dance with Tomie if he asks?" He is still smiling but I see the other thing lurking behind it, the small, hurt thing.

"Maybe," is all I can say, and it is only then I realize I have been looking for him too.

"I suppose you should try to form a preference. If you believe the council really honour them."

"You sound like me."

"Oh dear!" He laughs and my whole body nettles with need. *For what? To strike him? To kiss him?*

"So, you *have* settled on him then?" he asks.

I shrug and let it go, though I know he'll take it as an admission. But putting him right is too complicated. I cannot unravel the knot of feeling that is tangled inside me, that tangles further every time Wick looks at me, that is knotted around Tomie too. I cannot make him understand when I do not understand it myself. And I cannot let myself make a promise the council will break with their arbitrary matches. Not to Tomie, or him – or even to myself. Wick was right. I have never believed they honour preferences.

"Have *you* settled on Sally Mason?" I ask, trying to lighten the mood. I lift my chin towards the girl he danced with at Penn, who hasn't taken her eyes off him whilst we've been talking. But it does not have the effect I had hoped. He looks startled, takes in her doe-eyed expression, and his face twists like a child on the first day of school, drowning in words he doesn't understand. "She's waiting for you to ask her," I say, and it sounds like a cruel jibe, though I hadn't meant it to. He hasn't seen what I've seen, and I know it now. He hadn't realized she was falling for him.

"I didn't realize..." he says, his shoulders collapsing. He sits on a bench and I sit beside him.

"I hope..." Wick begins. "I hope I haven't let her believe..."

"That you *prefer* her?"

He winces at the word. I know what he feels – the mess and confusion of it all. How much have I let Tomie believe before I really know what I feel myself? How much do I hurt Wick without intending it?

"I'm sorry," he says. "I shouldn't have asked about Tomie—"

"How's your mother getting on? Father told me she's expecting," I ask, before he can go on, feeling for the right string to pluck, as if he were an instrument and I a musician.

"Growing," he says, both his mouth and eyes widening into the smile of a son who loves his mother and dotes on his siblings.

"You have a big family already?"

"Aye. Plenty to feed," he answers, warming to the notes of the song I've begun.

"My sisters are united already," he adds, "outside of Penn, so there's only the five of us ... until..." He doesn't finish the sentence.

"*Only* five," I snort. "I'd have loved a brother or sister. Your folks must really have preferred each other."

How full their house must feel compared to Wild Fell.

"Not at all. They hadn't even talked before the Declaration Ceremony. And I think Mother took some

persuading, but they like each other well enough now."
His eyes simmer with mirth.

Choose acceptance, I think.

"Do your sisters prosper?" I ask.

"Aye," he says on a sigh, "though we haven't met their little ones. It's impossible to cross the borders outside of the Virtue Season these days." His forehead wrinkles and I fight the urge to run my thumb along the crease.

I see Tomie then, his hand already out to claim me from across the room, his face full of anticipation – but a boy from school stops him halfway, and begins talking in his ear, gesturing wildly with his hands, their conversation silent.

Wick has seen him too.

"I better talk to Sally," he says, getting up to go and I don't stop him.

I dance under the stars with a boy from Foxfields who sweats throughout.

"What strapping girls the Penn girls are, must be all that food they hog," he says over and over. I watch the sweat bead and trickle on his forehead and try not to slap him – and all the while Wick talks to Sally Mason in whispers, my stomach crawling as if spiders are spinning their webs. When she puts her finger to the corner of her eye to pinch away a tear, I try not to feel glad.

The ball is almost over when Tomie appears again.

"Dance with me," he urges, breathless and plum-faced. He doesn't wait, just grabs my arm, sweeps me to the middle of the dance floor, pushing through the couples to the very centre of the crowd.

Something is different. Wrong.

"I'm wearing the comb," I say, a little embarrassed, tipping my head to let him see, but he doesn't look at me, only over his shoulder. "I looked for you," I try again, but Tomie only grunts and nods. He misses a step and I trip over his foot. "What is it?" I ask, trying to get him to look at me, stopping in the middle of the dance.

"Nothing."

"Tell me."

He looks at me then, his eyes crazed and red and I think he is about to cry.

"I didn't mean to," he whispers, clutching me like a lifebuoy. "Manon, you have to help me. I didn't mean to."

"What do you—" Councillor Torrent steps into the crowd.

"Subjects of Calde Valley!"

Councillor Torrent continues to walk through his subjects as if he barely sees them. He shouts over the music, and the instruments silence one at a time so the music unravels like a loosening thread. The dancing couples stop too as he nears them, like a ripple that reaches Tomie and I last. "I must call a premature halt to tonight's proceedings. Most of you have conducted yourselves with great decorum but" – he pauses, filling us with his unspoken words – "I'm afraid there's been an infringement of the Chastity Rule."

The whole crowd sinks. Gasps. Watchers circle the dance floor like a second stone wall. My heart thunders against my ribs.

Tomie.

"*This girl* is no longer chaste," Torrent announces, a crumpled paper bag of a girl being dragged on to the stage by a pair of hungry-looking watchers. She is blonde but her hair is dishevelled and covers her face. She could be anybody.

She's crying and yelping – dangling from the watchers' hands like a pendant from a chain. There's a gash on her lip that's bleeding. A shriek comes from the back of the room that can only come from a mother.

"There can be no doubt," Torrent says, as he reaches the stage and mounts the steps, putting his palm on the top of her head as if absolving her.

No. There can be no doubt. He hasn't allowed her to dress fully, and her dress sways unbuttoned from her shoulder. Her face is ashen.

"Name the boy," Torrent demands, mace outstretched, pointing to the crowd, but she only shakes her head, wracked with tears and strangled sobs.

The crowd has drawn itself tight, doesn't move. Tomie is beside me, the heat coming from him like a toxic breath.

"Come forward, boy. Take the opportunity to prove your preference for this girl. In the case of an overwhelming preference, punishment will be lenient."

He pulls the girl up from her knees, takes her chin in his hand and inspects her. She can barely stand.

"*Show yourself! Show yourself, I beg of you!*" the mother cries.

"We are not insensitive in cases of real connection. *Reveal* yourself and we will be merciful – as long as the bloodlines are pure." He pauses, expectant, but the silence seems to grow. Not one flicker reveals the boy.

"We *must* trace the bloodlines," Torrent says, letting the girl go, who slumps to her knees – eyes rolling as if she'll faint. "If you do not confess and agree to unite with this girl, she will be scaphised."

The word booms. It takes a minute to grab the meaning from where it bounces around my brain, attach it to itself.

It's a death sentence. She'll be sent out on the flood plains to starve, strapped inside a boat like an open coffin, pecked by birds, baked in the sun, dehydrate until she withers.

She looks down at us – her eyes secretly catching ours. Tomie's hands are shaking, still limply attached to my waist; his face has a sick pallor, skin stone-white, breaking with sweat.

"Save her," I beg in a whisper. I don't ask him to explain, don't allow the horror of the betrayal to touch me, think only of this poor girl, about to go to her death. But he shakes his head once, curtly.

I try to pull free. He digs his nails into my wrist.

"Time's up," Torrent says, and the girl is dragged away, her shoes making a vile scraping sound that tears through me.

Tomie grabs my elbow so hard I wince. I work at my voice, try to scream but his hands are everywhere at once. He heaves me into the shadow of the stone wall, pushes me down. All I can see is pretty leather pumps leaving the ballroom. And it reminds me I don't have my boots on. If I did, I'd kick.

And then there's no one left to notice, only Tomie's smooth hands crushing my throat.

Cedar and oak.

I struggle and hit, but he weighs me down, squashes my chest.

"I'll tell them about you," he whispers, his blonde hair wild. "Everyone in Penn knows what your mother tried to do. There hasn't been a verdict, has there? Think what they'll do if they know your mother is *flawed*."

I can feel the purple bruises breaking, around my mouth where his grip is so fierce, along my ribs from the pressure of his thighs. And one thought wails: if he'd asked me instead of her, would I be in that boat now? Didn't I almost give in on the moor?

The air thins and my vision blurs. He's struck me with something sharp – a sliver of stone?

And then he's gone.

I gulp, the air too crisp, pull myself up, graze my arms against the jagged edges of the wall – but I make my legs carry me to the water, which is a shimmering haze of blue-black.

The horizon seems slanted. The white boat is already a speck, the girl's fading screams are skewed by my dizziness. *I'm* screaming now – I think I'm screaming, but it doesn't sound right, it's just a husk of a noise, shrill and broken, as if Tomie's hands still strangle me.

"Manon!"

Mother?

She's reaching and running, shouting something that breaks into pieces and flies away.

I'm coming. Wait for me—

But she's splaying out into strands. A cold sweat – or something like it – trickles from the pain in my head. I feel cold.

"You're bleeding. We need to get you home."

It is a sea creature, black tentacles sprouting from its head, its face obsidian glass. It is not Mother, not Tomie. But my feet have grown into the riverbank, the silt climbing through me; the creature can't pull me on, though I want to go with it.

A shard of pain splinters my head, sickly sweet blood seeps on to my tongue.

The creature's hold is almost as tight as Tomie's, coarse and cold but gentle too.

"It's not your fault," it says as I collapse and drift in my own open coffin.

CHAPTER TEN

Sails Down Against
a Breathless Sky

The kitchen door is open, the heavy curtain keeping most of the mosquitoes at bay but struggling against the heavier heat. Wild Fell's thick stone walls should keep us cool, but the tin roof soaks up the sun and intensifies it, cooking us inside. There is no relief outside, no shade, only the open, sunburnt sky. The roof pops as the metal expands, a concertina of sound.

Father is outside working through the morning heat before it becomes unbearable. I can hear the tinny rhythm of his broad fork, scraping and lifting the last of the summer crops, soil falling from the tines like rain, the heaving sigh he makes between swings before he breaks into the hard crust of earth. It is a hard job and reminds me of all the times we have dug the same earth together in the dry heat and the driving rain, and I wish I could go out and help but Mother has expressly forbidden it. She looks at me from the kitchen as if I'm a glass on the edge of a table, and she is primed to catch me if I fall.

She is scraping freshly-pulled carrots for a salad – her apron smeared with streaks of red, purple and orange that bleed into the linen and dry into different shades of brown. The way she holds the knife makes me nervous, too close to the knuckle, and I'm glad I did not sharpen it recently, fearing she might cut herself. I picture the inside of the medicine cupboard and count the stock of cloth scraps boiled clean and laid out neatly.

"Here," she says, picking up a small glass vial filled with honey, "it'll help it heal."

She screws off the lid and the warm sweet scent plumes out. As I take it from her outstretched hand, I'm tempted to dip my finger in and lick the sweetness. But she means it medicinally and I'll be scolded if I do. I put my hand to my head, remembering the wound now, and the touch brings back the throb. But worse than the pain, is the beating shame of Tomie, which also returns.

I dab a little of the honey over the wound as instructed; it stings and soothes at the same time, and my mouth swims with saliva at the thick smell of it.

"I got it from Josephine Docke at first light – she's fierce, that woman. I'm to take her some of the preserves when they're ready," she says, gesturing at bowls of fruit laid out on the table. *If* I can get a script to go again."

She peeks at me to see if the glass has wobbled any further to the edge, judges it safe to continue.

"The streets are crawling with watchers," she tells me, her voice low as if they are listening. "Looking for that Tomie." She tuts, shakes her head, and wipes her eyebrow with her forehand, the only part of her hands that are clean. There is a dew of sweat across the skin when she has finished, which she wipes on her apron amongst the rainbow of brown. "The whole of Penn is paying for Tomie Samms. The whole of Calde Valley, no doubt," she spits, chopping the carrots into uneven slices that bounce and roll. "Poor girl," she says to herself with a soft sigh.

So they know it was him.

I pick up a strawberry from a bowl on the table, squash it between my fingers, and focus hard on the sweet stickiness of the juice, rather than think of the poor girl.

The table is full of fruit: strawberries, early damsons and ruby stems picked to make preserves. Mother must have been busy whilst I was sleeping too long – a whole day and into the next morning. It looks like she has picked everything we have grown, but she has abandoned it all on the table, swapping from one job to the other before the first is done.

"If it weren't for that boy, we'd be free as birds in the sky still."

When have we ever been that?

"What do you mean?" I ask, wondering what I've

missed as I slept. I want to know if they caught Tomie, and what they did to him if they did, but I cannot ask outright.

"Josephine reckons that carpenter's boy had promised to state a preference for her Rosie," she says. "And half a dozen others, by all accounts. No one has seen him since Foxfields. What they'll do when they catch him…"

"How do you know it was him?"

"Eyes of the wolf if ever I saw them."

I have not told her about Tomie – only that I slipped and banged my head in the scurry to get to the water when everything went so wrong, when all the debs and their parents were racing to see the girl scaphised or running the other way. But I'm sure she sees it somehow. It is in the way she says *that boy*, like she has reason to dislike him, though I'm sure she has never met him.

"What will happen to him?"

She stares at me, knife mid-air, carrots rolling to the floor.

"What difference does it make?"

What difference does it make? If I'd seen Tomie for what he really was, I might have saved her. If I could find *him* now, I might still save him.

"I need to see Agatha," I say, changing the subject. "I could get a script, take some of the preserves to the Dell?"

"I don't think so," she says, pursing her lips. "Not today. There was a messenger at dawn-up, came just as I got home. All debs are to stay on their own grounds until

Penance Day. The council fear a repeat of what happened at Foxfields. All freedoms have been revoked. It'll have to be me that goes back to Summit."

All I want in the world is to see Agatha. The only one who knows about Tomie and me, the only one I can talk to. "You'll have to wait for Penance Day," she says, the sharp-sounding words repeated so that I hear them properly this time.

"Penance Day?" I ask – more to distract myself than anything.

"More punishment," she says as if I should know. "You're to report to the North Nab at dawn-up tomorrow. You'll be allocated a job – it'll be hard labour in the hot sun, teach you all a lesson. Although there's only one boy needs to learn it, I reckon."

Where is he?

"And there's to be no ball at Waddow either," she says, tipping the haphazard carrots into a pot that's too small, adding precious water from a pewter jug, which she lets swill over the sides. "I'm surprised they haven't cancelled the season altogether."

Preferences are a privilege. Not a right.

I picture a pair of dark eyes that make my insides simmer and wonder. They surely will not let me have him and even if they do, how could I ever deserve him? How could I have let him believe I preferred Tomie?

"Your father will be wanting water," she says, holding out the almost empty jug. I get up sluggishly, body aching

155

back to life, take the jug and an empty glass to fill for Father. "Go carefully now."

The well is nearly empty, and the water comes up full of silt: brown and murky. It will have to be filtered and boiled before it is clean enough to drink. I did not realize how thirsty I was until I saw it – but I resist the temptation to drink.

I pour the last of the clean water into the glass for Father, fill the jug with the dark stuff from the well and take it into the storehouse. Father made us a filter from a small barrel full of rocks and sand. I pour the murky water in the top and watch it pool over the stones, put the jug under the spout and leave it there. It will take hours to come through.

Father has gone inside so I leave the filled glass on the windowsill, taking only a tiny sip before I do. Then knock on the window and see him wave in thanks through the criss-cross panes, but I do not go inside to join him, despite the growing heat.

My legs ache to run but the farm is too small, so I pace in circles instead, round and round with no aim, past the chicken coop that butts up against Father's small patch of crops; by the small tin hut that serves as Whinny's stable, and then to the doorless storehouse – an open mouth with Father's cart sticking out like a tongue, too big.

Through the stone arch that once had a gate, which rotted off its hinges long ago, I can just glimpse the lane that leads by the front of the house. I stick my head through, look both ways down the lane. It seems quiet, abandoned, filled only with the echoes of time gone by. I'm tempted to walk out, but then I hear the feet, marching on hard ground, getting nearer and nearer. An army of trees they seem to me, green and swaying, growing larger as they move towards me. But it is not a forest of trees, uprooted and tramping the lane, rather a forest of watchers who pass as one body, boots sounding an angry song, leather on flint. I shrink back from the arch, stand with my back against it as the vast army pushes on, so many a cool breeze stirs.

All debs are to stay on their own grounds until Penance Day.

I am stuck at Wild Fell with nowhere to go. It is the only place I have ever felt free, and now they have managed to make a prison of that as well. I walk down towards the elm, at the water's edge, and sit with my feet tickled by the sea. So much water and none to drink.

Father has been washing potatoes and has left them drying on racks by the shore. It is a good crop. What we do not eat, we can store for winter. And we have the rooster to breed come spring. We will have a better year next year.

They will have a better year, I remind myself. I will no longer be a Pawlak; Wild Fell no longer my home and Mother and Father's struggles will no longer be mine. I try not to remember it is my fault this year has been so hard; that my behaviour at the fence on the day of the pledges is the reason we had to give double to the claims in the first place.

I think of what Father said at the ball: you do not have to form a preference to find real love. I think of Mother's words too. Love has no place in our world. They are right; they both are. But I cannot accept it. Something in my heart fights no matter how hard I fight against it. And his eyes haunt me again.

The sun burns my forehead, dries the honey that is spread across the cut. The light bounces off the water, reminds me of Mother's quartz necklace – the one she lets me wear for the balls. When I see the longboat, I realize I've been looking for a smaller one – scanning for the boat they strapped her in. But this is not a skiff, it is huge, driving through the water and blotting the skyline. A watch boat. And there is another – and another with its sails down against the breathless sky, oars synchronized at the sides. The patrol boats always circle the waters, but not this many.

They are looking for Tomie.

"Have you seen her?" a familiar voice asks. It takes me by surprise, and my eyes are so scorched from squinting into the sun, at first, I do not recognize Agatha's father; I see only the green cloak that sends shivers down my spine, and I think Clint must have come for me at last, his report finally heard.

"Have you seen her?" he asks again, moving into the path of the sun so that I see him clearly. He pulls me to my feet. There's fear in his voice. Why is he dressed like a watcher?

He follows my eyes to his cloak. "I joined the watch. They're taking volunteers to search for Tomie. It was the only way I could search for her," he says in reply, eyes everywhere, as full as the sea. "Have you seen her?" he asks, tugging at the shoulders of my dress now so I think the seams might give way.

"No, not since the journey to Foxfields. Why?" I ask, anguish beginning to creep into my bones.

"She didn't come home." He sighs, letting me go and circling the spot, worrying his hair with his hands. It stays where he strokes it, soft and smooth, as if he has slathered one of Agatha's elixirs on it. But it is the heat that sticks it to him.

Flashes of the ball – stampeding pumps, dresses hitched up to the hip as debs ran to the sea, Tomie's hand on my mouth – come back to me, but none contain Agatha. Again, I'm sorry I didn't go after her.

"What if she had a seizure and can't get back?" I say, panicked by a vision of her lying listless and abandoned.

"Don't you think I've thought of that?" he says, seeming to shrink inside the cloak of the watcher. "I went to Foxfields yesterday. She isn't there. Two nights she's been gone now."

"But what other explanation is there? She'd get home if she could—"

"It's not a seizure," he says, his voice so sure it makes me turn cold. "I spoke to the Clines this morning." Colder still. "Alsis didn't come home either."

A chill crawls over my skin then. Sweat pools at my temples. I look out to the water, the wall of boats seeming to grow impossibly large, impenetrable. They are looking for Tomie, but they might find her.

"How could they be so rash? We have to find them."

"Aye," Barrett says, heartsore.

"What about Jaynie's Foss?"

"I've been. Nag's Bay, Wanderer's Ditch, even Wolfhole Crag – *nothing*. They're not there."

"What did the Clines know?"

"Nothing. They were as shocked as me. If someone helped them plan it, it wasn't them."

"What can we do?"

His face falls, as does my heart. I know the answer. Nothing. We can do nothing.

"I thought she'd have told you," he admits, shoulders drooping, hope sliding off them. "I thought you'd know." He pinches the skin between his nose, squeezes his eyes shut and breathes deeply, forcing back the pain.

"I can volunteer for the watch too," I say.

"You can't, you know that. Women can't volunteer until after their unions, and even then, you must bear children first – you must have done your duty."

"What can I do then? I can't just sit here. Get me a script and I'll search too."

"Only councillors can issue a script now. The best you can do is talk to people at Penance Day. If the debs know anything—"

"I'll find out."

I nod, take his hands in promise. It hits me then – it's been two days. Two days for word to travel further than the two of them could.

"Do they know she's missing?" I ask.

"Not yet – but when neither of them shows up for penance they will."

Agatha, Seventeen

"Happy birthday," Alsis said, holding out a sparkling silver bangle for Agatha to see.

She held out her wrist in answer, made her smile as wide as she could.

It was not just the gift she would treasure, but that look, the hope that she would choose him, the fear that she would not. Over and over, she had chosen him, promised herself to him, and yet he never took it for granted. His eyes always asked the question.

He slipped the shining thing over her wrist and spun it so that its beauty caught in the moonlight as it twirled. The touch of his fingers on her skin was familiar now, but it never seemed to lose its power. Her skin shivered and the heat came.

One end of the bangle was narrow and decorated with exploding rays that burst from an arc and looked like the sun made silver. And the other end swelled into an oval shape that must once have been convex but had been flattened out and carved with two letters twined together: *A* and *A*.

"Agatha and Alsis," he said.

"I love it," she answered.

"I wanted you to have something fine to wear to the first ball."

She was seventeen. Only a year away from their pledges and the start of their season. A life, she hoped, with the sweet, honest boy who had made her a bangle from a Lost World spoon.

"I can't wait," she admitted, spinning it round again.

"I wish we could build a house here," he whispered, "stay for ever."

"Why don't we?" She laughed.

Jaynie's Foss was their place. They had made it so. No one patrolled here though they were supposed to. But the path was so overgrown with hawthorn, it was almost inaccessible. Only if you fought your way through the tangle of thorns and risked a few scratches on your forearms, were you rewarded with a path lined by skeleton trees that led to a clearing, shielded from view by sheer rocks on all sides. And in the centre, there was a warm pool that filled up in winter.

Children came to swim during the day. But at night it was all theirs. Sometimes they would bring a picnic and feast. Other nights she would lay in his arms and look up at the sky, up through the rock walls that framed the changeling blue so perfectly. She would wonder at the stars that had glittered there long before them and would glitter there still, long after they were gone. Stars that predated Calde Valley and its council. And the Virtue Season.

But that night, she wanted to swim.

She waited for him to kiss her first, for him to run his finger up her arm where the bangle had come to rest, the knotted *A* and *A* lit by strands of the moon. She waited as he traced her collarbone up to her chin and pinched it between his finger and thumb.

Every time he kissed her it was this second, this fluttering moment, she enjoyed the most: the brief second before his lips touched hers that stilled her heart every time. She wanted it to last for ever, for every moment to be so full of promise. It was the place she wanted to live.

But this kiss was going to be different. She was going to make sure of it, to turn it into a new kind of waiting, one that would erupt into something more. A birthday gift to herself. She knew what she wanted to happen. And why it had to be now.

Their season was coming but, with it, the certainty of Alsis was drifting away. He felt it too; she had seen it in his eyes and felt it in the strength of his embraces. For so long, she had expected their season to be their beginning. But now it was almost here it felt like the end. There would be dancing and dresses and nights lit by starlight. The things she had always imagined. And there would be the way it felt to be seen in his arms. But not once, in all that dreaming, had she imagined the doubt that was starting to consume her, which was becoming a begging, nagging thing inside her chest. She did not doubt that Alsis would choose her. She knew their preference statements would match just as she knew he would dance with only her. But she did not know what the council would decide.

So, as the rain fell between the rocks, into the rippling pool at their feet, and the moonlight broke into shards on its surface, she let the kiss grow, until there was only one place for it to end.

"Let's swim," she told him, unbuttoning the faded brass buttons of the doublet she knew he had worn just for her, one that she had never seen before. It was smarter than his day clothes: a watery red, stiff and unworn, at least by him. It was the one he would wear to dance with her at their first ball. And when they danced, how much joy it would bring to remember this secret moment.

At first, he stopped her, caught her hands in his, a startled look in his eyes, but that look soon gave way to the thing that lay behind the fear, the thing that had been there that first day in her kitchen, that had been there ever since. The caged thing, the thing she was about to set free.

The water was warm and flowing and made them truly part of each other; carried them towards each other on their own current. It had always felt that way between them, as if being separate from one another was unnatural, and their bodies longed to be made whole, one by the other, like overlapping waves breaking. And that night, under the canopy of stars and midnight sky, they were weightless, bleeding into each other as if they were liquid, seeping together the way water claims the rain as part of itself.

"Love me after for ever," she told him.

"And before, and in between."

CHAPTER ELEVEN

Debris of the Lost Cities

The Penn Vale debs are marched up the North Nab by watchers who form parallel lines at either side of us. It almost reminds me of a ball. Almost.

The ground is baked hard and it is steep, the sun a tireless beast, though it is only the morning of Penance Day.

My foot catches on a loose rock and I stumble. The watcher nearest to me – a woman with hair shorn so short I cannot tell what colour it should be – shoves me up again and I glare at the floor instead of at her, fearful I might strike back.

At the top of the climb, the hill opens into a flat expanse of parched grass, with white tents scattered across it, the biggest of which is for the councillors who stand in its shade, fanning themselves with concertina paper. There was no walk for them this morning. Their horses graze in a makeshift paddock, a small square hemmed with temporary struts and rope barriers.

We gather under the canopy of seemingly endless sky, squinting into the blinding sun and the watchers are antlike, swarming all around us, and in-between too. We are siphoned past tables where watchers are taking attendance. These, at least, are shaded and offer a temporary respite from the beating sun.

"Manon Pawlak," I say as I get to Brack's table. He scrawls a tick against my name, two fingers curled around the pencil instead of one.

"You look half-starved," he scorns, harpooning his incisors with the beefy length of his tongue. He doesn't remember he is the reason why I'm thin now, that it was he and Clint who took double from us in the claims, the rooster too.

"I can pull up crops, and I've driven a plough horse. I know seeds. And I can cook."

He smirks sideways as if he doubts it, balks so hard a little phlegm rattles in his chest.

At least I can hold a pencil.

He sucks his teeth.

"You can work the line," he barks, pointing up to the top of the Nab, the very top of the moor. Another short, steep climb that is no match for me, as hungry and thirsty as I am. "There's a heap of old stone underneath the ground, *foundations* or something, they called it. It's being dug up for the new building at Castle Hill."

He bites his lips as if to stop himself talking further and I think back to the hospital Tomie mentioned, what they are up to. "You can help pass it down."

Stone is more precious than ever now the forests are so depleted by drought fires and ash dieback, and the last working quarry is spent. No wonder they have us digging it up. Everything in the valley is reclaimed and reused.

"If you can handle the weight of a single stone, that is," Brack grunts, poking my forearm with his pencil, spittle clinging to his chin as he laughs.

"I know better than to eat the rooster," I mutter as I march up the hillside rubbing my arm, glad when my breath becomes shallow with the effort and vents my anger, my voice carried up and away.

When I reach what seems like the top of the world, the debs stand in two separate huddles – girls from boys – like groups of repelling magnets, each afraid of the other. Since the season began, they have moved closer and closer, finding their way beyond the barrier that has always been as tangible as the fence at school. But Tomie has driven them back from each other. They are frightened.

I join the girls with only a nod, and they peer back just as silently, eyes made permanently wide by what they witnessed at Foxfields. We have seen people cleansed, but never scaphised. I know how it must simmer behind my eyes too, so I keep them low, barely greeting anyone.

"That was close," Bertie huffs, pushing her brother's

cycle at her hip. It is a three wheeled thing – two at the back, one at the front – and is made of scrap tyre-less wheels with rusty spokes, bits from a salvaged leather saddle. She wedges a stone under its front wheel as a chock to stop it rolling and fights with her dress as it's caught by the wind. She is so out of breath she can barely speak.

"I was almost late," she chokes, and though she smiles, dimples scooped out of her cheeks, her eyes betray the terror of what might have happened if she had not made it in time. She tucks herself into our huddle, breathes hard through her nose.

"What happened?" she asks when she gets her breath back, pointing to the wound on my forehead. I touch it as if remembering, feel the sticky layer of honey that has not quite hardened.

"Tripped getting out of the cart on the way back from the ball," I lie. "Mother's going to take my dress up for Stone. The hem's a disaster waiting to happen."

Bertie flicks her eyebrows, disinterested in such a banal explanation. She is breathing normally now, and with the calming of her breath she seems braver too. She risks a quick, furtive glance across the moor to see that Torrent is sitting astride a chestnut mare, eyes everywhere at once as if every councillor were incapable, every watcher incompetent, and every deb unvirtuous.

I am not flawed.

"She's counting her stars, I reckon," Bertie whispers,

nodding towards Rosie who is standing outside the circle by herself, face turned grey since I saw her last. I remember what Mother told me, that Tomie had feigned a preference for her too. I try a small nod in answer to Bertie, but it is too large, and I feel as though I'm overacting in a play. "It could have been her in that boat instead of Geneve," she adds, forehead creasing.

Geneve. It is the first time I've heard her name, and I feel like I'm swallowing it, as if it were a chunk of something raw and sharp.

It could have been me.

"So you got assigned to the line too?" I ask, kicking against a deadly wave of fear in my stomach.

Kick. Kick. Kick. Geneve, Geneve, Geneve.

"Aye. We'll be purple as beets by lunch and my only hat has been given down to my sister. We'll have to ask Agatha to grind some calamine if we want to look presentable for Stone," Bertie says, a little of the excitement clinging to her despite everything. She looks around. "Agatha not here?"

I shrug. I am relieved. If Bertie has not heard about Agatha's escape, no one has. Then I see Torrent, down from his mare and talking to Reade. They stand either side of Brack, who points out names on his list, flapping the pages up and down like the jaws of a snapping animal, until Torrent snatches it and inspects it.

Bertie does not know. But they are about to.

"Did you get to dance with Matthie?" I ask Bertie to

quell the rising panic, but I keep half my attention on Torrent.

"No. He danced with Tabithe twice," she says, a spiteful little look thrown over her shoulder at the girl herself. "I'm sure he was about to ask me, but that's when Councillor Torrent got up and—"

There is a gap at the end of her sentence that is so large, so full of horror.

"There's always Stone," she says.

We are man-handled into a line by faceless watchers, who have their hoods up against the glare of the sun. They arrange us with our backs to Torrent so that I do not see what happens next or what orders he gives. And the stones begin to come. The diggers bob up and down, swinging their picks side by side, unearthing them. The swoosh and strike of metal is percussive.

I'm not surprised to see Wick Flint flinging a pick at the earth as if he wants to split the world in two. The stones begin to reveal buildings from the Lost World, slowly at first, then quicker and quicker. They appear in long geometric shapes that must once have marked the façade of a house, or the places where one room ended, and another began. The circularity strikes me. How these stones will be stacked into new formations, at Castle Hill, a new world from the old.

I stand next to Bertie and a steady stream of rocks is passed from hand to hand, loaded into carts and driven down the Nab. It is easy to lose myself in the rhythm, the drag and drop of stone through fingers. Then I see a little speck of black stalking towards us, like a black bird with no wings. It bursts up the hill, bigger and bigger and I almost shout her name—

And then I see. It is not Agatha, but a miniature of her. It is Wren.

"Excuse me, sir," the miniature Agatha says in the long thin voice of someone who has cried themselves hoarse, and Torrent looks down at the pale blonde girl whose face is so like her sister's. "I've been sent for my sister who can't come."

Clever Wren.

"What's her name?" barks Torrent. He is back astride the mare, making Wren look even smaller.

"Agatha Curlew," she answers simply, looking up with her hands cupped to her eyes to shield the sun.

"*All* debs must report for Penance Day," he says, yanking his reins together when the mare begins to circle. He locks his hands at the bottom of his stomach, pulling the reins so hard the bit must bite the horse's mouth, but it yields, stands perfectly still. "No exceptions. Go back. Bring her."

Wren hesitates.

"Her sister's a decom, not a deb," I say, stepping out of line, which causes a flurry of stones to falter to the floor behind me as the line continues to pass them. They clink as they knock against each other. "Has she been unwell, Wren?"

173

Wren only nods.

"Agatha Curlew," I say slowly so that he notes the name, thinks back to the list, which, by the way his mouth curls, I'm sure he does, "has seizures. She cannot work immediately after. But Wren can work in her place. She's as strong as me."

Torrent snorts.

Wick has stopped digging – they all have. Their picks are silent. I feel him looking at me. It is a strange sensation. Warm and cold. Pure and dark.

"She'll come when she's feeling better, won't she?" I ask Wren, begging her to play along with only a glance.

"Aye. Perhaps this afternoon – she'll be better by then, I reckon."

Torrent jumps down from his horse, which shakes its head as he grabs the reins in one hand. He tugs so that the mare brays, but it is soon quiet. Torrent steps towards Wren, who closes her eyes as if she expects a beating.

"Join the line," he snaps, shoving her hard, and she hurries over, stands in line beside me.

"Well done," I whisper as the stones begin again, a constant stream that mimics the seconds ticking. My arms begin to feel heavy, skin chafes and cracks, arms burn red from the sun.

"Wake up, lazy animal," Brack says when I stumble and miss a step. He pushes me back into place like a puzzle piece. Wick's axe pauses. Clint, who is guarding the diggers, kicks him in the shin, hard and swift.

For hours we stand in the line, passing an endless stream of rough stone, but the diggers only unearth more.

"I don't think I can do many more," Wren murmurs, lifting her hands between stones. Hot-looking blisters have formed all over her palms.

When the sun is at its highest, Clint calls lunch and I carry the weightless girl, drooping with dehydration, forehead red and raw, and feed her water from a ladle. There is a tent for the debs too, with a table of over-ripe fruit and bread.

Wren swigs thirstily and I take some too. We eat the bread and fruit whilst the councillors eat chicken legs and swig wine.

Wren and I sit on a scratchy patch of grass outside the back of the tent where its shadow is cast over us.

"Where do you think she is?" I ask her quietly, checking over my shoulder for the nearest deb or watcher.

"Away from here," she says, yawning. She looks so young and, for the first time in a long time, I see her as the small child she is, hug her in close until she falls asleep with her head in my lap and a hunk of bread still hanging from her hand.

"Do you want company?" Wick asks, and he sits beside me without an invitation.

We sit silently, eat with an automatic appetite. His hands are blistered too, arms swollen with effort, stained with mud and rivers of sweat, but he does not complain.

"I never get *this* view out on the water," he says

cheerfully. "Do you see? The two green glints out there. It's Stone."

I follow his hand to the line at the edge of the world where, if you squint, you can just make out Stone Hamlet and its two towers, topped with shimmering green. From where we sit, there seems to be no water between them and us at all, as if the two counties are met by land. The valley, and the tremendous expanse of water, seems to have been stitched up.

"Copper," Wick says triumphantly.

"Why is it *green*? I thought copper was brown."

"The rain turns it green over time," he says.

"The only rust I've ever seen is brown," I say, and he laughs.

I glance at Wick, the way his sweat-soaked hair seems to suit him, curling away from his forehead, and his bay eyes that are a furnace of feeling. I might never fully understand him; he has trained himself to hide his heart so well.

"I should have warned you about Tomie. I never trusted him," he says, the sad notes of his voice making my heart as sore as my hands.

"It's not like you knew what he was capable of. And it's hardly your job to look after me."

"I wish it were. Though I know better than to try," he says.

A single beat stretches. The hairs on my arms stand on end.

"You couldn't have done anything. I was completely blinded by him. I should have seen it—"

"The eyes of the wolf?"

"You couldn't have known what he'd do," I offer.

"But I'd been watching him. At the Penn Ball he danced a lot, with so many girls who all seemed taken with him."

He had watched me too then.

"And then at the market, I saw him with that girl, Geneve. He gave her something, like he did you."

He says it so matter-of-factly. I remember Tomie giving me the comb that day, sliding it into my hair.

He is looking at the grass intently, plucks up a blade, puts it to his lips and blows a shrill note.

"Why didn't you tell me?" I ask, stroking Wren's sleeping face but looking at him, at the side of his face that is turned away from me.

"I didn't know how. And I thought you'd be angry. You never seem to trust me. I thought I'd only make it worse."

I do not admit it, but I know what he means, how I would have fought harder to be with Tomie if he had warned against it.

"Does everyone know about Tomie and me?"

"Of course not. Nobody does," he says, reaching for my hand where it rests on Wren's shoulder, but he stops before he takes it, lets it fall in his own lap. My hand fizzes. "When I think about what could have happened if it were you instead of her…"

It is me who takes his hand, gently, mindful of the blisters we both have. His hand is warm and strong, even if it is as rough as pumice. So what? Mine is too. We are both workers, he and I.

"It could have been."

He looks at me now, bold and fierce and brave.

"I would never have let that happen."

When he smiles, his face opens like a gateway he is letting me through. And the feeling that rushes through me is not what I felt on the moor with Tomie. It is a wild thing.

"I didn't prefer him," I say, the truth tumbling out like a hurriedly wrapped gift. "I've always wondered … what it really feels like. To be in love." I look deliberately at Wren rather than him, at the soft skin of her nose that has burned and will peel. "I wanted to try it on somehow. Like practising. I know it doesn't make sense. It was foolish."

I risk a look. He has dropped my hand now and is looking down at the ground. I want so badly to see his eyes, I think about lifting his chin, but watchers are crawling and even though it would not be wrong given we are debs, somehow, in the shadow of everything, it is not right either.

"I never had to wonder."

"I wish I could be so sure," I admit. "It has never come naturally to me."

He does not speak, but I can see him juggling the

words. He has always known. His parents have been so happy. How could he understand what I feel?

"Do you ever imagine a world where we're free to choose, where there is no Virtue Season…?" I ask.

"Without decommissioning? Without 'flaws'? I think everyone imagines that."

"It kills me to think that's how they see her." I search his eyes. Is that how he sees me?

"Theirs is not the whole truth," is all he says.

"Do you think it will ever be that way? A free world?"

"If someone could prove the council wrong. But it works too well, doesn't it? The fear of extinction. No one wants to test that theory."

"Agatha did. She was treating more and more sick children. Why are they getting sick so easily if the bloodlines are being purified?"

He considers for a moment, his forehead creased.

"Everyone in the valley feels that 'flaws' are a half-truth at best and a downright lie at worst, and worse than that, everyone suspects the council know it. But it's one thing to know it and another to prove it. We need to ask what purpose the season really serves, and how do we do that when—"

"They teach us only from the Mythics, and limit what we know?"

"They tell us the border wars almost drove us to extinction, so they put up walls to stop an uprising. But all it really does is divide the counties, stop us uniting against them. They take our resources, keep us hungry. We don't have the means to fight. Or to question. Or to trust each other."

If I could live in a world without fear, in a world where nothing could be taken away from me, where I could never be taken away, I would love this boy, cast a line into his sea. I don't say it, but it's bursting from me.

"I found this when I was digging," he says. He brings something metal from his pocket, which he cups in his hands to shield it from view. He is grinning from ear to ear. "Do you want to play *What Is It?*" he asks. I think of Agatha – all the times we played this game as children, when Father had dug out some Lost World treasure from the ground.

He hands it to me, and I look at it closely, hiding it between Wren's body and mine so no one sees. It is a metal spiral with a sharp spike at one end, the metal crusted with rust.

"Told you rust was brown," I say, and he smirks.

On the other end of the spiked twist is a hollow "o" which must be some sort of handle. I turn it over in my hands, the sharp end sticking out, the heel of the "o" in my fist.

"So?" Wick asks, impatient, smiling. "What is it?"

"Seed pricker?"

"Water drill?"

"Hoof pick!"

"Back scratcher!"

We both laugh and it feels fine, like a song we are singing together.

"I think," he says, "it's a weapon. So that you might fight the Tomies of this world your own way. Like only you can."

My chest swells with pride. I tuck it into my pocket with one hand, tuck Wren's hair behind her ear with the other. That hook I had imagined in my chest yanks a little with him beside me.

"They look alike," he says.

I nod, smiling, but now I'm thinking of Agatha, lost and running.

"She's gone. Alsis too. I wish I knew where she was."

He tenses beside me.

"I might have an idea," he whispers guiltily. "He was asking questions, at the Penn ball..."

I sit up ramrod straight. "Questions about what?" I whisper sharply.

"About the Drift – an island in the sea," he admits sheepishly, picking at the dry grass again. "I told him it's just rock – nothing grows there. It seemed like idle chatter – he doesn't even own a skiff let alone a boat that could row out that far. I never dreamed—"

"How long can they survive?"

"If they make it, there's a freshwater pool they can drink from. They could survive a while. But..." He hovers over the words. "There's a stretch of water, we call it the Pull, where the undercurrent is so strong even Father and I struggle to row through."

"So, they'll capsize and drown before they reach the Drift?"

"Or starve. Even if they make it through the Pull, they'll be trapped without food. There's nowhere to go from there."

Drown or starve. Those are the only fates Wick can foresee and the immediate sickness in my stomach seems to confirm it.

Wren's forehead is wet with sweat and she's murmuring — I can guess what her nightmares are.

"We could take them food—"

"Impossible. Since Foxfields, there are patrol boats everywhere. More longboats than I've ever seen. We'd be caught."

It snaps. The line I had cast.

"You should never have told him," I seethe.

I wake Wren and help her to stand. She is confused when she sees Wick, but I do not give her time to ask questions. I stalk away, dragging her behind me like a heavy rock, leaving him shipwrecked, an abandoned skiff.

The stones come rolling down the line again. Drown or starve. Drown or starve. It repeats until it is an echo.

CHAPTER TWELVE

Pheasant's Eye

Penn House is empty: a cold, gloomy place, changed since the night of the ball. It is silent and still. The only people who come here outside of the balls wish not to be seen, to make a report or barter for a bigger share of the claims.

I emerge from the wheat field that protected me from view and am greeted by a goshawk on the lane, picking at the rotting corpse of a hare, its orange eyes afire, grey beak stained and dripping red. It flaps its wings and squawks as I pass but does not abandon its prey. Even the birds know hunger here.

It mocks me, as if it knows what I am about to do. As if it knows I must fail. This is the only place I might find out what they know about Agatha and Alsis. If I can get into a councillor's office—

I don't know what the end of that sentence is. Search? Beg? Lie?

A tall, pillar-like man with receding hair is giving instructions to a team of watchers. He reads from a list and each one nods and leaves in sequence, like fragments breaking away from one body.

All debs are to stay on their own grounds.

I have stashed my emblem patch in my basket and try to pass them with my eyes up. *It is permitted*, I tell myself, hoping they will believe my lie. They eye me but do not stop me.

I follow the path to an open door and am led into a room I have not seen before. It is not as grand, nor as decorated as the ballroom. A receptionist sits at a desk and is leafing through a heavy ledger, arranging a pencil just so, perpendicular to its edge.

"Good morning," I say, smiling brightly, hoping to get her onside.

"You're up early," she says, yawning and leaning both elbows on the desk, lacing her hands together under her chin so that her face rests on a bed of fingers. I cannot bring myself to frame the words I need to say – words that will either rescue or condemn Agatha.

"I'd like to speak to a councillor," I gulp, not knowing how the words will come, what I'll say when she asks me why.

"Ah, you're here to make a report," she assumes, to my relief. "I see. Well, you'll have to fill in the form first – and I can't promise you'll get to see a councillor," she says, retrieving her pencil and rolling it through her fingers as if to warm it up. "Depends how serious it is."

"I'll only tell a councillor," I whisper. "Please. It is important."

She raises her eyebrow, which makes me squirm.

"That's not the way it's done. You fill in the form. It gets assigned to a councillor and then it's investigated. You'll be contacted."

I think of Clint's report, perhaps still waiting to be assigned. Investigated. For a moment, I think I could swipe that too. The receptionist pushes the form at me, offers her pencil.

"I can't write," I lie. She rolls her eyes and takes back the form.

"You say it, I'll write it."

"No," I bluster. "I will only speak to a councillor. It is about the boy from the Foxfields ball. I know where he is."

And maybe because my lie hides a truth, she believes me.

"I'll see what I can do," she says after a pause and disappears, leaving me alone in the small room, waiting.

The room is exactly square, the white wooden floor scuffed where so many people have walked, every report made seeming to have ripped its skin off. The walls are made of thick stone, so the room is cool and yet sweat runs down my back in rivulets. The receptionist's footsteps click–clack into the room before she does.

"The councillors have been summoned to Castle Hill," she says, sitting back down, tucking herself under the desk. "You'll have to make do with Brack."

"I'll come back," I venture, desperate to avoid the brute of a man, but his shadow is already reaching down the hall for me.

"You're here now," he spits, appearing from the corridor, almost filling it. "You might as well stay."

As soon as he speaks, he turns back, with the absolute certainty I'll follow. I look at the receptionist for help, but she is arranging the ledger and pencil again, avoiding my gaze.

I follow.

"Sit," Brack says when we get to an office where the desk is stacked with files, arranged in several disorganized piles. I scan the room for any clue. The name plate on the desk says *Councillor Reade*. The walls are lined with similar files, neatly stacked, endless lines of them and I think of the people they represent – see them as if they are standing by the dipping stool or waiting to be branded at Castle Hill.

Where is my file?

"How are your hands?" Brack asks, a ripple of humour forming between his brows as he perches on the desk.

How is your conscience? I wonder. I'm just an insect to him, a tiny ant indistinct from all the rest. But he is no better than me, just a villager, who has bartered his morals for a share in the claims.

"They'll heal," he says, wafting his spade-like hand as if any answer I gave would be unimportant. "You have some information for me?" he asks, trying to sound like Torrent. It doesn't suit him. He only sounds ridiculous.

"I have some information for a councillor."

"Sit," he barks when I continue to stand. I sit, fanning my dress out grandly. He places his feet either side of the legs of my chair.

"I will only speak with a councillor. Is Reade here?" I risk, putting my basket on my lap and placing my hands on the handle to keep from touching him.

"*Councillor* Reade. He's at Castle Hill. They all are. There have been hearings every day since the Foxfields incident, trying to find *that boy*. And as if that wasn't enough to deal with, another idiot local boy has decided to abscond." He snorts and grimaces, his tongue sticks out, too big for his mouth. "You make your report to me."

Some boy. So, he knows about Alsis. Does he know about Agatha? Perhaps I was lucky to stumble on Brack and his loose tongue.

"I don't think you have the authority to hear it," I say, quiet and controlled. The black of his boot crowds the corner of my eye.

"Make your report, or *I'll* report *you*," he says, his voice a whole language of hisses. He shoves my chair with his foot. It tilts back and almost falls. I grip the arms ready for impact, but it rights itself.

"Don't waste my time – you told Maisie you knew where the Foxfields boy was."

"Only because she wouldn't let me through."

He stands, smiles, crouches down with his hot face close to mine.

"I could have you dipped for wasting my time. And you know debs are supposed to be housebound. *Why are you here?*"

"I will only speak to a councillor," I insist, breathing hard into his face, refusing to look away.

Brack narrows his eyes, strokes my head as if I'm a pup, closes his fist down the length of my hair, then puts his lips close to my ear. I shiver.

"Pawlak," he says, turning towards a shelf across the room, inspecting the neatly packed files with all the drama of a schoolboy in a play. My breath catches in my throat as I open my mouth to protest, but a familiar crest catches my eye on a piece of parchment amongst the chaos of paper and I let him carry on with his melodrama. The single piece of paper has two shining towers embossed in silver at the top of the page. The crest of Stone Hamlet. The academics' crest. I snatch it soundlessly as Brack runs his finger across the files, moving through the alphabet.

L, M, N, O—

I conceal the page behind my basket so I can read whilst Brack's back is turned.

My eyes slip across the parchment.

As per my previous … it is imperative you cease the decommissioning process … damaging the gene pool … purity is a fallacy. It must end now—

The letter is addressed to Torrent, but it is on Reade's desk. *Why?*

"P," Brack trills, pulling a file from the shelf and my stomach flips. He sits in Reade's chair, makes a show of reading the file, tracing his forefinger along the words with a flourish.

I stash the letter in my basket, cover it with the linen cloth.

"Clint has been jawing about this for weeks. He *saw* your mother jump. It says so right here. And yet, here it is, marked as resolved and filed away."

Resolved?

My shoulders, heart, lungs all feel light.

"This should have been signed by Torrent for it to be marked resolved. And yet it has not. What a puzzle."

Councillor Torrent, I want to say.

He stalks around the desk and leans over me again, traces a crescent shape around my undamaged cheek bone with his thumb. It burns even without the branding iron.

"She *fell*," I say, shrill with fear. I sound like a desperate bird. I think of the goshawk on the lane.

"Why is Councillor Reade helping you?"

Councillor Reade. I know the name Reade. I've seen him.

Small man packed with muscle. Mace unused.

He was at the fence that day. But it was not him who beat Alsis. I remember the reluctant look on his face, the eager faces of Clint and Brack, snapping at his heels. *Why is he helping me? Is he?*

"Do you know how you get to be a councillor, Manon?" Brack asks, the sound of my name on his lips appalling.

I nod. "You have to be united to a councillor's daughter or born a councillor's son."

Brack tuts.

"There is another way. It so happens that Penn is a councillor short just now. Moore died without a male heir, and his daughter is not yet uniting age. So his seat is dormant. Isn't that a shame?"

He is waiting for me to do the sum.

"Reade lied on this report. Buried it without it ever appearing before Torrent. If he were exposed as corrupt ... which he clearly is, that *would* be a service to the council. I will be commended" – he smirks – "and promoted. Moore's seat will be mine ... or Reade's."

"There were other witnesses."

Brack tsks. "The fisherman and his son? Gillam and Wick Flint?" he reads. "No boy would ever lie for such a pretty thing as you during the Virtue Season, I suppose." He runs his thumb over my bottom lip, which makes me imagine the chink of his bone on my teeth. "Who do you think Torrent would believe? You'd be decommissioned for your flaw, of course – but I'd make sure you live. You can come and work for me. You could be mine. Every councillor deserves a housemaid."

"I'd rather die," I seethe, pulling away from his touch. "I'll tell Torrent myself." My fists are clenched so hard I can feel my fingernails piercing my palms.

"Brave words, but I think not. All right – I've got another suggestion. You tell me how Reade coerced you into breaking the chastity rule with him, and I put the file back on the shelf. You stay anonymous. Your flaw need never be revealed. You won't be decommissioned – you or your mother, just quietly forgotten. I get my seat on the council for exposing the scandal. You get to complete your year as a deb. Shame though, you'd have been a good housemaid," he says, squeezing my chin. "Go on. Say it. Tell me what Reade did. Tell me—"

"What are you doing in my office?" Reade demands, striding in, brisk and urgent, his boots loud on the wooden floor. "Who's this?" he asks without looking at me. "What's going on?"

Brack stares blankly at Reade but offers no explanation. He does not shrink but his face clouds like a sullen child caught with stolen toys, unapologetic but cowed.

"No one – time waster. I thought you were at Castle Hill," Brack says, clicking his tongue. I almost laugh at his lost chance. But I have lost mine too, to have Mother and me spared.

"The meeting was cancelled," Reade mutters, searching through the detritus of his desk. He sees the open PAWLAK file in Brack's hand, and his face is like an abacus, slotting the beads to one side, adding it all up.

I see the brief look of panic, but he covers it, a wrinkled sheet quickly smoothed.

"Is there a problem, Brack?" he asks, gesturing at the file with the tip of his nose.

"There's no signature," Brack says, throwing the file across the desk. It comes to land half hanging over the edge, sending another folder swirling to the floor. Reade picks them up, shuffles them into some sort of order, and inspects my file, as if reading it for the first time.

"Hmmm, that's odd," he says, flicking the pages back and forth without meeting Brack's eye. "Well, there seems an obvious solution. Let's take the file to Torrent, get him to review the evidence. He won't be in the finest mood – on top of the Foxfields incident, it seems the boy who absconded has taken a young decom with him."

Agatha. Now they know.

"He's already mounted a search. Watchers are being redeployed – including you. But, if you *must* have his signature…" Brack looks mildly astonished to have been outmanoeuvred, but Reade is already stepping out of the office, the file tucked under his arm.

"No, I… Very well, councillor." Brack nods curtly, brow knitted, and allows his gaze to rest once more, full of fire, on me before marching from sight.

I turn to Reade. *I still have a chance,* I think. "My friend is missing," I say, the words coming as if from far away, quashing my other, burning question.

Why has he helped us?

"The decom with Alsis?"

"She has a name. Agatha. Please help her."

"She's beyond help," he says, the pheasant's eye flowers stitched on to the chest of his uniform flashing red as he turns. I wonder to myself. *Where have I seen those flowers before? Growing on the moor? Mother would never let me sow them.*

"What if you could find her before Torrent? You could bring her back – say Brack made a mistake with the lists, say she was here all along."

He laughs, an honest sort of bitterness in it. He does not trust Brack.

"He'll squeal about you and your mother the first word I say against him."

Again, that question. *Why is he helping us?*

"Enlist him then. He only wants promotion. Promise him the vacant seat on the council in trade for his help. Make him an ally."

"And have him on the council? He'd betray me in a heartbeat. His only loyalty is to himself."

"Please. I can't fail her – not when I've escaped what she didn't."

I choke on the words, my throat swims with tears, and I feel the truth of it to my bones.

Reade is quiet for a long time, turning it over in his mind.

"Let's say I could try. How would I even find them?"

he asks, his face so stern and stiff, I believe he will help, no matter the cost.

I take a deep breath. "I know where they are."

☽

I open the door of Wild Fell as quietly as I can. It creaks but no one hears. Mother is in the kitchen with her back to me, clanging pots and pans in chaos. Father is outside as always. I sneak up to my room, hide the letter I took from Reade's office behind a loose brick in the unused fireplace, desperate to read it more fully, then come back down loudly, as if I have just risen.

Mother is making yeast: pouring starchy water into jars with a little flour and sugar at the bottom, which clouds as they fill. Soon, they will begin to fizz and bubble, and reduce into the sticky, porous extract that makes bread rise.

"You're up late," she says, looking up with a smile that carves shapes like brackets around her mouth as she fills the last jar from a pan she holds in both hands.

"It was a hard day yesterday," I answer, sitting at the table and tying scraps of linen over the open jars. She only nods and carries on working, though I see the way she looks at me, the concern that worries her eyes.

I try to imagine her as a deb, wearing the same dress that I wear to the balls, twirling in the arms of a man she hopes to unite with. It seems impossible: that she could ever have felt that way, the way I fight never to let myself feel. In my mind, she has always been this old, has always had skin around her jaw as soft as dough. But for the first time, I understand – somewhere within myself – the wound that has rested in her eyes, so long misunderstood.

I think of the red flowers stitched into the lining of her coat. *Pheasant's eye.*

She looks up as if she senses me watching her, a doubtful look in her eyes, and I'm so sorry for all the times I judged her, all the times I hated her, I almost cry.

"I'll go up to the Summit, see if I can trade some of this yeast for milk or water," she says, sighing a satisfied sigh. I don't tell her that people won't trade for it until it's properly fermented, which won't be until morning.

Soon, Wick will know what I've done. What will he think of me?

The memory of his face, sitting abandoned behind the white tent comes back to me, the hot scald I seemed to have left on him painful to think of. And I'm sorry for him too. I've judged everyone harshly.

"Tell me about you and Reade," I say, as gently as I can so that she won't startle, hardly realizing what I am asking. She does startle. She looks up from her work, wipes her hands on her apron and her eyes turn to steel. Her face transforms, as if a mask has fallen away, and I can see her as a deb now, the cloth of age falling from her, as if she's taken off her apron and stepped into a different time.

"Between the last ball and the Declaration Ceremony," she mutters, almost as if she's heard my question. "There was a moment when I was so sure he would choose me."

Between the last ball and the Declaration Ceremony, when longing is at its most desperate and the risk seems to have dwindled to nothing. Promises have been made. Hearts stolen. And there are no more chastity checks.

"We were both from Foxfields. I knew him always. And I always expected we'd end up together. It seemed as true as the sky being blue, or the sea being tidal. But he chose someone else. A councillor's daughter."

Power over love then.

"He covered for us … after Clint's report," I tell her, wanting to ease the pain that has washed over her, and yet it seems to pain her more.

"Perhaps he thinks he owes me a debt. He did make me a promise after all. I would never have … otherwise … not if he hadn't…"

Father's anemones grow in my mind but are thwarted by the more virulent stems of pheasant's eye. The extent of Mother and Reade's relationship dawns on me and I feel sick, the sourness rises in my throat.

She reaches into the pocket of her apron and retrieves a plaited band. It is an inanimate thing – a simple ring with three twists of metal – but I can see its worth reflected in her eyes. "Your father gave this to me," she says, holding it out to me, her face drawn with shame and my stomach volleys. *Does she mean Reade?*

"Trent made me a promise I couldn't accept. Not then. Not when my heart was so broken."

A sigh of relief convulses through my lungs. Trent gave it to her. *My father.*

"I kept it, though I could never bring myself to wear it. Wearing it meant giving myself to him. And I could not. But all these years it has been there. Waiting for someone to do its sentiment justice. It should have been me, and I'm so sorry it wasn't. Take it."

"It is yours," I say, pushing it back at her, as if I could push back time.

There are tears brimming in her eyes, but they are full of something like relief too, as if opening the wound has also closed it.

"Promise yourself to someone, Manon," she begs. "Really truly promise yourself. Make a different choice than I did."

"It was hardly a choice... What choice did Reade give you?" I am surprised when I hear it, the sympathy in my voice.

"No. It was not a choice for me. I did not choose to lose myself in it. But I believe it is for you. You see this thing coming for you. You know it waits. And you are ready. *Fight.* Make the choice your father made, to have an open heart, to accept."

Father's words in her mouth are strange.

"Let this ring remind you to make that choice every day."

There is a deeper fear than not finding love. It is a fear of finding love and having it ripped away from you. This fear is what has stalled my heart for so long, what has kept me from giving it away.

"Is he my father?" I ask, my voice begging and broken. Everything I've held back erupting.

"As truly as he has been my husband. He gave his heart to you just as he gave it to me. When you are loved by Trent Pawlak, there is no room for doubt. You are his because he wishes it so." She chokes on a sound – half laugh, half sob. "And because I believe it is true."

It is an answer. And yet it is not. She does not know. She cannot know. So neither can I.

I cannot bear the pain in her voice, the ringing sound of doubt, so I put the ring in my pocket – an undecided choice – and leave the room.

I want to give myself fully to someone, the way she could not. I can even see his winter-dark eyes.

In the garden, Father is busy picking Whinny's feet. He has her hind leg on his knee and is scraping her hoof clean.

"Father," I manage to say before the sobbing comes and I run at him.

"What on earth is the matter?" he asks, letting Whinny's hoof fall to the floor, the miniature pick too.

I cannot speak. I just fall into his arms and let him hold me, overwhelmed with gratitude that he chose me too. That he let me be his. And that he makes that choice every day.

Father.

CHAPTER THIRTEEN

My Very Soul

The air is turning cooler. Rapeseed is being harvested, and a flaxen cloud of dust catches the early winds. Yellow fronds scatter like fairies through the open window of my room. It tastes sharp and syrupy, tickles the back of my throat.

There has been no news from Reade. Still. I am beginning to lose hope. Except hope is a stubborn beast. I hope she is alive. I hope I can trust his word. I hope...

I am sitting in a chair wearing the Penn red dress for the Preference Ball at Stone. I feel as if I have awoken from a strange and terrible dream and cannot get my bearings.

It has always felt like Mother's dress, each time I've worn it. I have always felt wrong in it, as though the very warp and weft of the cotton found me lacking. It is too pretty and clean for me to sully it.

She is cleansing my skin with a sponge, and I try to feel the cold lick of the water, but it does not touch me. I have become detached from myself, a shapeless thing, waiting for Calde Valley to form me in its image. I know now what I want, and with that knowledge, I have so much more to lose.

I am not ready to face the end of the season. Or make my choice. And have it denied.

"You must go," Mother begs, a command in her voice that does not belong to her. She sounds more like me.

"Why?" I croak, too tired to speak.

"Because they'll come for you if you don't."

I remember the night on the water as if living it for the first time. It is her words that echo through me.

If we are clean, virtuous, we survive.

But I think of the letter secreted in the fireplace. I haven't taken it out; haven't read any more than those few lines in Reade's office.

It is imperative you cease the decommissioning process ... damaging the gene pool ... purity is a fallacy. It must end now—

"There's no choice," I stammer, "is there?"

I see the truth of it in her eyes. Her fear that I will not survive a loveless match, that I am too like her.

"I know what you feel but, believe me, it *can* get worse," she says as she is lacing up my field boots, my foot resting on her knee as she crouches by my chair. It reminds me of Father picking Whinny's feet, and I hold on to a sob.

When she has finished lacing my boots, she stands behind me, and takes my hair in thick sections, tries to rake through the endless knots. It has grown so long since Agatha last cut it.

"I think we'll leave it down," Mother concedes with a sigh, letting the heavy lengths fall against my back, and I think how I must look. Boots, unkempt hair. Ghost face. Hardly fit for a ball. Unlikely preference.

"It's your best feature," she adds, standing to admire the gift she gave me.

"I can't go," I say, limp.

"You *can*," she says, bending down and running her thumb over my cheek as if trying to smudge the pain away. "Your season has been so full of hurt, worse than anything I suffered. But you're stronger than me, Manon. Much stronger."

There is strength in her eyes as well as the fog. *Why have I never seen it? Has it not always been there?*

"Though this world has made you feel it, you are not flawed. Not in the same way as me. I'm not sure whether it's right to even call it a flaw. It is only this place that makes it so." She waves her hands and, at first, I think she means Wild Fell, the place I love so dearly. Home. But she means Calde Valley. The place where only the council's truth counts. "You have something of your father in you."

"My *father*?" I ask, hearing the pitch of my voice rise in anger, not sure who she means.

"Trent," she says with a small smile, her cheeks

flaming, which makes me feel ashamed for invoking Reade. "You have something of Trent in you too. And you'll make the best of it, no matter who you're united with." Her smile is so in earnest, it makes me want to hug her. I don't know why I don't. "I was lost for a long time. I pined for another life, but it was never mine to pine for. I was wrong to cling to it."

She kneels by my chair, holds my chin in her thumb and finger, looks at me intently.

"There is no other half that will make you whole, my love. Remember that."

I cannot tell her that there is. That I have found it. That I should have known long ago. She cups my face with both hands then, and I feel like she is holding me together. I do hug her now, close and tight.

A breeze drifts in, framing her in yellow fronds of wheat. Her red hair blows loosely around her shoulders, and she looks so youthful, strangely peaceful. Something has mended inside her — she has pieced herself back together, fragile but whole.

"I *hated* you for not loving Father," I rasp, my heart catching fire as quickly as a parched field, and the words come by surprise, swift and true.

"I know. I'm sorry. I promise you I am trying. After what happened, I *see* now... I see what I have. And I *want* it. I will fight for it. But you must promise me something. You must fight too, and you must try to accept love, wherever it looks for you. Don't look the other way."

That loose chain, floating for so long without anchor, seems to pick up slack and tighten in my chest, for me and for Father. How long he has waited for her.

"I will try."

☽

When the water came, Stone Hamlet was completely submerged, the Mythic says. Only the copper-topped towers of the sandstone schoolhouse leaped free of the waves, green orbs floating on the sea.

But the water receded, and the councillors were able to claim the land back, a victory by their own making and not the hands of fate, or so they would have us believe. They made the schoolhouse habitable again, reclaimed the buildings that satellite around it, just when the Virtue Seasons were beginning to build back a population and the land was much needed by the growing numbers.

But its position is precarious. The schoolhouse perches on the very edge of the shoreline, threatening to dip back into the sea at any moment.

The council insists the water is stable, but they insist a lot of things I don't believe.

It is far in the distance, in the mouth of night, across the water. Somehow, Mother and Father have got me to the dock at Fishes Fields. Now they are gone, ferried across ahead of the debs, who wait for their turn.

"The Preference Ball," Wick says, somehow managing to lift the gravity from the words, making the ball at Stone Hamlet sound trite. I know the notes of his voice now, the way I know the notes of Father's songs that unfold like a cherished memory each time I hear them, and I don't need to turn to see the mirth in his eyes.

The last time we spoke was at Penance Day, and I haven't forgotten his part in Agatha's escape, just as he hasn't forgotten my anger at him. But he didn't mean to show Alsis the way. And what would be the point of spiting each other now, when it is the last thing my heart wants to do?

"The Preference Ball," I mimic, for there is little else to say.

He stands beside me as we wait for the boats that litter the water in readiness for us, filling with debs and sailing away. The fishermen who live in the fields and fish the water have been commandeered for the night. Some of the boats are only big enough for three or four debs, whilst others fit ten or more.

"That's ours," Wick says, pointing with proud eyes. "Father's skiff."

It is one of the bigger boats, a great white sail not yet hoisted. Wick chews his lip nervously as he watches debs climb in, as if he's worried their weight will sink it. I recognize Gillam, ready with his oars, and try to smile, but it is a hollow, flat thing.

"This one must be ours," I say, as the smallest of all the boats lands at our feet, only big enough for its captain, Wick and myself. No more. We will be alone as we row towards Stone. Wick looks at me as if for permission to help me in, but I get in unaided and hear him laugh.

"My Manon…" I half hear him whisper to himself as he takes his place next to me, the boat rocking with his weight then steadying when he's seated. My insides rock too.

"How long does it take?" I ask, already feeling seasick.

"Half hour or so."

Half an hour of weightlessness, sitting so close our thighs touch, with only the captain's presence to disrupt this stinging need. But he has his back to us, facing the night.

Wick reaches for the oars then remembers himself and drops his hands guiltily.

"Habit!"

We set off, and the stars reflect on the water, the sparkle seeming to pierce the surface, like darts sent down from the sky.

"Are you going to state a preference?" he asks, blunt as ever. I shake my head like a horse flicking a fly with its tail, but a small smile crimps my mouth nonetheless.

"I don't know if I care enough," I say, regretting it when his jaw tightens.

I feel as though I am growing towards him, and he towards me, so that we must meet in the middle and tangle like tree boughs eventually. And I am terrified of the endless pain when the axe severs us.

"You're letting fate decide?" he asks, smiling through a hard mouth.

"I don't want to hope for something I might never get, and I won't be the council's fool."

Like Mother.

"Are *you* going to state a preference?" I ask, too curious to stop myself.

"Aye," he answers as if it's as obvious as breathing. "I'd like half a chance. Maybe they really do match people with their preference. It's better to have half a chance than none at all."

"And what if they don't?"

The soft heft of skin between his eyebrows puckers and he drops his hand in the water, leaving a white wake behind his fingers.

"That is why the balls are so important. So that we may know love, even if we may not keep it."

"So you can torture yourself for the rest of your days?"

"Is it torture to know you are loved? Even from a distance? Beyond space and time. Love does not die if it is true."

"That is my fear," I answer, and there seem to be no more words. The last stitch in my heart holds. "It makes me queasy," I admit, feeling the turn of the waves in my stomach. "The boat." I don't know if it's the boat or the weight of our discussion that churn inside me; I think perhaps it is both.

"When I was little," he confesses, "I was sick every time I got in." He wipes his hand against his thigh and dips it in his doublet pocket. He brings out a glass vial, twists off the cap and hands it to me. "It got so bad, I felt sick even *before* I got in," he says, closing his eyes in mock shame. "Ginger oil. Works every time."

I put it to my nose, but it reminds me of the tea I make for Agatha when she feels nauseous, and doesn't calm my stomach.

Stone Hamlet comes into view: a vast, ancient building dominating the skyline like a great bird spreading its wings. It perches on the edge of the water, watchful with so many candlelit windows.

"We'll get to see the great relics," I say as I let Wick heave me out of the boat, the tendons of his hand flexing against mine, his strength and mine as one.

"Father said they have maps of the Lost Cities," he says. "That's how he knows where the deepest water is – he memorized them in his season. I reckon he didn't dance at all that night but just stood looking at the maps!" I can imagine him doing the same.

He talks of his father as if he talks of the man he wishes to be. I loop my arm through his, like trying on Father's coat – too big and heavy but warm. He is startled but walks on, a smile pressed deliberately thin, but threatening to widen into a grin. We see the watchers, endless numbers of them roving between the debs, pushing and shoving and issuing warnings through gritted teeth.

"It is because of Tomie," he says. *And Geneve*, I think.

This is not to be a ball like the others. He unloops me and we walk stiffly on apart.

We enter the stately building through a stone archway and emerge into a courtyard. The debs are standing as if to attention, as if on parade. The white dresses of the Stone debs, symbolic of the paper that is produced in Stone, stand out in the dark. Those who dare, whisper to each other, pointing at the carved heads that frame the doorways or counting the windows. The building is old, ancient – the grandest building I have ever seen.

Through an open door, candlelight spills, framed in stone.

"*Relic Room*," I whisper, hearing Wick's answering awe. The door leads to a long narrow room, the ceiling of which is painted red, with decorative mouldings dividing it up – white veins in the blanket of blood red sky. There are huge, coloured windows – though some are cracked or have been replaced with boards.

The debs are funnelled through and take it in turns to marvel at the precious objects recovered from the sea-soaked palace: a fragment of a painting showing a man in a great floppy hat, peering up in wonder at a pair of bleeding feet, spikes pierced straight through them.

"The council didn't invent punishment then," I joke, and Wick snorts, breaking the spell of silence so that everyone looks at us.

"They found all this here," he says.

"You would have loved school," I answer. It's sad that he never got to go.

"Imagine, all this underwater. Do you mind if I look for the maps?" he asks, and I shake my head, watch him stalk off with one purpose, through a door to another room.

It is the books that captivate me when I find them in a glass display case, books from the Lost Cities that are foxed with brown stains, pages permanently rippled by the water that was their home. They are beautiful things, not like the Mythic with its humble leather binding. These have gold spines and neatly typed font, so small you have to squint to read it. The pages are incomplete, ripped or the text washed away.

My eyes fall on a book that has been left open as if the reader has just set it down for a moment.

"*The world may laugh*," it says. And then there is some damage, a torn part of the page. "*My very soul demands you: it will be satisfied, or it will take deadly vengeance on its frame.*"

I follow the lines with my finger, fill myself up with them. They seem to have been written by my own heart. The words I have always longed to say out loud.

They echo inside me. That chain in my chest pulls so tight it is painful, deliciously so. A cold crust peels away within, wrenches open a small space for Wick to crouch in. The last stitch unpicking. I know it is me he sees, his soul searching for mine, and I want to show him more, even if it means a lifetime loving him from afar—

"You like books?"

She is all grey, the woman who speaks from a seat tucked into a corner, so shadowed I hadn't noticed her. Her hair spills over one eye, which is highlighted silver in places, and she has an explosion of lines around her colourless lips, like the pattern of lines that radiate from stars. She looks at me expectantly, but with a friendly eye.

"I've never seen books like these. It makes you wonder."

"Does it?"

"About the Lost Cities. The lost knowledge … about what else they knew and what the councillors know."

I barely know why I say it, except that she seems almost a prophetess, her eyes like the crystal balls the soothsayers use. She glares at me, her eyes glassy and uncertain, but then she comes to stand at my side and touches the top of the cabinet as if I've asked a question and she's pointing something out. She looks at the watcher leaning on a door jamb at the other end of the long hall, bored.

"You're an academic, aren't you?" I say, barely loud enough to hear myself.

She slides the glass and removes the book as if to allow me to look more closely. Her hands are spotted brown, and I imagine all the books she has touched, as if each page has left its time-worn mark on her.

"These are only half of what they found. There are more. Books they don't want you to see. Books they won't let us tell you about."

She smiles but it is as grey as the rest of her. Tired and empty. And yet there is something tempting about the way she speaks, as if it is an invitation. She doesn't meet my eyes as she says, "Books that tell the truth."

"I found a letter ... back in Penn, it had the academics' crest..." I take a breath, desperate, suddenly, to *know*. "It said that *purity is a fallacy*—"

She drops the book, and it clatters against the glass cabinet.

"Be careful, old hag. I'll have your job," the watcher booms.

She replaces it in the cabinet and slides the glass closed again.

"Safe and sound," she tells the watcher, and he goes back to his indifferent lean. Quietly, like a breath, she says, "We wrote to each of the chief councillors. They won't listen to us. They won't hear the truth."

"What is the truth?" As though she has been desperate to tell someone, anyone, for all this time, the words spill out, barely a whisper. I look at the books, as though she's pointing things out to me.

"The decommissionings have nothing to do with flaws and everything to do with control."

I wait for my stomach to surge but it doesn't. Because I knew. I have always known.

"Genetic inheritance is complex, but they would have you believe flaws are *bound* to be passed on. We're only at the beginning of our research, but the evidence is clear. And there's so much we're yet to understand." She grimaces. "We are so far behind what our ancestors knew. Much of it comes down to chance. Two healthy parents could have ten healthy children and only one the council deems flawed. But it doesn't matter. By their regime, all are condemned."

It is too big. Too much.

I point at one of the books, as if asking about it.

"So flawed parents don't always pass on their flaws?" I ask, wishing for any other word, not wanting to use *their* language. She looks at me sharply, as though she knows why I'm asking, what I fear, and her answering smile is warm.

"There's just as much chance they'll pass on their strengths as their weaknesses. I suspect, if they were allowed to have children, they could have a completely healthy child. But it's more than that."

"What do you mean?"

"Purity is not just a fallacy – *it breeds weakness*. We have told the council so. They won't listen to us, they shut down our research. All the while the gene pool gets smaller and children less resilient – we've never seen so many childhood illnesses. So many decommissionings."

"Purity is *harming* the bloodlines?"

"It's an oversimplification but aye. Every time they decommission someone, they suppress not just the population, but its genetic variation too; they strip something vital from us all … diversity. They are recreating the very scenario that almost ended the world."

Anger is not the right word. Rage, fury: they are somewhere akin to what I feel but the blistering, burning thing that starts in my stomach and fires out in all directions has no name, no beginning or end. And I don't think it will ever burn out.

Agatha is gone, who knows where. Mother and I live in constant fear. *And they know.* All of them. Every Chief Councillor is in on this secret. And not one of them has acted.

"They're not here..." Wick sighs as he arrives unsuccessful from his quest for the maps. I jump and the academic shrinks back to her corner. He doesn't see her. I try to pretend she isn't all I see. "They were getting damaged by the light apparently. They've taken them to Castle Hill."

I look past him to the academic, who sighs deeply, the weight of Calde Valley's shame unfolding in the sound.

I could tell Wick, but what can he do? What can either of us do here, at our Preference Ball, under the steady stare of hundreds of watchers?

"At least there's dancing," I say, and his face opens, as if some joyful liquid has washed through him. I offer him my hand and he pulls me away, the hooks in my chest pulled painfully, gloriously tight.

Take my anchor and moor me with you.

☽

In the ballroom, the music plays but the floor is almost

empty. At first, I don't understand why and then I see the watchers, so many they outnumber couples. They stand so close that they breathe the same air. Some couples dance still, awkward and silent, holding each other at arm's length.

Bertie is standing on the other side of the room, silently asking something of a boy I think must be Matthie. But he is shaking his head, determinedly, arms folded across his chest like a shield.

"Shall we?" Wick asks. "It's our last chance."

He is right. The next ball is at Castle Hill when the union matches are announced. If we aren't paired, we won't be allowed to dance together. It is now or never.

"By the rules?"

"Even if we may not keep it."

He takes my hand in his and we begin to move in time to the music. It isn't long before we are joined by our own watcher, a woman from Stone who glares at us fiercely. I think of Wick's words in the boat. *Beyond space and time.* I know without doubt what torture it would be to love him always at a distance, without ever having the promise of this touch. I wonder if I could do it without being driven mad.

I wish I could believe it is as easy as choosing him, that I will write his name on the preference statement as he will write mine, but I cannot trust the council's word when I know the world they have built is a sham, when I know they have told the worst lies.

The preference statements are made in a room called the atrium, which is topped with a glass roof that lets the stars peer in like spies.

There are two neat lines: one for girls, one for boys. Wick joins his queue and I mine, and we shuffle forward, synchronized, as preference dockets are posted in huge metal boxes at the front of the line. No one talks, except through quick glances that are their own conversation.

The councillors stand watching from a gallery above, sipping from pewter tankards, and gently applauding as each deb scribbles the name of their preference on their docket. Chief Councillor Torrent is there, nodding and smiling, the grand benefactor. He is buttressed between the chief councillors from Waddow and Stone, who jovially slap him on the back or whisper in his ear. He flinches and scowls, his eyebrows a heavy knot, his nostrils flaring. I think he'd like to shove them back, shield himself with watchers who would force them to keep their distance. I search but cannot see Councillor Reade.

The line ticks on, a countdown. I am behind a girl wearing the pearl white of the Stone debs. She has a look about her, the way all the Stone folk do, a crystal-clear focus. Wisdom. They are not allowed to read the books – they read the Mythic, the same as we do, but perhaps there is something about living amongst the ancient artefacts that gives them clarity.

It almost seems possible, to imagine leaving Penn and coming here. Perhaps here I would not crave the things I had lost. I look across to the boy's line, trying to pull a name from their number. But I only know Matthie.

Tabithe and Bertie are not far ahead. Tabithe gets to the head of the line first and looks over at the boys with a flourish, as if considering her options one last time. Several of them look back at her. She bites the pencil, and smirks then shrugs as if it is meaningless. As if she really doesn't care who she chooses.

Bertie is next, and she hasn't seen what I've seen, or perhaps she has seen more, and understands better. She has as much chance of being united with Matthie as Tabithe after all. She is counting on it, fidgeting restlessly, her feet translating the urgency in her heart. Everyone in the line knows what she will write. Even Matthie, who bears it with open malice.

The two girls disappear out of the far door into the darkness to board boats as girls and boys once more, the fences re-erected until they are demolished for ever at Castle Hill.

All too soon I am at the front of the queue. Wick's queue has moved ahead slower than ours, so I am spared the glare of his eyes. But I can see him in my peripheral vision: the firmness of his stance, the set of his face, his unswerving nerve.

I'm handed a docket that has a space for my name and one for the name of my preference. And then there is another option, a box that says "no preference" beside it. It almost makes me laugh. I think of all the preferences I have that aren't this one: the choice to wait until I am older or am sure. The free will to choose who I want, how I want. There seem to be so many preferences, the words are ridiculous. And yet there is a lure to them, a world where I just shrug, the way Tabithe did, let it happen around me. Perhaps that would be for the best.

I pick up the docket, crouch over it the way I used to do in school, fearful of people seeing. The paper is coarse, like holding Wick's hand. I flit from one thought to the next. Fractious. And in the end, it isn't a choice at all, but automatic, mechanical, the pencil moving on its own.

And then it is done, and already in the box behind me. I cannot be sure what I've written. It seems hidden, even from me.

I don't look back because I can't bear the pain of doubt in his eyes.

At Castle Hill, we will know.

Agatha, Eighteen

At first, Agatha thought it was the leaving coming again. But then the pins and needles crazed through her arms and legs, and her vision clouded. This was not the leaving. It was something else. Sight and sound bucked and reared and

ga
llop
ed
aw
ay
into
    un
            end
ing   night.

"Feeling better?" her mother asked, her foot pressing the pedal of her spinning wheel as she spoke.

Agatha nodded and inhaled, coddled her cup of ginger tea, the edifying scent calming but not quelling the dizziness.

She had told Mother that she'd swooned in the heat

and Miss Warne had sent her home, though she knew she must tell her the truth before the watchers came, which must be soon. Miss Warne was bound to report the seizure she had had at school.

Instead of making her pledge as a deb, Agatha would be making it as a decom.

There was a calm suspicion in her mother's eyes, but Agatha knew she would wait for her to be ready, and she was grateful to her for it. She knew how fear would bloom in her mother's eyes, how it would not be for herself, but for Agatha, and, worse, for Wren who was barely eleven.

She had grown used to the leaving, but the new thing was different. It was an unfamiliarity that rose in her stomach, a smothering weakness when she woke on the floor, sore and aching, disorientated. Sometimes she was injured: a bruised eye, a cracked tooth or a swollen cheek that she invented excuses for when people asked. And always the lingering queasiness.

Gradually, others had helped. Her family. Manon. Alsis. Somehow, she felt she had let them all down by allowing Miss Warne to see.

Mother continued to spin her wheel, her movements a melody. Agatha was exhausted, and wanted to stay in that moment, familiar and easy, the noise of the wheel a whirring music that made her feel like an infant on the edge of sleep, in that safe space where Mother was watching.

She picked at a loose seam of her dress, pulled it a little

further apart. It had always been her favourite, as green as moss with a white lace border along its hem. It had patches on its patches, but it was pretty and soft. And soon she must only wear black.

Perhaps she would gift the green dress to Manon. It would suit her. There had been some spite in the thought, though she was fighting it.

"It's coming apart," she said, knowing Mother would think she meant the dress. But it was. Everything was coming apart like those stitches, one thread at a time, and she could not pull the thread taut much longer. She did not cry but the tears burned somewhere else. In her throat, in her gut.

"It will mend," Mother said.

"Not this time." Her voice was hoarse, stretched thin by holding back tears and fear and anger and everything else between.

Mother's pedal stopped rocking, and her hands fell in her lap. She looked at Agatha with concern but did not speak, only waited in that way of hers. Still and patient. If it had not already been shattered to pieces, Agatha's heart would have broken.

"They are coming for us," she said.

People think it is the pain that makes decommissioning so brutal. But Agatha already knew that the shame was worse.

☾

The judgment had been swift. Everyone in Penn knew

that the decommissioning had been scheduled for the end of summer, only weeks before the pledges.

And now she was to wear the black dress too. It was the only completely new dress she had ever owned – or was ever likely to now. She put it on, little expecting how it would drain the colour from inside her too. She had not then become the blackness – she was neither the darkness nor the light but grey, somewhere between.

She had to see him. But she feared he would only see the dress when before he had always seen so deeply inside her. So, she had avoided him.

Ever since the hearings that wrote her fate in ink at Castle Hill, she had been numb. She wished she could be angry, that she could rage at the world and everyone in it, but the anger had not come. And nor had the sadness.

Wren needed her. Father needed her. Even Mother needed her. They would both be branded at Castle Hill, both have the operation to tie their tubes, but only Mother would ascend to duty immediately and be assigned who knew where. Agatha would see out the Virtue Season.

She found him in the barn, milking, his fists too fierce, the goat straining at its rope.

Wren and Mother were carding wool, the chiff chaff sound of the brushes angry, even from the barn. Even the sky was enraged: orange and red.

As she walked towards him, she lifted the dress so it

222

wouldn't swish on the floor. He looked up anyway, as if he sensed her there and she stalled, caught in the moment before again. Though this time it was not the moment before he kissed her, but the moment before he saw the dress and realized the truth.

His eyes narrowed, a strange expression on his face, as if he did not recognize her. He had known it was coming. But seeing is believing. The look on his face was not disgust. She knew that look. She had seen that look already from the women at the Summit who feared her. To them, she was a creature now.

"Come here," he said, standing so brusquely his stool tipped over.

She didn't move. "I'll come to you then," he said, striding towards her.

"Stop," she begged. "I can't. I've come to say goodbye."

He shook his head.

"Do you think they can stop me loving you with a dress?" he asked, and he did not ask permission this time but took her forcefully around the waist and pulled her close, almost as close as he did once at the Foss.

"What can love do now? Now that I must be this?" she asked, trying to pull herself out of his grasp, both body and soul, not succeeding at either.

"It makes no difference," he insisted, gritting his teeth, refusing to let her go, his arms rigid around her.

"You have to let me go," she begged. "You have

to see that it does make a difference. It makes every difference."

"Not to me," he answered, kissing her so hard it felt like a fight she was losing.

She told herself this would be the last kiss, that she would do him the favour of letting him go, but even then she knew it was a lie. She would let him continue to love her. Because she would let herself continue to love him. As hopeless and sorry and useless as it was for them, she would eke out their tiny forever for as long as she possibly could. For the next year. Through the Virtue Season. And beyond.

She could not begin to talk of the end. Because there would be no end. That was the cruel twist of it. They would spend their lives trying to say goodbye when they had known long ago such a word was not in their shared vocabulary. There would always be some part of themselves that clung on, fingers and faith grasping at one awful lost promise, their love like granite.

The council should have taken her now. If only to give him half a hope for his season.

"I hate Miss Warne," he whispered into her hair, clutching her to him, so she felt the ferocity of his words as a warmth against her face.

"I don't," she answered, breathless, soothing his face with her hand. "It's not her fault. She did what she had to do."

"I don't see how. Who would have known? What did

she have to lose?"

She let herself imagine it. A world where no one knew, and they united, and he protected her for ever. And she did hate Miss Warne then. A little. And then a lot.

"They would find out eventually," she said in a desperate whisper.

"I would never have given you up like that."

She heard his words as a threat. Not to Miss Warne or even to the council. But to him. He would never give up. There was something in the rock-solid set of his shoulders that scared her. A new sort of danger, a danger she wanted so much to protect him from.

"I made you a promise," he whispered, the words stroking her face more softly now.

"You cannot keep it."

The whole world became a whisper. A silent place.

"I don't know how to break it," he said, and he put his forehead against hers, breathing her in. She listened to the sound of him, the sound of his honest heart.

"Love me for ever," she asks him again.

"And before, and in between."

"We need to say goodbye."

"Can you?"

She wanted to, she thought. She wanted to want to. But a more urgent need dethroned the first and she pulled his mouth to hers, led him to the stacked hay in the corner of the barn, and began trying, at least, to say goodbye.

"Not until it is time," she admitted as he kissed her

neck, sorry and ashamed because she was not strong enough to let him go.

Yet.

PART THREE

"Man selects for his own good;
nature only for that of the
being which she tends."

Charles Darwin,
On the Origin of the Species

CHAPTER FOURTEEN

The Ground Falls Away

Not much remains of the castle for which Castle Hill was named. Only the keep, crumbling and windowless, has survived. It stands on top of a mound that spews from the earth like a green boil, fifty-two steps curling around the side of the hill like a snake constricting prey.

At the bottom of the hill is the Annulus, a great circular building that has been built to frame it all. It is the only building in the valley made completely of glass and steel and it peers out, as if it has eyes, reflecting the sea, and the debs and the valley behind us. It serves as the council's headquarters and is where they hold the hearings and the final ball of every season.

"One step at a time," Father says as we start the journey upwards. He feigns a smile, but it is only a shadow, not real. Even he feels the gravity of today.

We climb slowly, a pack of debs and their families

slithering and shivering upwards. The railings that line the steps creak away from their fastenings in places, forced further by the crowd. They will give way one day and, when they do, the fall will be deadly. I push the rail a little further, test it. But it doesn't take me down.

The sound of so many feet on stone carries memory. This is where they branded her. This is where I watched. There is still no word from Reade and the silence sounds like grief knocking. Soon, I will have to admit that Reade has broken his word, that she is truly gone.

As we climb, the rest of the land around Castle Hill and the Annulus appears acre by acre. The Annulus is hiding a huge building that is being erected on the other side of the hill, made from burnished wood, so vast and black even the Annulus is dwarfed. The building looks like it has eight long legs, like a spider. *A hospital*, Tomie had thought, *though it looks more like a tomb*.

At the top of the steps, we spill into a cobbled yard, a round space with a high stone wall encircling it. On top of the wall are the ramparts where soldiers once stood to protect the castle from attack. Now, it is where the watchers stand guard, a human cage.

The keep towers up from the courtyard and is a perfect square, except for a corner of stone that has fallen away. At its centre is a black arc that was once a door. They say that's where prisoners were kept. Now it is where the chief councillors stand on a platform that reaches around it, hands on iron balustrades that are missing in places, rusting and flaking in others. Their grey cloaks flap like hawks' wings.

One by one, debs leave their families and join a circle in the centre of the yard, sheltered from the wind but whipped by a whirlwind, nonetheless.

"Be strong," Father says, but his lip wavers, his hand lingering in mine.

"I'll see you soon," I say into his ear as I hug him tight, hiding my fear against the stubble of his cheek.

"Aye. And there's the binding supper. I'll be eating your butter pie before I know it." He smiles, that shadow smile again.

I had not thought of deserting him to Mother's food until now, and the thought of him pretending it's the most delicious food he's ever eaten for her sake makes me smile, a ghost smile like his, but it fires his into something real. He's right. There is always a supper between uniting families ahead of the unity ritual. It is tradition for mothers to welcome their new daughters by preparing the meal together. The smell of pastry, sweet and buttery in my mind, takes me away from the castle, and fills my mouth with watery hunger. I couldn't bear to eat this morning.

Father kisses my cheek, pulls me into his familiar warmth and releases me.

"Good luck," Mother says, fiddling with the lace trim of the faded red dress I am wearing for the last time. She worries it so much I fear it will unravel. I take her nervous fingers, still them with my own, and hope she doesn't notice how mine are shaking. Her eyes are misty, and I fear the fog that might engulf them again.

"I'm OK," I say, a lie I don't mind telling – for her sake and mine. "Go to Father."

"Remember," she says, "you have to *try*." She pinches my chin and joins Father where he stands against the wall. He folds his arm around her, as if tucking her under his wing, and she puts her hand on his. My hope for them stretches into the space between us as this last stitch of time gives way.

Tonight, I will leave with my betrothed's family. Their home will become mine. This is goodbye.

I take my place in the circle of debs and wait. I don't notice the girls either side of me or the boys who face us. I don't search for Wick. I look at the leather pumps I have been forced to wear and imagine swapping them for my field boots as soon as this is over. Running as fast as I can towards something, towards someone.

The last debs join the circle and Torrent lifts his hand to an already silent crowd. He opened the season, so it is he who will conduct the declarations. He stands on the platform around the keep, tall and looming, the blackness of his eyes magnified.

"Debutants, it is a proud tradition that you continue. If your preference is matched, you are blessed. If not, you must remember your duty and be glad of your unions for they are in the service of our kind. Our purpose is not self-gratification but the sanitation of the species. We must work together to rid ourselves of contamination, make ourselves pure—"

Purity is a fallacy. My heart beats the words.

"Before I begin tonight's Declaration Ceremony, join me in thanks as we say the Dedication Prayer."

Do my lips move? Does the crowd make a sound? The world has gone mute. Even the wind has lost its whistle.

"Joelle Cook of Penn Vale, stand forth."

Joelle – the smallest boy in our year with hair that worries his eyes – looks back at his parents stiffly. His mother gestures with her hand and moves as if she's pushed him onstage.

"Your preference was not matched. You will unite with Annalise Dixon of Waddow who stated no preference. Stake your claim."

Joelle's eyes smart, though he is silent. He looks across the circle at the girl he must have preferred, a mouse of a girl whose mouth falls open, chest heaving. She preferred him too. It's obvious. He drags his feet as he crosses the circle to claim his mate, who takes his hand like you'd hold a hot rod, and they stand side by side.

Couples are called out quickly – moving in blurs outside my vision. Time and again, the preferences are not matched. People are united outside their county. The hunger in my stomach grumbles into my heart. I try not to count the debs as they dwindle or take note of who is left.

"Matthie Dunne of Stone Hamlet, stand forth,"
Matthie looks bleak, his eyes red–rimmed, his preference
lost already. I look for Tabithe, who has been joined by a
boy from Foxfields. She is not blithe any more.

Matthie takes a step inside the circle, lifts his chest,
takes a huge breath to ready himself.

"Your preference was not matched. However, there was
a preference stated for you and the bloodlines are pure. You
will unite with Bertholamay Kane of Penn Vale."

There is a soft gasp that I know comes from Bertie and
he collects her like she is a piece of bobbing flotsam from
the sea. Poor Bertie – she will spend her life as Father has,
pushing a giant rock uphill, crushed by the weight as it
falls against her time and time again. The worst torture
in Calde Valley is not the claims or the seasons; it is not
the dipping stool or even the decommissionings, it is the
myth of preference.

"Wick Flint of Penn Vale, stand forth."

My ribs seem to clutch my breath, hands around my
lungs, but my eyes find his without effort, as if my gaze
and his share one path. His whole face is flexed tight, jaw
tense, eyes scared and small. It is not his face at all, not
the face of the boy who trusts the rolling sea. My heart
stammers. I feel tired to my bones. The blood is loud in
my ears.

"Wick Flint, you stated a preference that was matched,
and the bloodlines are pure. You will unite with Manon
Pawlak, also of Penn Vale. Stake your claim."

I feel my finger write his name again, the pencil fluid in my hand, how easy it was to form the letters, as if they came right out of my soul. I see the breadth of his smile, the automatic speed of his step, but my body becomes solid and the ground falls away. I have fought for so long against the strength of this love, the fullness of it breaks me. It is too big, too strong. I feel dizzy. Gasp for breath.

I hesitate. And he sees.

☽

In the grand ballroom of the Annulus, everything is bigger than it should be. Windows and doors, tables and candelabra: they are all too big.

"Even the chickens are fatter than at home," I joke as the music begins.

The councillors lead the first dance with their Madams, to show off their model unions: an example of what we should aspire to. I catch sight of Reade, not dancing but standing with Brack between two tall pillars that look like guards. They are talking in whispers. My heart thumps. But the dance continues, the debs join, and Wick and I are compelled away by the music, which takes us into the crowd.

We haven't spoken since the announcement. His disappointment is palpable.

"I'm sorry," I say. Our feet move, the practised steps stored somewhere by muscle memory, but we do not float the way we did before. "I was just surprised."

"I understand," he says, and I know he does, in part. "It takes time," he whispers.

I need to tell him he's misunderstood. That I want this. But not here. I will not convince him with words.

The dance floor fills when parents are invited to join the dance and dresses paint the floor like brushes on canvas. Mother and Father come dancing towards us, smiling contently. A weight has been lifted from them. They know I will stay in Penn, live amongst good people, and for them, that is enough.

"Joy and hope," they say together, words that seem to boom and echo before the steps of the dance lead them away.

Joy and hope. It is its own sound, so many voices repeating these words to their own loved ones, and it becomes a dance of its own, with its own steps.

"Joy and hope," I say to Wick, feeling the smile fill my cheeks, though I know my eyes are uncertain.

"Joy and hope," he returns – polite, censored. I feel panic spread through me.

"I am looking forward to meeting your mother," I say. I have found my way before by talking of his family.

"And she you." If I didn't know better, I'd think he was concentrating on his steps.

"I hope the children will not mind me. There is room at Walker Clough?"

"They will not be inconvenienced." He smiles and there is a secret in his eyes, something he wants to share. He is holding back again, and I am desperate to reach him, to close this distance he seems insistent on maintaining.

"What is it?"

"Nothing. There's plenty of room is all," he says, the closest he's been to a grin since the dance began. It makes me smile too, though I do not know why.

"That is good. They won't like their new sister if they have to give up their rooms."

"They will love you," he says, and I know he wants to say the other thing. The thing he has never said. But he does not.

"Will we never understand each other, Wick Flint?" I ask, tracing his jaw with my thumb. The music lulls us closer together. It is a part of the dance where we are joined. He puts his forehead against mine, whispers the lyrics softly. And we sail.

> *When I was faithless, I believed in you.*
> *When my heart was empty, I trusted yours.*
> *When I was barren, I hoped for you.*

He murmurs the words, so soft on his lips they are almost a kiss. But the dance takes him off in one direction and me in another so I cannot answer.

CHAPTER FIFTEEN

Farewell, Fire Angel

Cayte is at the kitchen table at Walker Clough, which is to be my new home. She tips a lump of dough out of a bowl, which lands with a *pfut*. Her dislike of me clings to her like a close-fitting dress, uncomfortable and itchy. It is an ordinary enmity. Her son is the favourite, I can already tell. She punches the engorged dough so that it implodes and wheezes. Strands of her hair fall around her face and stick to her forehead.

"I promised Father butter pie for the binding supper," I say. Though I have asked for leave to go to the summit to trade for the ingredients. Though I have more I want to trade for, and have packed a few items I won't miss.

"It's not for a week," she says, "it'll go off."

"A ruby pie then," I struggle. But she does not protest further. She seems relieved at the prospect of having her house to herself, free of my irksome presence. She can put me off for a little longer.

"Is there anything you need?" I ask, but she looks at me as if I'd be incapable of achieving such a thing and shakes her head. So I leave her to prepare for the supper, guilt seeping through me. She is pregnant and though she is not showing, I know she feels queasy often. There are so many things I could do, but she won't hear of it and I don't know how to placate her, just as I don't know how to bring her son back to me. But it feels like winning her approval would help. The two of them are alike.

Gillam and Wick are long gone by the time I pass the jetty – but Rubin and Stela are hanging over the edge on their tummies, dangling tin buckets into the water. They don't bring up fish, only sludge and silt.

"We should put some stale bread in."

"Bacon would be better," I offer.

They look up as I pass, eyes wide, unsure of the creature in their midst – perhaps I'll swallow them whole like a sea monster from the stories Wick and Gillam tell them when they come home from the sea. They knew a sister would come at the end of the season and have forged their own myths around me.

"Bacon," Rubin mimics, his mouth lopsided as he thinks. The children have not been sour, only shy. If I can get them onside, it might help with Cayte.

I walk through Jaynie's Foss, though it is not the most

direct route to the Summit. It is a peaceful walk, good for reflecting – like a fairy dell, or so Agatha always told me, with its tangled trees and pond in the rainy season. And all I think of is the letter. And what it means.

When we were small, before the need for scripts and the fear of the watchers, we roamed free here, swimming on our backs and staring at the sky. It was ours alone, or so it seemed. Back then it was framed by leafy boughs and fractured sunlight, but an ash dieback crackled through it and now the sky bleeds through the charcoal statues of skeleton trees. It isn't a place of freedom any more, but a memory of innocence long gone. The stone walls remind me of animal skulls now, stripped clean, and though the ground glints silver where the sun shimmers against the edges of limestone scraps, they no longer seem jewel-like but jagged, metallic – like the swords of watchers.

I stride to the end of the lane with my eyes on my feet and arrive at the edge of the Summit. It is bustling with debs shopping for the binding suppers. There are new faces, as there always are at this time of year, girls from across the borders, strangers who are met with suspicion. The women of Penn eye these foreigners with apprehension and greet them with a wall of whispers where I am greeted with a kind eye and favourable tongue. I have never been friendly with the women of Penn and yet, suddenly, it seems we are the best of friends.

"Morning, Mistress Manon."

"Joy and hope."

"To think ... a Flint!"

"How many young you will have!"

"Strong girl. Good match."

They treat me like a goddess. I am one of theirs, a Penn girl, united with one of theirs. And Wick is one they all know and love. I am not newly arrived on their shore, here to take the food they have grown, the boys they have borne. But the way they treat me only makes me feel like a creature, dragging entrails of seaweed behind me. I am not used to it. And it makes me feel conspicuous, as if I could only let them down. But I have decided on Wick. It gives me hope that I could be what they want me to be.

There is a crowd around the carpentry. I push closer and see wiry Mrs Samms at the centre. She wears her hair tucked in a cap, but little wisps fight free, the colour of Tomie's hair. Blonde and thin.

"You can't do this," she is yelling, waving a piece of paper at no one in particular. "This has been in the Samms family for generations." Her face is white with the tracks of tears. A knot of local women soon tie themselves around her to witness her despair or to hold her fast in it. The watchers are anonymous, hoods raised, only their hard mouths visible, smirking as they leave. One stays, lurking at the edge of an alley that runs between the carpentry and a shop that sells herbal remedies.

"Have they found Tomie?" I ask a woman ahead of me. She is old, her shoulders pulled down by time, her face a tangle of lines.

"No. They'll be taking the carpentry from them."

"You can't do this," Mrs Samms continues, but her voice is weaker.

"As punishment for Tomie?"

"Not officially. They'll be giving it to a newly united couple. There's a shortage of homes. There always is. This happens every year."

Does it? I wonder how many other atrocities have bypassed me before my own season began.

"They have no right to keep it. Tomie isn't here to inherit."

My throat fills; I could spit fire. *How long before they take Wild Fell?*

"Where will the Samms go?"

"To the scrappers." She squeezes her lips together and swallows, but the thunder that rolls through me cannot be sunk as easily.

I think of the salvage yard at Waddow. Furnaces for the Lost World metal skimmed from the sea, hotter than the eye of a drought fire. I think of the people who work by those seething fires, beating the metal into useable lengths, tipping it into moulds. Before long, they too melt away, destroyed by the heat of the fires.

Mrs Samms is tidied back into the carpentry, like a dangling thread tucked away by the women who have surrounded her.

Mr Samms is inside. I can see him through the window. He hasn't come outside to fling his fury at the world as she has. He has simply continued his task and is bending over his lathe, foot crashing against the pedal whilst the rest of him is as still as rock. I remember Tomie, so proud of the skills he learned from this granite man, and I think of the mirror he made that hangs so heavy in my satchel.

And then I see him.

The figure I first mistook for a watcher.

This face is not the face from the moors, the one I longed to touch. It is old, papery, grey and flat. His cheeks are sallow. Though it is certainly him, the same fiery glint in his eye. A whisper of himself as he watches and cannot intervene. His cloak is dark green and the hood has fallen only far enough to know it is him.

No one else sees him, and he is gone before he sees me.

I follow him, trying not to make a sound as I stalk down the narrow passage, through the vapours of flax and milkwort that effervesce from the herbal seller's window.

He sneaks through a wooden gate at the back of the carpentry. There is a sound like dry, rustling leaves, a slam, and then quiet. But when I creep into the yard seconds later, he is nowhere. Gone. There is nothing but four walls and a backdoor to the carpentry. I try the handle, but it's locked.

I wonder how the watchers have not found him if his parents have been hiding him here. Surely, they have searched here – his home. If he was here all along, someone would have told.

I'm about to leave when my toe catches in the dense mat of bindweed that erupts white and pink all over the ground. I bend down to free my foot from the knots of vines and realize it is not the vines at all, but the metal arc of a handle. A trapdoor, almost invisible. That is why they have not found him.

The hinges creak as I pull. The door folds back on itself and I manage to lay it down quietly before I step into a forgotten cellar.

It smells rotten, like strawberries left in the sun. Fungal. Dark.

But he is there. I hear him breathing.

On the last step, the blackness gives way to a flicker of candlelight, barely enough flame to light his face. He sits on a pile of hay sacks, his log legs drawn into his arms so his knees touch his chin. He has pulled the green hood back and his blonde hair – which always touched his shoulders – has grown longer and has been made darker by dirt.

"Tomie," I mutter.

"You found me. Clever you," he says, sour.

"You've been here since Foxfields?"

He nods, barely perceptible, irises burning amber in the candlelight.

"What is this place?" I ask, and he snorts as if the answer to my question should be obvious, which it is. I have seen a cellar before. But I don't know what else to say. He coughs, the sound rattling in his chest.

The tiny room is damp and as closed as a coffin. Anything put here would rot, even Tomie it seems. The walls are wet, and it seems like the slime that lines them also lines his lungs. I can't bring myself to turn and leave.

"I saw you," he says when he gets his breath back. "I knew you'd follow me. I let you find me."

"Why?"

"I wanted to hear your voice."

"Aren't you frightened I'll give you away?"

"Will you?" he asks, but I do not answer because I do not know.

"Did you hear about the carpentry?" he asks.

I nod.

"What will I do?" he says, his voice a half-sob, and it catches me by surprise. It is not his parents he thinks of but himself. Though they have shielded him and risked their lives, his only thought is what will happen to him when they are sent to the scrappers. I move away from him, suddenly aware of how close we are.

"You didn't help her," is all I say.

"Who?" he asks, looking up with vacant eyes. He fiddles with his fingers as if he's counting or stripping wood. *Who? How could he ask who?*

"Geneve," I whisper, the sound of her name unbearable. It seems to bounce against the walls. "You might have saved her, and yourself."

He snorts, a childish sound, and it makes me turn and mount the stairs.

"Manon, wait! I'm sorry. I am. Please don't leave. I only meant that I could never have saved her. Do you really think they would have let us unite?" His voice is young, soft, he sounds so like Rubin or Stela begging Wick for a story that I pause. But I keep my back turned to him.

"I was scared, Manon," he mutters. "Haven't you ever been that scared?"

My heart sinks. I think of Mother, of Agatha, of Wick and Geneve and Stone – most of all, and the academic. The fear I've felt has been a black flower, with petals that keep on opening. I will never find its centre.

I do turn now, to see if the look in his eyes matches the sorrow in his voice and am gratified to find it there. A curtain of shame has fallen over him. He let her die and he is sorry for it.

"It doesn't bring her back."

"I know," he says, voice weary. He sounds like Mother when the fog takes her, the words automatic. "What will I do when they're taken? They'll find me and—"

"And you'll pay for what you've done. It is only what you should have suffered then," I hiss.

"I suppose so."

A hint of regret spasms through me.

"Farewell then, fire angel."

I feel as though he has tied a lasso around me and is pulling me back.

Don't listen. You cannot trust him.

"I meant what I said that day. I did want you," he says.

"Then why did you do it?"

"It was she who had the eyes of the wolf," he adds with a lopsided attempt at a smile.

"You're blaming her?"

"No. Not entirely. We were dancing. It was nice. And then it was something else. But she began it. I swear."

"You could have said no."

He stands up, moves towards me on the steps, turns me to face him and something of what I felt on the moor wakes. The hairs on my neck have not forgotten his touch.

"Would you?"

There is no space between us now. He stands very still, as if he thinks moving will scare me.

His hands fall to my hips. "I did want you," he says again. "I still do."

And then his lips are on mine. He tastes earthy and salty, and his arms and hands are everywhere. Then the scratchy hay sacks are at my back, and he is on me, heavy and tempting, and it is dark, and no one would ever know.

But it is Wick I see when my eyes close, staring at his breakfast instead of at me whilst I long for the intimacy of his eyes meeting mine, and it is him I am kissing, not Tomie. It is frustrated and angry and needy, and a pang of guilt and shame spreads through my chest.

I push at him, fight my way from under him.

"I can't," I whisper as I untangle myself from him and stand. "I am uniting."

"Who with?" he asks, sitting up. He looks more himself now, powered by me and my weakness for him.

"Joelle Cook."

I don't know why I lie, except that I cannot say Wick's name in this place. In this darkness.

"Go then," he mutters. "Leave me to rot."

And I do.

☽

I remember why I came to the Summit and head to the blacksmith's forge, my legs as hard as the iron he hammers on his anvil. I had wanted to impress Cayte by getting her a gift. That is how this day had begun. But her dislike of me seems less urgent now, and even merited. I see myself as she sees me. Weak and unsure, my heart easily turned.

The heat of the blacksmith's fire spirals out from the wooden hut. When I am just outside the door, Reade comes crashing out, his grey cloak flapping around him, and something inside me snaps. Where has he been all this time? He was meant to find her and he has done nothing.

I fly at him, claw at his face. He stills me gently, trapping me until I am calm, then puts his finger to his lips and pulls me into a narrow passage.

"You didn't help her," I say, the sting of salt at my throat, in my eyes. "You abandoned her—" I sob, unsure whether I'm talking about Agatha, or Mother.

Not a day has gone by that I haven't waited for news, desperate for any sign Agatha is alive. But each day has brought the sure conviction that Reade has betrayed me.

"I *tried*."

"Really?" I say, disbelievingly.

"Yes. You have to believe me – I wanted to help. It's all I've ever wanted. To be a friend to the people of the valley, to you and your mother. To make up for what happened between us." His words are tentative, he waits for my response.

"I know you chose someone else," is all I admit to knowing.

"It wasn't that simple. I thought I could change things by being in power. That need was greater than what I wanted for myself. I was too young to know then that it takes more than one man—"

"What happened to her?"

He looks over my shoulder, back towards the forge, then again to me. He's frightened, I can see that now.

"I was losing the council's trust. Torrent was suspicious … of my lenience, my opposition to … his plans."

"*What happened?*"

"Brack was listening that day. He knew about your friend. Agatha. He knew where she was, knew I'd offered to help. He threatened to expose me to Torrent but, worse … you and your mother."

I feel sick, dizzy, as the realization hits. "You traded her. You gave her up to *him*."

"I did it for you. For your mother. Brack agreed to keep your secret if we gave Torrent…"

He blinks, his eyes full of their names that seem to stab him.

"Agatha. Alsis."

"All he wanted was a seat on the council. He didn't care how he got it."

I am not like this man. I recognize nothing of him in me.

"I'm not proud of what I've done—"

"You did it to save your own skin."

"I did it to save yours!"

He lowers his head. His guilt is nothing to mine. I trusted him. I put her in his hands. And he delivered her to the council. I will never trust him again. "Where is she?"

"Why must you know? What can you do for her now? It will only torture you."

"It is torture not to know."

"She has ascended. That is all I know."

"Please."

He swallows, looks down again.

"Torrent has her. She is his housemaid."

He had said it would be torture. And it is. But the thought of him so close to her, the memory of what he did to Miss Warne, it is not a helpless feeling, not acceptance. It is too violent. I need to get away from Reade.

"The boy is a prisoner at Castle Hill."

I hardly hear him. My skin goes cold.

"I have to see the blacksmith," I say, the weight of one more word too heavy.

He blinks. Nods as Brack rounds the corner, puts his hand on Reade's shoulder.

"I know the blacksmith is your brother, Reade, but he's slow, that one." Brack tuts, holding a dagger out to inspect its sharpness. It slices through the sun's rays, hurting my eyes. "He does a good job, though." He takes a single ringlet of my hair and cuts it to test the blade. There are emblem flowers etched into the blade. A councillor's dagger.

"We have to be at the hearings in an hour," Reade says, a friendly note in his voice. He walks away, leaving Brack by my side. I watch him go, wondering how he turned into the man he is today if what he said was true, if all he ever wanted to do was good. I wonder too what this new alliance with Brack means, why they are here together, and who will usurp the other and when.

"I haven't forgotten you," Brack tells me when Reade is out of earshot. "I'm just biding my time. All good things come to those who wait."

Agatha, Eighteen

"Are you ready, miss?"

It was a strange thing for the masked figure to ask, and in such a sweet, soft voice too. She had not expected the man who wielded the iron to sound like a man at all but some livid, growling beast. It was even stranger that she nodded; aye, she was ready for the hideous torture he was about to inflict.

It was his eyes that chilled her. Through his mask they were obsidian, no white around the black pupils. The weight of responsibility had turned them to stone. No one knew who he was underneath, and she wondered: does he? How far had the iron become an extension of his arm? How many brandings were on his skin?

Castle Hill was warm that day, but the sky had been clouded over, summer fading into autumn. Agatha felt much the same, her old self fading from her. It was as though the whole world was there, assembled to witness as she and a line of others were paraded on the castle keep like puppets in a play. But the valerian tea had worked, in part. It had muddied her senses enough that the screams of those who went before her were muffled, and the eyes that watched her were indistinct and hazy.

"The blood of the impure must not be allowed to taint our progeny," Torrent boomed, his arms out wide as if he were trying to contain the people inside them, his voice an angry vapour. "With this sacrifice, you safeguard all our futures." He beamed, his eyes distended in her dreamlike haze, his face stretched long – mouth pulled at angles, teeth clenched and venomous.

She knew where she was, noted the curved shape of the rampart walls that clutched her inside them like a cupped hand and shielded the rest of the world from view. This was the place they should have announced her union. This was the place where the debutants stood for the Declaration Ceremony at the end of the season. And though she would join them, it would not be as one of them. She would watch from the outside, bear witness to the life she had never once doubted would be hers.

The sky was mottled, the clouds like silvery bruises on its lifeless skin. She was thankful she could not make out Manon or Father or Wren. Or Alsis. The crowd was as liquid as the sea. These people were her mooring, and she was glad the valerian kept them far from her.

When Agatha was little, she could never watch the branding iron as it touched the skin. But there had been no escaping the screams, no matter how hard she covered her ears or buried herself in her mother's belly. And now that scream would be hers.

As she got older, she forced herself to watch because it felt like defiance. A way to honour them, to look into their eyes and silently say, *You are not that which they accuse you of.*

The decoms lived amongst them. Anyone could apply to have one. They were servants or fieldhands or they scavenged the sea and brought their finds to the council. Or they taught the dogma of the council like Miss Warne. But they were tightly controlled and at night, they would report to a watcher's house. Or worse, a councillor's.

"Mark this girl so that all may know her failing," Torrent called as the iron was brought down.

It was the smell that hit her long before the pain. The sweet burning smell of bacon. But the pain followed, sure enough. It woke and was searing, slicing along her cheekbone and filling every part of her. A sheen of sweat coated her back, and she felt the fragility of her bones, so weak they might implode. She didn't cry out but took the cry inwards and it buried itself in her, a feral thing. Contained … for now.

She was quiet because somewhere inside the misty blur, she knew her sister was watching, knowing her own day would also come. Wren would mark each moment of her sister's pain and those moments would come again and again in nightmares and fearful daydreams. Agatha would not show her sister the agony that waited.

When the iron was taken away, and the acrid smoke

had risen to the sky, she saw it on the crest of her cheek: the red-hot scar that would forever sit at the corner of her vision, colouring the world in shades of mauve. The pain cut through everything else. Silent tears stung as hot as the iron, and she slumped to the floor, exhausted and raw. She let the watchers tidy her away, dragging her by the arms to the end of the line of the other new decoms, all on their knees as limp as empty sacks, weeping and moaning. And the branding iron lifted again behind her. But Torrent's gaze lingered on her. For a single moment she felt powerful, meeting his gaze with all the ferocity she could muster.

"Such beauty," she thought she heard him say, so quiet it was barely audible. He blinked hard then and gathered himself, straight as a dart, and turned his eyes to the crowd. "You have done your duty," he repeated, and she thought maybe the valerian was playing tricks on her hearing. "The people of Calde Valley thank you, child."

For a second, she dared not look up and show the world her new face, and buried it in her hands, careful not to touch the raw wound. But then that thing inside her, made small but not extinguished, rose, indefatigable and she pulled herself up to standing. The crowd stilled. She felt their eyes on her and welcomed them. She looked directly at Wren, at Manon, at Alsis, the way she had not dared to before, and was fired by the anger in their eyes.

"I *have* done my duty," she struggled to say. Her

voice was hoarse but echoed through the silence. "But who amongst you is not flawed?" She looked directly at Torrent. "Who does not harbour some secret shame? I am so much more than you can imagine. I am no more flawed than you."

The crowd held its breath. Torrent scowled, and before the blackness came, before the watcher struck, she saw the way the truth of her words rippled through the crowd.

When she was brought home, there were two more scars, which sat either side of her belly button: tiny nicks that healed too quickly, the skin forgiving faster than she could. She wondered how they could be so small and so large at the same time. Because these small wounds represented the everlasting pain of being a decom, the pain of never being able to have children.

☽

Alsis ran his finger over the milky-pink scars on her abdomen and she shivered. His fingers were cold, and the skin was still sensitive. Although the wounds had healed, the nerves underneath seemed to hum at his touch.

They had been at the Drift for two days, and he had touched every part of her new body. But it was these marks that fascinated him, that he came back to again and again, as if he were trying to rub them away. His touch woke the hunger in her stomach, and the grumbling groaning feeling seemed to follow his finger underneath her skin, down through her belly. There were so many different types of hunger. And now she knew them all, she thought.

The wind whistled around them, through the cold shelter of the cave. The blankets they had brought were sodden, the food long gone. Water dripped from stalactites above them. Everything was wet. They hadn't been able to light a fire.

"We'll row on soon. Find land," Alsis said, but she knew they would not. Even if their boat hadn't been damaged by the Pull, it had been a hard enough journey with full bellies and eager muscles. Beyond the mouth of the cave, the roar of the waves was a waiting serpent, and she knew that the longer they lay like that, the weaker they would get. And yet they continued, tangled in each other's arms, talking as if the world were all theirs to roam.

"There's no hurry," she said, and every ounce of her wanted to believe it.

"I wish we had tried sooner… Before…" His thumb was still trying to smooth away her scars.

"It was impossible then. Besides, I'd go through that pain every day to get to this moment," she said. It was true – being together again like this, even for a short time, she could almost pretend it had never happened, that the iron had not fallen. Despite everything, there was still a small creature of hope inside her that thought things could have been different, that the life she mourned might materialize, whole and healed and beautiful.

She let him search her eyes, feed his empty belly on the complex truth.

"I would go through that and more to take the pain away and give you back what's yours. I know you wanted... We wanted..."

It was not just him she had lost. It was *them*: their children. It was as cold as the ocean and as deep.

"But we are together," she said.

He put his head on her chest, and she kissed the top of it. His hair smelled like home. Of fields and animals and hard work. She inhaled it, framed it in her mind, a gallery of him.

"They are coming," he said, and she felt warm tears land on her skin, heard his breathing hitch. He was giving up too. He would always have had to in the end. Even Alsis could not defeat the council. "I saw the boats."

"How long?"

"An hour at most."

This was it then. These were their last moments. She had imagined them often. But never let herself believe they would come.

She thought of that first kiss, the hope inside it, and of all the hopeless kisses after, when they knew this was where it would end. It seemed like every kiss had been a countdown to this last one.

"Never be sorry," she told him, stroking his hair, feeling her own tears slide down the back of her throat, swallowing them.

"I will *always* be sorry," he said, lifting his chin to look at her. "No matter what happens, I failed you. But I won't fail in my promise. I will always love you."

"Then don't fight," she pleaded. "When they come, don't fight any more. I want to remember you like this." She smoothed her finger over his eyebrows, adding the sensation to the gallery wall.

He didn't answer, but she heard the bitter sigh. She imagined that he was breathing her out, slowly but surely. And one day, he would breathe for someone else.

"Alsis?"

"Aye?"

It took every ounce of her to say it.

"Try to love when you unite," she whispered, hoping the poker of white-hot heat that seared as hot as the branding iron did not shudder into her voice.

The last kiss was so sweet and bitter and tender and rough, she was sure she would never forget the feel of it, or the current of need and the desperate sadness that convulsed inside it.

There were so many different types of hunger, and here was yet another, she thought.

An hour at most, he had said. Let it be enough. Let it be enough to last for ever.

CHAPTER SIXTEEN

Manon's Leap

Walker Clough is two miles from Wild Fell. It is strange to think it has been there all this time: an easy, flat walk across scorched fields, a scramble over a couple of twisted old stiles. There is even a makeshift path that leads from one door almost to the other, the meadow grass trodden down by people beating a path to the Boot or the Summit.

It is early evening, just before the sky steals the sun, and Gillam is giving me a tour. Wick is sitting on a bucket he has upturned on the jetty, mending nets.

Rubin sits beside him, fiddling with the twisted strands of a discarded net the way his big brother does. Only his holes seem to get bigger, and he frowns. Though he does not ask Wick for help, he stares hard at his brother's hands, hoping to prove himself as worthy, without admitting defeat.

Stela is dangling her dolly, Mirabelle, on the edge of the jetty, making her feet walk along the boards whilst her own feet dangle in the sea, and Cayte is in the kitchen preparing supper. She whistles as she works, and the sound casts a spell over us all.

Gillam speaks of his home as if it is another child.

"My grandfather built the cold house," he says. "That's where we keep the barrels."

It is not a huge plot, but it is twice the size of Wild Fell. The main house faces us, and then there is a row of connected buildings that turn a corner at one end, making an L shape. The main house is made mostly of stone but has patches of brick that look like badly stuck plasters where parts of it must have been eaten by time.

In the middle, in sight of the kitchen window where Cayte's head bobs in and out of view, is a square-shaped knot garden, edged with corrugated sheet and planted with herbs. And there is a patch of wild grass on the open side of the L that could be ploughed and planted. It occurs to me I might have something to offer the Flints that even Cayte would be happy with. And, as Gillam talks, I make a mental list of all the seeds I need to fetch from home.

"My own father and I fixed up the holes in the big house," Gillam says. He is not as good a builder as he is a fisherman. Father's pointing is much neater.

We have walked the longer length of the L now, past the main house, and turned the right-angle so that we pass the cold store he spoke of. Adjoining it is a stable that houses a gelding called Jack. I stroke his nose as we pass, and he whinnies. We are facing the jetty now, and the sea beyond it.

It is a calm day, the blue-grey water is inanimate, as if you could pick it up and pull it over yourself like a sheet. I try to map the world anew from this angle, so close to home yet so different, the landmarks moved. Castle Hill is visible from here, as it is from everywhere in Penn, but it seems closer than it does from Wild Fell. I try not to think of Alsis locked inside and focus on the new building instead, enormous, with legs that crawl out on all sides. The strangeness of it. The question.

"This is what I wanted you to see," Gillam says. "You're not to stay in the big house when you unite—"

"Father," Wick says. "Not yet."

His father's eyes are full of excitement, and I think of birthdays in this house, imagine him bursting with secrets until he explodes and gives in, giving the children their presents too soon, his glee as he watches their faces light up into reflections of his own. He bites his lip as if to stop himself speaking, and looks at Wick.

"Son, *show her*," he instructs, almost dancing, but Wick lifts the nets, showing why he can't.

"In a minute," he answers, working at the holes with impatient hands. He doesn't look at me.

Gillam looks like he might show me whatever it is himself but sighs, apologetic, waves his hands.

"It's always hard at first," he says, tutting and turning back towards the main house. He looks at Cayte through the window. "She was hard work after the Declaration Ceremony. But I won her round!" He chuckles, his grin as cheeky as a child scrumping apples.

He links his arm through mine, which reminds me of Father – and makes me yearn to tuck myself into the crook of his arm and walk this way with him.

"He'll come right soon enough," Gillam says, which makes me look at Wick who is folding the nets up now.

"He's disappointed with me," I say, unable to stop myself confessing my worst fear.

"No. He's just… Well, it's not for me to say. He must speak for himself."

He winks, squeezes my arm, and goes into the house. Cayte has been watching from the window, her face stern, her shoulders moving up and down with the motion of kneading or washing, or some other chore she has been using as a channel for her vexation. But she smiles when she meets his eye, her shoulders relax, and Gillam's stride quickens as if he might leap through the window to get to her sooner.

I wander around the knot garden in squares: patch of grass, Cayte's kitchen window, cold store, stable, sea … all the way round and back again. And all the while Wick bothers with the nets, arranging and rearranging them in a lidded box at the mouth of the jetty until they fit, and the lid closes, and he can't put it off any more. He stands with his thumbs hitched in his pockets, his back to the ocean and his hair ruffled by the wind.

Leap, Manon.

"Come and see then," he says, walking towards me.

"Father thought you should have a proper home," he adds, blushing, leading me towards the building that has the stable on one side and the sea on the other.

The little house, *my* house, I think with wonder, is a one-storey building, about as big as the stable and the cold store combined. But it is a pretty place, built with a border of red brick with grey stones like honeycomb crammed inside it. And it has a corrugated iron roof that reminds me of home. I long for the sound of rain on it already.

It might have been a pig barn or a storehouse but has a freshly painted yellow door, not garish like buttercups but soft like meadow rue. The smell of paint fills the air.

There is a small path that leads to the front door, edged with upturned bottles, and there is even a spindle tree, its orange and pink berries budding around the door.

"Your father is very thoughtful," I say as I follow Wick to the front door, breathing heavily. I could cry for this kindness. It is more than I could ever have hoped for and now that I have it, I dare admit it is what I have hoped for all along.

"He's a practical man. The main house is a bit cramped with three children in one room, and you and I were to share with them otherwise. He wanted some peace, I reckon."

He pushes the door handle, brushing against the spindle tree and knocking a clutch of infant berries to the ground, then hovers in the doorway, stalling for time. Nervous. I will not fail him this time. I am ready.

"Welcome home," he says, swallowing, and letting me pass. "It used to be a smokehouse, but it hasn't been used for years."

His nose wrinkles as he tests the air for any lingering smell. But there is only the smell of the sea, and the fresh paint, and the mint growing in Cayte's garden.

Inside, it is cool and dark, with only one cracked window to let light in. The wind whistles through the tubular grooves of the roof, a musical house.

He follows me but leaves the door open as if I might want to escape, and finds his way through the dark automatically, retrieving some candles from a drawer in a table that sits in the very centre of the room. He lights the candles, and my home unfolds.

The small table is made from a length of crooked driftwood that has been balanced on tree stumps. There is a handmade stool either side, one for each of us, and a kitchen of sorts along one wall, though it is just a tiny stove, a tall cupboard set into the wall and a basin for washing. The cracked window has no curtain, and I am amazed to find I long to sew some. I will go to Mother when I can and beg her to teach me. Or ask Cayte.

There is a pallet in one corner where we will sleep. Together.

Everything is arranged in pairs: two bowls, two plates, two sets of knives and forks, all laid out and ready to use. There is even a vase in the middle of the table, though it is empty. When this is our home, I will fetch anemones for the Pawlaks in spring and fen violet for the Flints in summer.

How long have I known where to find his flower? When did I notice it growing at Wolfhole Crag?

"Where did it all come from?" I ask, thinking of the dented tin plates I've brought from home, embarrassed to unpack them. The two on the table are porcelain from the Lost World, with faded bluebells all around the rim. Wick shrugs, as if it is nothing. When he must know it is everything.

"No one barters like a Flint."

I fiddle with the pots and pans that hang about the stove and imagine our life: serving the fish he brings home, eating hungrily, and, if my stomach has a heart, it leaps and falls.

"I don't know how to thank Gillam," I say, my voice thick.

Something catches in Wick's throat too, an unspoken thought. His feet scratch restlessly against the floorboards as he shuffles, as uncertain as I am.

"It is not grand. We can eat at the house – you don't have to cook for me."

"I can cook," I say, laughing, as if it should be obvious, my mind flicking through the pages of Grandma's recipe book already.

"Did your mother teach you?" he asks, his voice warming, the cork coming loose.

"No." I snort. "She wasn't a natural. I was forced to teach myself. That or starve."

"I should've known," he says, smirking. "Is there anything you can't do?"

He looks at me properly then for the first time since Stone, his lashes sweeping his eyes, and my heart sways and swells. But he stays put, holds back.

"It's unlucky for a house to have no name," I say.

"That's what Father said. I told him you'd decide." He bites his lip, scoops the floor with his foot. "I never expected you to choose me. You understand that? But I *hoped* – after Stone—"

"We meet again," Gillam says, coming through the open door, backside first. He is carrying the casket I brought from home. It is not large or heavy and he easily manages to fit it through the doorway, but he makes a show of heaving it about as if it's laden with treasure. He sets it down on the table and the crockery clatters. I'm tempted to rescue the fragile things but resist. They aren't mine yet.

"I thought you might want your own things – make it home," Gillam says. "The lad's done a good job building it, but it could be prettier," he adds with that side smile, a special smile he reserves for poking fun at his son.

So, it was Wick – not Gillam – who did all this. It was Wick who built me a home.

"What do you think then, Mistress Flint?" Gillam

asks, giving me my new name the way the women at the Summit did. It is not yet mine, but it hovers in the air as if I could snatch it. I want to.

"It's beautiful," I tell him, meaning it so fully. It is all beautiful: the house, the name, and Wick. He is the most beautiful of all, standing with his face turned away from me, and his chin dipped.

"Aye. It was worth all his hard work, even if he did neglect his job all summer," Gillam mocks. "Supper's ready," he says, closing the door. I wait to hear the handle release and turn to Wick, disbelieving.

"*You* did this?" I ask, and Wick looks at me slowly, his eyes broiling.

"Just in case," he says, hooking his thumbs through his pockets again. I step closer to him, between him and the table, and unhook his thumb, stretch his palm against mine, and splice my fingers through his. A shared pulse beats between us.

"I thought you regretted choosing me," I confess.

"Never. I just wanted you to choose me for love, not because I was the only option."

I cup his cheek in the palm of my hand. "I never had an option when it came to loving you. As hard as I fought it..."

That smile he has been forcing down is finally freed. He puts his hand on the small of my back where it seems to fit so well and pulls me towards him so that our hips meet, and I feel a hot rush through my stomach.

"I am sorry," I whisper.

"For what?"

"That I didn't show you how I feel."

I bring his mouth to mine with my finger and thumb on his chin and taste him: copper and sand. It is feathery at first, his lips brush mine, tickling, testing, and then it is deep and warm and full. His hips press harder against mine, the table taking my weight, and my hands answer as if it's a question, pushing against the top of the table so that my hips rise to meet him. There is hardly a way to be closer and yet it isn't close enough. The pulse in his chest beats against mine.

"Supper," Gillam shouts from the main house.

There is a violence to our parting. As if my body gasps; as if it's left a wound that throbs. I thirst for him. And supper is long.

☽

I sleep in Wick's bed, which he has forsaken for a pallet in the parlour. Under his sheets, I envelop myself in his smell. How deeply it seems to fill me, how real he seems to be. I imagine tiptoeing down the stairs, waking him from sleep, peeling him out of his sheets, the dark hairs on his arms and thighs, the journey my fingers would make over his chest. I do not sleep but I dream: feral, desperate dreams of him.

☽

Cayte is pouring hot water over raspberry leaves, the sweet steam puttering around her. She gives me a side-eye as I roll out the pastry for Father's butter pie but smiles when I catch her. The kitchen is full of the sweetness of ruby jam, heady yeast and the tart freshness of lemonade. I have already made a ruby pie, though the oven is crowded with Cayte's baking and it sits on the counter waiting its turn.

When she is busy peeling potatoes in her rocking chair, a bucket catching the curls as they fall, I take the chance to leave the gift I fetched from the blacksmith. I know she will not thank me for making a scene of it, so I put it by the sink where I know she will see it. It is a baby's rattle, made of iron, with little ringing bells on one end. I gave Tomie's mirror for it, knowing I could not give such a useless trinket to Cayte. Trading it made peace with Tomie somehow. He is not my responsibility. I owe him nothing. Though it makes me sad to think of him alone in the dark.

Wick appears just as I'm putting the pie on the window to cool, fresh from the sea and as rough.

"Come out with me," he asks through the window, a needful look in his eye. I look at Cayte as if for permission and she nods.

"But be back in plenty of time."

☽

"In you come," Wick instructs from where he stands inside his two-man skiff. The wind worries the little boat, and it strains at its mooring. I step too heavily and it lists, taking me with it, but he holds me fast, one hand either side of my hips like he's planting a tree.

"Sit. I'll teach you to scull," he says when the boat stills, smothering an infuriating grin.

"Is that something I want to learn?" I ask. "It sounds sinister."

I sit on the narrow board that Wick tells me is called a thwart and pick up an oar as if I know what I'm doing. I'm pretty sure it's the right way up anyway.

"Well, it's a whole lot more fun than drifting," he answers. It makes me think of Agatha. She always called me a drifter, until that day at school, which I cannot bear to think about. I think of the letter from Reade's office instead, which has been tucked in my basket since I came to Walker Clough, asking to be taken out and read aloud. I think about what the academic said. That our children would stand as good a chance of being healthy as any.

Wick unties us and pushes us off with his oar. When we're clear of the jetty, he dips his oar in the water and pulls back with both hands. I try to mimic him without studying him too closely and find the cut of the oar through water is a similar release to climbing or running. My arms strain with effort. I like it.

When we are half a mile from the shore and Walker Clough seems shrunken, a watch boat pulls up alongside us.

"Where are you going?"

"Nag's Bay," Wick answers, all politeness, lifting his oar arm to show his emblem patch. "Mother wants shells for the binding supper – to decorate the table."

He lies with ease.

"My mother had to have *ferns*," the watcher says, chuckling. Even watchers are amiable during union week, especially to the boys, who they treat like warriors, returning with their bounty.

My strokes are shorter than Wick's, so we move lopsided through the water and make slow progress.

"Let's fix this wobble," he says, putting one hand on my thigh and stretching my leg with the other. His body leads mine. "Plant your feet against the footboard. Push against it," he tells me, and I push as hard as I can as he takes his hand away. Cold pools there and makes me angry. But we row on, swifter and truer than before.

"It's so vast," I blurt out, a shiver in my voice, "haven't you ever been scared?"

He shrugs.

"The water's the only place I *don't* feel scared. It's the only free place in Calde Valley. You can go as far as you like, as long as you bring back fish," he says, chuckling again. "No watchers or councillors or debs whose heart you want to win anywhere in sight. It's the best job in the valley. Not many folks get to see what I've seen."

"You mean the Drift?"

His hand stills on the oar and he rests it on his lap. Water trickles from the end, puttering back into itself.

"I'm sorry about that," he murmurs. "I should have said it sooner. I wouldn't have told him if I'd known why he was asking," he says with a sigh. "Maybe they made it."

I could tell him. But I prefer to let him believe. And I cannot bear for him to know what I did. Or about Reade, and how he is tied up with us. I want him to believe I am Trent's daughter, without doubt. I wish I could go back to a time when I was so certain.

"I'm glad they went in a way."

"Why?"

"Sometimes you have to fight even though you know you can't win."

If it is a test of the idea growing inside me, he does not fail.

"Aye."

He smiles and picks up his oar. In the sunlight, his skin is honeyed umber, tanned by the summer months at sea.

"The only place I feel free is on the fells," I say. "I've climbed them all. Though everyone laughs at me for it."

"Let them laugh. You belong in the wilderness," he says without mocking. "It suits you."

The last petal of my heart opens. *He sees me.* Not the Manon who needs rescuing, or the Manon who is flawed, but the Manon who runs wild. He will never attempt to tame me.

"What's beyond the Drift?" I ask, feeling like Rubin, begging for a fairy tale. Not something from the Mythic: the silver birds that flew; the metal caterpillars that thundered through underground tunnels; something real, a tangible hope that there's something else out there.

When he answers, his heart seems as full as his nets.

"Nothing but never-ending water."

And there it is. There's nothing there. I think I always expected to run away from Calde Valley, always thought there would be something else out there, a place far away where your choices are your own and nothing is claimed, not your land nor your body.

We row on silently until we approach Nag's Bay.

"We can moor her up here," he says, and catapults himself over the edge of the skiff, spraying me with saltwater as he lands thigh deep. He shoves the boat on to the stony bank, and I step into the lick of the water, stowing my boots in the skiff, leaving my feet bare.

We sit on a blanket, eating in comfortable silence, hugged into secrecy by the cliff that reaches around us. It is the bay of childhood once more. No dipping stool, no watchers. The world is busy with union week. It looks the other way.

"You don't remember me from school, do you?" Wick asks, splitting a piece of pie, crust crumbling to the ground. It catches me off guard, but I am glad he is talking again.

"You didn't go."

"I did. At first, though not for long. And I remember you," he says, shoving a piece of meat in his mouth, discarding the pastry. He puts his thumb up in approval, takes his time chewing so I have to wait for what comes next, which I do with sullen impatience. He's about to take another bite when I scowl and snatch the pie, shove it whole in my own mouth, grinning. He laughs.

"Do you remember the union game?" he asks, a crease of embarrassment sliding across his brow as he speaks with a full mouth. *"Who's your preference? Who would you unite with?"*

"Aye," I answer, feeling like a child on the school yard, cheeks warming.

"We used to spy on you through the fence. When your turn came, my heart would turn inside out waiting. I so hoped you'd say my name. Even then. But you would always say 'I have no preference' and skulk off to the dead oak."

"Ask me."

"It's silly."

"Ask me," I say, poking him with my foot but he shakes his head.

"I've decided…" I say, teasing him the way he teased me, speaking in ellipses.

"On?" he asks, his eyes full of the burn of the late sun on the water.

"A name for the house."

"Oh?" he asks, feigning disinterest.

"Manon's Leap."

I let his eyes burn through me for a moment, the eyes of the wolf, delicious and savage.

I watch the slow parting of his mouth, his chest rising and falling.

"I like it," he says.

The only sound is our breathing, the rolling sea, the soft autumn breeze.

I kiss the edge of his mouth, tempting him to me, knowing exactly what I want, and what he wants. I feel the way his lips turn into a smile and am gratified that they will come as I bid them. And then we kiss as we did before, need meeting need. Equal and honest.

It is as though we are on the edge of a precipice, dangerously high and soaring downwards, but we let ourselves fall into the abyss. Dark and warm. Safe in each other's soft landing. Flesh sinks into flesh until our bodies are as fluid as the water that carried us here, a giant stirring wave crashing inside us both. There is a way to be closer after all. And it is this.

☽

"You have brown eyes," I tell him, my chin propped on his chest so that I can look deep into their feathery tones.

"Have you just noticed that now?"

"Gillam and Cayte's are blue."

"Stela and Rubin's too. I'm the only one with brown." It all makes sense then. The academic's words, the letter, the truth. And I have to tell him or I'll go mad.

"It's just like she said." I sit up, tidying myself. "The academic. Things aren't necessarily passed down."

Wick sits up too, fastens his buttons, frowning.

"What academic? What did she say?" he asks, alert.

I look at him, desperate now to tell. Even if it means

he looks at me differently.

I pull the academics' letter from the basket of food, pass it to him and he reads, still and silent. I ready myself too, as I knew I would have to if I shared this secret. I fasten my dress, lace my boots, ready to row back to the house. And for what comes next.

"It's all a lie," he says when he's finished.

"A downright lie." His words from penance day. "They know. And they do nothing."

"I knew it but … to see it in black and white. All those people decommissioned—"

"Torrent has Agatha," I blurt out, not daring to tell him all when his eyes seem to ask.

"How do you know?"

"Councillor Reade told me."

He draws a sharp breath but doesn't push me further. He looks down at the letter, thinking.

"What do you want to do?"

"I have an idea. But…"

I cannot say it because I don't want it to be true.

"But it means risking this," he guesses.

If anything could make me turn my back on Agatha, it would be his love. I wish we could stay in this happy ever after. He does too.

The pain turns his brown eyes almost black. But he doesn't argue. Just waits and listens as if my words are his own breath.

"Even if we do nothing," I say, "Brack has not given

up, he told me so at the Summit. We will unite, but he'll still come for me."

"When we least expect it."

He pulls me close, and I feel whole. So whole, I can't believe I'm about to shatter us both.

"We will never stop looking over our shoulders," he says into my hair. I look up at his eyes, a match being struck. "We have no choice then."

"*This* is our choice," I say, letting his body warm me. The only one that matters.

Agatha, Eighteen

Frederika lays out Torrent's uniform on a chaise at the end of his bed, as if she has done it a hundred times before. She works methodically, splaying the arms out, smoothing the creases, a well-rehearsed routine. It is a ghost of the man who fills the room, even in his absence.

When she is done, she turns her attention to a little desk of trinkets – nothing much at first: a leather purse worn thin at its corners; a small wooden box with the letter "H" carved on the lid. From her place on the bed, Agatha sees something she recognizes from long ago through a window, when her world was so different and her friend was always at her side. A jewel encrusted crown. Red stones for Penn.

"His Madam's desk!" she gasps, clambering over, and Frederika nods as if it should have been obvious.

"I thought she died," Agatha wonders aloud.

"She did. But he has never forgotten her, never got over her. It's why you're here."

Her back is turned as she dusts each item in turn, but Agatha understands. She had noted the resemblance between herself and Frederika, both blonde and slim. Both with briny eyes like the Madam whose desk Frederika dusts. Torrent's Madam.

"He likes her things kept just so," she says as Agatha watches.

Her mind goes back to the day on the Drift when Reade and Brack came for her, the way Brack beat Alsis whilst Reade held her back, the seizure that has left her tired and weak. Sore to the bones. Resigned to her fate here.

She hugs herself whilst Frederika lifts each object carefully, marking its place with her pinkie finger. She dusts underneath each item then lays it back down exactly as it was. She picks up a small glass vial, as blue as sapphire, and so faceted it twinkles in the sunlight coming from the window. This kind of glass could only have come from the artisans in Waddow. Frederika takes the stopper off and hands it to Agatha. It is full of a liquid that smells sweet, like fading summer roses.

"It is your turn to wear this. It's not enough to look like her. You must *smell* like her too. Although the bottle stays here – you must make your own. I'll teach you how."

Agatha will replace Frederika and yet this woman has been nothing but kind. Agatha knows she could make the perfume in her sleep, but she nods in thanks, and sifts the smells, one from the other. Not roses after all, but orange and bergamot.

"Where will you go?" she asks, setting the perfume back just so, as Frederika had told her.

"They've stationed me with Councillor Brack."

"*Councillor* Brack?" Agatha asks, dismayed.

"It was his reward – for discovering you."

And Frederika will also be his reward, Agatha thinks though she does not say it. Even the thought makes her heave with fresh hate.

"How long have you been here?"

"Eight years. He found me working for a seamstress when Hope died. He had brought her unity dress to be fixed to bury her in. I had the misfortune to look like her."

And now he wants rid of the woman he took on a whim, to replace her with Agatha – how dispensable the life of a decom is.

Frederika is beautiful. She has fine lines around her eyes and grey webs at her temples, but there is a dreamy softness to her skin when she is bathed in sunlight, as she is now. She is sepia.

"He won't hurt you."

"He already has."

Frederika holds Agatha's gaze for a moment, as if she wants to hug her. But she takes her hand instead and plods through the house with Agatha lagging like a pet on a string. She shows her the bedrooms no one sleeps in, three different parlours, all richly furnished with oak and velvet, and a pantry so full of food, Torrent and his servants could not possibly eat it all. It is more, even, than the feasts at the balls.

They go to the bedroom that is to be Agatha's. Frederika stands at the door and gestures inward. It is a large room with half panelled walls and a picture window that looks over Torrent's ornamental garden. The bed is draped in expensive blankets and is overflowing with pillows. It has curtains hung in all four corners, with tassels fringing them.

"You mustn't wear this now," Frederika tells her. She tugs at the black dress that has become Agatha's skin. "There's plenty in the closet," she adds.

"Yours? I couldn't take them," Agatha says, aware that this must have been Frederika's room, her bed, her closet, until this very moment.

"Of course not. Mine are packed. These have been chosen for you. Choose something and come down to dinner. He wishes you to be presented when he arrives home from the hearings."

Frederika does not sound angry or sad – just tired.

"Wear the perfume." She points at another glass vial on Agatha's own little desk under the window, before leaving her alone. Agatha wanders to the desk and picks up the perfume absentmindedly, dabbing her finger to its neck, then to her own. It is a pretty smell, but it is tainted by this place, and this man.

She thinks of her mother, longs for her warm embrace, her comforting eyes. But it is a struggle now, to remember them, to believe they ever existed.

When she turns the key in the lock of the closet and the door swings open, it is the colour that finally brings tears stinging to her skin, washing the numbness away. She did not think she had any tears left. Not after the Drift. But here they are, wild in her chest, fast in her throat.

It is so long since she wore colour, that seeing the vibrant greens, reds, oranges, blues all in a row is jarring. It is a clothesline of loss, of decoms' lives taken from them, hanging loose. She touches each one, imagines putting them on. She will not escape the black in this house. She will become it at last. A creature. His creature.

☽

"Very pleasing," Torrent says when she arrives in the dining room.

She has chosen a navy dress, the closest to black she could find so that he might not forget who she is. It has a full skirt and a scooped neck and mother-of-pearl buttons on the sleeves, but it is the plainest dress she could find.

"It needs something," he says, touching his neck with his finger, and then tapping a velvet box that is laid on the table in front of him. He is still wearing his leather gloves, and he tugs them up at the wrist as if checking they are secure, before picking up the box. He crosses the room in quick strides and opens it just in front of her face.

It reminds her of Alsis. Of the bracelet that was taken away from her. She wonders if Torrent really does believe she is Hope.

283

"Do you like it?" he asks, taking the trinket from its box, a strand of gold with a ruby stone hanging from his gloved fingers.

"It is for a Madam."

"Of course it is."

"I am no such thing."

He clenches his teeth. She is ruining his game. But he stands behind her, undeterred. She hears fabric chafe as he removes his gloves so he can fiddle with the clasp, and she forces herself to be still whilst he puts his hands on her, though every pore objects. His bare hands graze her collarbone, and she draws breath at the sight of them. But before she can turn and face him, he has put his gloves back on and she cannot be sure what she has seen, if she has seen it at all.

"Sit," he tells her, pulling out a chair. She does, though she does not thank him as she knows she should. He goes to sit down on the other side of the table. There are other servants, all decoms, who serve them from fancy platters. She has seen watchers, from the upstairs window, guarding the gates. Already, she is mapping out this place, which is a palace to him and a prison to her.

"I hope you are pleased with your room," he says, taking a silver fork and stabbing it into a slice of pork. It makes her queasy. It is too much like human flesh.

"I would rather be at the Dell."

She half hopes he will strike her, that reminding him of what and who she is, what he himself made her, will force him to send her away. But he just scoffs, the way an impatient teacher might scoff at a child struggling with basic sums.

"You will not talk of your old life here," he says, pinching the bridge of his nose. "I have offered you a fresh start, where none of that unpleasantness exists. This is to be the *last* time you raise the topic. Do you understand?"

"Will we talk of you then? Of Hope?"

He shakes his head and rolls his eyes all in one gesture. "You do not say her name. You must earn that right."

"I thought I was to *be* her."

"You are but a shadow of her," he barks, slamming his fist on the table.

"Why keep me then? If I am only a pale imitation?"

I am not afraid of him. She repeats it to herself over and over.

"Because…" He pauses.

Because a shadow is better than nothing.

"Since you are insistent," he tells her, putting his hands together, his elbows on the table. "Let's talk. Let's talk about the boy in a dank cell, screaming to be let out, to be allowed to unite."

"You're lying."

"I heard it myself. 'My blood is pure, I will unite, I will obey.' I think that's how it went. I might be paraphrasing." His eyes are shining. "Oh, and 'I never loved her'. That was my favourite part."

He picks up his fork as if conducting.

"He gave you up, Agatha of the Dell," he says, stuffing a forkful of cabbage into his mouth.

"He would never."

"Oh, but he did. In the end, he valued his freedom more than he valued you."

She forces herself to be calm, if only on the outside.

"So why is he still in a cell? Why didn't you free him and let him unite?"

"You know why. Because we don't need the blood of that boy, sullied and unclean, polluting our gene pool." He pulls a face. "I should have drowned him at the cleansing."

She watches him eat, watches his hands.

"It's not polite to wear gloves at the table," she says, her voice as dark as midnight. He puts down his fork, pulls the wrist of his gloves up tighter, the way he did before.

"It is *my* table."

Agatha clamps her teeth together, feels the tightness creep along her jaw.

"Take them off."

"Enough," he says, standing up and shoving the table so that it makes a sickening, scraping sound. He unlaces his mace from his belt and walks towards her.

He holds the mace to her face, to the scar he condemned her with. The spikes crowd her eye.

"I have tolerated your little outbursts till now. But you

286

are in *my* house, and you will learn to behave, or you will be *made* to learn."

No, she thinks, trying to keep her breathing level, fearing the pain but resolved to it. She will only ever *pretend* to have learned, cost what it may.

☽

The sun creeps around the thick curtains that keep day out and Agatha has slept – not soundly, but deeply. Her dreams have carried her from the Dell to the Drift and back again, and she wakes heavily, her limbs slow and sluggish, remembering afresh where she is.

"Who's there?" she asks the drifting shadow that lurks here then there, disturbing the silence with the clink of a tea tray, the ring of a spoon on porcelain.

"Frederika."

"I thought you were gone." Agatha yawns, though she tries to be alert, which is almost impossible as she leans against her too-soft pillows. There is a glad feeling in her stomach at the sound of this cheerful voice, a thankfulness there is something sweet in all this bile.

"Torrent thought it wise I stay. Help you settle in." Frederika beams, as happy to be here as Agatha is to have her stay. It is one more day she does not have to go to Brack.

She perches on the bed with a teacup in her hand. Agatha wonders where Frederika slept.

"Ginger," Agatha breathes, taking the cup and sipping. "It's my favourite."

"I know. A friend told me."

She puts her hand in her pocket and pulls out a folded piece of parchment that looks like a list of groceries. Agatha can just make out a few words. *Bread, eggs, chamomile, mint…*

"Brought by some Summit urchin this morning."

She means the children who deliver goods across Penn in exchange for food or treats. Agatha wonders if it could have been Wren – clever Wren who darts across the valley unseen and unnoticed – and wants to ask what the child looked like, but Frederika is too quick.

"My order apparently." She shrugs. "Though I don't remember making such an order. I definitely did not write this list," she says, flapping the parchment, which makes a sound like a bird's wings. "A whole basket of food. Every item on the list. Just so," she says, gesturing as if ticking the air.

She unfolds the paper, revealing the neat script of a hand she recognizes on the other side. It is not just a list. It is hiding a letter, with one word on the outside. *Agatha.*

"And I definitely didn't order *this*," Frederika says as she unwraps the parchment altogether and hands the hidden note to her. There is only one word in Agatha's mind just then. And it is as red and wild as the girl who owns it.

Manon.

CHAPTER SEVENTEEN

Strobes of Fire

"You *do* belong in the forest," Wick says when everyone has arrived, and I fetch him in for the binding supper. I have put on the green dress that swishes to my calves and a fur-edged pelisse that Mother sewed for my union trousseau.

"Have you sprung directly from the hills, my love?"

He is sitting on the jetty, his trousers rolled up to his calves, his feet dangling the way Stela's did this morning. He squints at me in the glare of the moon.

"Do you like it?" I ask, hitching my skirt up so it doesn't spoil as I swish towards him. "I thought I should dress as a proper wife ... just this once."

"Mm, suits you," he says, his eyes conflicted in the same way mine must be. Just this once is all we have.

He lets me pull him up, so he is standing close, our bodies touching, and traces the rabbit fur that lines my collarbone. He follows the V-shape, his touch as soft as the fur itself, and breathes me in, holds my scent in his chest, and I know he is thinking of tomorrow, of Union Day.

"I want to remember this," he says, kissing me with trembling lips. I can taste his sorrow.

"There'll be a good view of the firecrackers from here," he whispers, pointing at the empty sky over Castle Hill. He slides a hand over each of my shoulders and turns me towards the imaginary streaks that will light the sky at midnight. One arm moves around my front, and he pulls me close so his lips are pressed against my ear.

There are no stars, only a black canopy of never-ending night and the autumnal moon like a face: peach and blushing.

"We can watch after supper – Rubin and Stela love them."

"Whinny was always scared of them," I answer, snatching a look at Jack in his stable. His nose is poking out of his stall, but he looks half asleep.

I do not admit how those strobes of fire scared me too. Back when they signalled the end of a victorious season and a step closer to my own. I could not have known then how I would feel now, what we would be preparing to do. I could not have predicted that this season the firecrackers might signal our victory and a new hope.

"Are you ready?" I ask him. His cheek brushes mine as he looks at the night sky, his thumb stroking my collarbone.

"I am." He sighs, sad and determined all at once. "And I'm hungry." He laughs. "You?"

"As a wolf."

$$\mathbb{D}$$

The binding supper is a celebration, a time to invite friends and family and feast on all the council has provided for us: a joyful union, a hopeful future … a chance to change the world.

No one needs a script for the binding suppers. No one cares who goes where. The skyline is free of watchers.

Joy and hope after all.

Everyone I love has come to Walker Clough. Mother and father, Barrett and Wren. Even the Clines. There is a joviality to it. It *is* a celebration. We are stronger this way. We feel it. Even if that feeling wars against the absence of Agatha and Alsis, who are here even though they are not.

"How many?" I ask Wren, who is sitting at the table with a pile of parchment scraps, counting and sorting them into two piles, the way she used to sort Agatha's endless labels.

"Ten more who will help."

She puts a slip on the top of a pile and takes a deep breath. I know she is counting the other pile, the debs who have refused, whose slips said "no".

"There will be more," I tell her from across the table, with a confidence I do not feel.

The table should be laid for a banquet, but it is strewn with parchment and maps instead. The valley drawn out in inky lines. Cayte has prepared the feast, but she has arranged it on the counter, only picked at between tasks. Wren gets up, takes a bite from a chicken leg, and leans back on the counter, a crease growing between her eyes. She wipes her mouth on her sleeve.

"There will be more," she parrots, masking her anxiety poorly.

There is a clank of metal on metal as Father drops a tool on to a growing pile.

"There *will* be more. Of course there will. Have faith."

"Aye. The call has gone out. People will hear," Gillam adds.

Father is sharpening tools at a wheel that he's managed to squeeze into one corner of the kitchen, the stairs leading up behind him. He pumps the pedal and leans forward to push the steel against the stone at just the right angle. His face is twisted in concentration, his forehead a map of new lines, and there is a pile of angry-looking farm tools at his feet: forks, hoes, knives, all sharper than they have ever been before.

"One valley with no borders," Mother says, biting the end of her thread and dropping a finished garment into a basket at her feet. Mother and Cayte and Mary Cline are all sewing, squashed on to a bench that runs the length of the back wall of the kitchen, each with a basket to catch their work. Mother is much faster than the other two women. They look up, perhaps surprised at the resolve in her voice, the clarity of her words. Cayte pats her abdomen between stitches as if soothing her unborn child. *It's all going to be all right, there is nothing to fear.*

"The watchers will be too merry to patrol tonight," Barrett says from where he is standing by the open door, framed in moonlight. He is wearing his green cloak, watching and listening for others of his kind. "They have families too. If not friends." He sighs, sad and distant. I realize now how others must have seen the trade he made. Since he volunteered for the watch, they will be wary of him, keep their distance. Even though they have always known him as a good man. Only we are in his confidence. Only we know his motive. To anyone else in Penn, he's just another watcher, grasping at a bigger share of the claims. I feel guilty for him. It is yet another sacrifice in his lifetime of sacrifices.

Wick and I are sitting with Gillam and Henry Cline at the other end of the table from Wren, puzzling over hand-drawn maps. The kitchen has become a living and breathing thing, coughing up sound. Metal grinding on stone, the seamstresses' lullaby as they laugh and tell stories of their seasons, Wren rustling with parchment. We have become a many-eyed monster, working separately but together.

"Are you sure she is there?" Barrett asks from his station at the door.

"Reade told me so himself."

"It could be a trap. You said yourself he can't be trusted."

"These were brought by Torrent's own maid," I tell Barrett, picking up the instructions. "She stands with us."

"How do you know this ... Frederika ... isn't taking information straight to Torrent?"

Everyone is silent, all considering whether it could be true. I grab the parchment, and stalk to his side, take his hand between mine.

"I *know* because I saw it in her eyes. She wants this. Many want this, Barrett, not just in Penn but all over the valley. The counties are coming together at last to put an end to their lies."

"You don't know her."

"I know *Agatha*. So do you. Who else could draw this all out so precisely?"

He looks at the map of Torrent's house and garden, taking it in his hand.

"She was always writing in notebooks," he says slowly. "Medicines. Herbs – illustrations of them all. Descriptions of what they do. Potions and tinctures."

"Not 'was' ... she's not gone," I say, putting my arms around him. "She's coming home."

I sit back down and smooth the map out on the table. There is a map of Castle Hill too – and its prisons, stolen from Torrent's office by Agatha and Frederika. It might have begun with Wick and I, but it is the two of them who have worked to bring us this chance.

"I'll go for Agatha. Torrent's 's ordered a sack of grain. I'll pick it up from the Summit and deliver it," Father says, as sparks fly up from his stone. "If an Agatha-shaped package happens to fall on to the back of the cart whilst I'm dropping it off … well…" His voice is almost smothered by the shriek of the wheel, but his mirth is still loud and it makes me smile.

"Frederika knows every decom in the valley," I add. "Every blacksmith's boy, every weaver's girl. If a tool falls in their path…"

Father smiles at me, my echo of him.

It is not just Father who will have a poorly packed cart come Union Day. There are others who will lose their cargo, others who are sharpening their tools.

"It might work," Gillam says, his voice steady but small. "It's Union Day. Everyone is travelling … it will be chaos."

"It *has* to work," I tell him.

It was easy to rally them all. Everyone in this room has a person they love who has been threatened by the council. Even Cayte, who worries most for the child inside her.

Rallying the debs has been harder. Now that the season is over, most just want to get on with their unions and bury their heads – especially those who were granted their preference.

Rubin and Stela tumble in, Rubin with his wooden boat and Stela with her dolly Mirabelle. They are packed to the gills with parchment, torn pieces secreted inside socks, up sleeves, tucked into the backs of their collars.

They start to shed them like trees shedding leaves, and I gather pieces up from the floor, cheered by a note from Bertie that says: "Of course. You can count on me. I am with you."

Three answers when only one would have done. Perhaps she has realized what a mistake it was to choose Matthie already.

"Well done," I tell the children, hugging first Stela and then Rubin, who wriggles free and puts out his hand instead. "You are our best weapon," I tell him, shaking his hand. And it is true. These small children, who cannot know the importance of their work, have wandered the length and breadth of the valley with fragments of rebellion tucked all over themselves. Stela's eyes shine with pride and Rubin's shoulders square. He looks at Wick, who smiles and applauds once.

"Can you get us into the detention block?" Gillam asks Barrett, who is staring out to sea. Gillam stares at Barrett's back in frustration, unwilling to trust this man who seems so distracted and despairing. He does not know Barrett like I do, the man who lost his wife, his daughter – who survived all that…

"We'll get in. I'll say you're coming in for questioning."

"And if they ask questions?"

"It's Union Day – you said it yourself. They'll be too distracted."

"And we have this," I tell Gillam, sifting the blank parchment from the pile. It is Torrent's own letterhead, his black petunia embossed over a silhouette of Castle Hill. It has even been signed at the bottom and needs only the name of the prisoner, and his infraction, to be added to the dotted lines. It is another gift from Agatha and Frederika. A stroke of genius.

"What crime have I committed?" Gillam asks.

"Stolen a barrel of fish?"

Everyone laughs, even Barrett, who is lured away from the door and into the fold of this makeshift family. Father gets up from his wheel and the men laugh and joke together whilst Mother, Cayte and Mary pass the food around, finally feasting on the dried fruits and ruby pie we laboured over together. Wren plays with Rubin and Stela, sitting Mirabelle on the toy boat and sailing them both off to some imaginary place whilst the children laugh.

"I wish we could go for them," I tell Wick quietly when the others are happily eating and talking.

"We are debs," he tells me, and we hold hands under the table. "That is our part."

He squeezes my hand and my heart stutters. It is only a part now. It is a game we are playing for one last night when it could have been real.

"Right – the firecrackers are about to start," Cayte says brightly, which makes the children jump up and run. Rubin snatches his boat from the floor and Stela grabs Mirabelle. Wren runs after them, ruby pie staining her cheeks and chin. A child at last.

At the end of the jetty, Wick and I sit and watch, my dress rolled up to the knee and my feet soothed by the water. His feet tickle mine beneath the ripples.

"This union has been sanctioned by the council, in the service of all our futures," he whispers, putting his arm around my waist as the firecrackers light the sky. His voice is not mocking as he repeats the words of the council. They are in earnest: though it is a different future he talks of, not the one they intended. I rest my head on his shoulder, melt into him. I wish for this moment to last for ever.

"Do you, Manon Pawlak, give yourself to this man?" he asks me.

"I give myself," I say. "With thanks for the council's grace," I add with a wry smile. "We will find our way back to each other."

"Always."

CHAPTER EIGHTEEN

Fearless and Unashamed

A storm is brewing on the morning of Union Day, the world caught in the breathless moment just before it comes. A lukewarm wind sweeps through the tunnel that will lead us through the glass and steel walls of the Annulus, into the last and grandest ballroom of the season: the amphitheatre at the bottom of Castle Hill.

The debs wait to be called for the Union Ceremony, in the whistling dark of the underpass. I stand with Bertie, who seems to have aged since we last spoke.

"Where are they?" I ask her. She has linked her arm through mine and will not let go, though I confess, I do not want her to. "They were supposed to be here by now."

"They *will* be here," she promises, but her eyes do not trust her words and flick too quickly away from mine.

Debs from every county wear newly sewn white

cloaks with hoods drawn – a flight of white hawks with their heads pulled into their feathers. There is no telling one from another.

"Almost every deb in the valley is with us," she croons. She holds the letter I sent her, the same letter sent to every deb we could reach and, as I look around, many hold them like daggers. It reminds me of the way we held the pledge letters at the start of the season, but this is different. This letter contains eleven names of people they know. People who should stand here with us, beside us, but who have been segregated, who have been branded. The season's decoms.

I have a letter in my hand too. A letter I stole from Reade's office.

"Agatha," Bertie reads from her letter, practising what we have planned. I hold her more tightly, this brave, bright girl.

"Agatha," she whispers again, and the word seems alive.

"Are you sure you want to do this, Bertie?"

"I've never been so sure of anything."

"What about Matthie?"

"He doesn't love me. He never will. I want the chance to find someone who will."

"You will," I promise her and try to make my eyes more certain than hers.

"Agatha," we say together.

There's a beating of drums like canon fire that echoes

through the tunnel and Torrent's voice soars above us, its own lifeforce. This is it. It is time.

"Debutants, welcome to the culmination of the Virtue Season. You have conducted yourself morally, chosen your mates. You are worthy of this honour. Will the boys please step forth?"

The drums beat again and the boys march forward whilst the girls wait their turn. We watch them disappear into the open sky, a mouth of light at the end of the tunnel, their footsteps another layer of percussion. I know the sight that awaits them, every adult in the valley compressed into galleries that orbit the amphitheatre; every councillor's eyes glaring from a podium so high you have to look up.

"You are no longer boys but men. It is your duty to bring fruit to this valley."

I saw it last year, from the galleries that rise into the roofless sky. This year, *my* year, I can see little but the darkness of the tunnel, but I know that watchers will march the boys forwards, line them on either side as they make their way down the avenue towards the centre of the amphitheatre.

The drums cease, but the boys' feet continue to beat: a rebellion in time ahead of us. The girls, still crowded in the tunnel, begin to stamp too. The sound amplifies. I try to imagine the look on Torrent's face as he wonders what this is, but I cannot see him, can only hear his voice as it booms towards me.

"Silence!" Torrent cries and a ripple goes through the tunnel as the edges of the crowd is pushed and shoved by watchers. The debs' feet still as one.

"These unions have been sanctioned by the council in the service of all our futures," Torrent continues, unwavering.

I think of Wick's smile, the way he said these words last night as firecrackers lit the sky, and how it will please him to hear them now.

I give myself. Always.

I think of how these words will strike fire in his chest. They set a fire inside me too.

Together, the debs begin to speak with one voice, one aim.

"Agatha, Ardem, Bo."

The name of every decom in our year, one for each deb to fight for. Our voices fuse together, rise and echo back. It feels familiar. But wholly new.

"Enya, Hunter, Jewel."

Torrent raises his voice. "May your unions be blessed by the coming of children. Let them be pure and whole."

"Logan, Lewis."

"Girls, it is time to take your place in our society." His voice carries, sound and true. If he is ruffled, he covers it well.

"Nora, Patrick, Sawyer."

Manon. Manon. Manon.

The rain starts as the girls leave the darkness of the

tunnel, but we are sheltered in our white hoods and don't feel the cold spots on our skin. We look down, watch the grey floor become spotted black with rain.

"You are no longer girls," Torrent shouts, though his voice is uncertain, wary. The change of dress has not gone unnoticed. These are not the white union dresses with flowers down their backs. But he continues, sticks to the script. "You are women. Our future is in your hands."

Your future is in our hands.

Almost every white-clad girl in the valley loosens the ties at her neck, sweeps the white cloak over in one deft pirouette as if the cloaks are dancing as one, revealing the other side. Where there was a sea of white, now there is only black, only darkness. The cloaks sewn by Mother, Cayte and Mrs Cline – by other mothers across the valley – turning us into black sea. We raise our changeling hoods and disappear. And yet we do not. Now, more than ever, we are here, loud inside their silence. They see us. All of us. Finally.

I look up at Torrent. Now I see the shock in his eyes, the fear on his lips. It is almost enough to have humbled him. But we are not done yet.

As we have turned ourselves black, there are those who have turned themselves white, those who should never have been forced to wear black. And these white figures weave through the blackness and stand ready. I do not have time to count but hope there are eleven. I hope Gillam and Barrett and Father have succeeded.

Torrent looks around at the councillors from each county as if communing an idea. He checks watchers like he is counting heads, and they raise their swords as if he has given the command. More appear from nowhere and surround us.

Torrent has a hold on himself now. A slow smile hovers on his lips, creeps up to his eyes.

"An amusing stunt. But one that can only disrupt and delay … and for which your leaders will pay. But now is not the time. This is a time for union. You were born for this moment."

I knew he could be counted on. He thinks this is *his* plan.

"As is traditional, the first-born male will commence the unions."

Wick's eyes find mine.

Where are they?

"Wick Flint of Penn Vale."

I cannot help but think of the Penn ball as he steps through the corridor of green watchers.

"You will unite with Manon Pawlak, also of Penn Vale."

I walk towards them, every eye on me, every breath held. Even mine.

Torrent looks relieved when he takes my hands and puts them in Wick's. He believes he has won, that our protest is done, that we have nothing else to offer.

"Do you, Manon Pawlak, give yourself to this man?"

I step forward. Take Wick's chin in my palm, kiss his lips.

"This is your right. These children are our hope!" Torrent cries. "Do you take—"

"No."

I take Wick's hand in mine, and we turn to the crowds together.

Please be here.

My voice rings out. "I do not give myself to this man. I forfeit my right."

I scan the white hoods but see only shaded, colourless eyes.

Torrent growls, grabs my wrist and there's a metallic glint that sends a mirror shine dancing everywhere, from every gallery. Sharpened tools glisten in almost every hand. They are an army of farmers, traders, fishermen, children. And decoms.

I wish I could find Father and Mother, or Cayte and Gillam in the galleries, know that everyone is where they should be.

The watchers stare up at Torrent, their hoods falling back as they tip their heads to look upward at the podium, which makes them look small and wanting. They wait for Torrent's command, but it does not come. He knows they are outnumbered. With so many prepared to fight, the losses would be too great. We would come for the councillors first. To wage war would be to write his own death sentence. Torrent lets go of my wrist, stalls the watchers with his hand.

"Entertain me then," he says, gesturing as if giving permission. But the smile he intends to be patronizing is a grimace.

"I forfeit my right," I say again. "Until that right is the right of all."

A lone black hood falls, a lone voice, scared and unsure. "I forfeit my right!"

Bertie. Darling Bertie.

"I forfeit my right!"

"I forfeit my right!"

The words carry, then explode. Hoods fall and eyes are raised, fearless and unashamed as debs join the cry.

A figure in white steps forward, slow but sure. It is her. They did it. My heart fills.

Agatha kisses my cheek, and I see her eyes, liquid pain, and I know something has gone wrong. There is no time to ask what. She turns to the crowd and lowers her hood, her long hair taken by the wind.

"Every one of us is flawed," Agatha shouts as loud as her voice will carry. "I have done no wrong and I demand what is my right: the right of each and every one of us." She looks at Torrent and his stony expression meets hers.

Alsis steps forward from the gallery and makes his way through the crowds. Gillam and Cayte are there, and the Clines behind them.

But Father is not, and Mother is rushing away.

Something has gone wrong.

Alsis's smile as he walks towards Agatha is pride and

love and pleasure and pain. I try to focus on that, on what we came here to do. They join hands at the altar, but there is no one to say the words.

Torrent is still as the other councillors' eyes flick between themselves.

"Do you, Agatha Curlew, give yourself to this man?" I say, hearing my voice as if it is outside me. There are cheers from the crowd that build with every word.

"I give myself."

"Do you, Alsis Cline—"

"This is heresy!" Torrent yells, finally finding his voice. "We cannot permit this union." He moves between Agatha and Alsis. "She has ascended. She is barren!"

"Who made me that way? Heresy is what you have done to us. To our children. You know they sicken. You know they are weak. And yet you do nothing to help…"

This is my moment. "It is because we are so few," I add. In my hand I have the letter.

"It is you who sicken. You are still children yourselves," cries Torrent. "What could you know?"

"It is true!" A voice sings out. I know the sound. It is her. The grey woman from Stone. She speaks from the galleries, her ancient voice resounding. "We have been warning the council for years. The decommissionings are a threat to the health of the genetic pool."

Whispers and then cries travel through the crowd. But my eyes are locked on those of one man.

Reade looks at me, a clever glint in his eyes that fills

307

me with horror. Not evil. Not selfishness. *Conviction*. That same conviction that led him away from Mother for a seat on the council.

He leans over and whispers to Brack, who sniffs and nods, a pucker of a smile at his mouth.

"It is true," Reade says, silencing the crowd as he stands. "We have received warnings from the academics at Stone. But to say we have ignored them is a falsehood. Members of the council have been lobbying for a research project," he declares, looking at Torrent meaningfully, who seems to pale. "Several of us believed the academics. This belief is not one shared by Councillor Torrent."

"It was I who commissioned the new hospital!" Torrent roars.

"You intended it as a prison, to rehome the decoms and alleviate the burden on our resources."

Torrent blinks.

"Do not attempt to deny it. The council has opposed you at every turn and yet you have forced it through—"

The councillors nod, to save themselves from a sinking ship and Reade's voice is so earnest, I almost believe him, that he is the saviour we are waiting for. There is that trick of his again, to make me believe. But he has betrayed me before. And Brack's shadow beside him gives me reason to doubt. And to fear.

"If you listen to these lies, we will all perish," Torrent protests. "We must weed out defects in order to ensure the lives of the next generation!"

Agatha walks towards him and, very gently, takes his hands in hers. I see her slip her fingers under the rim of his gloves.

"It is over," she tells him quietly. "The decommissionings were never about flaws, were they, councillor?" she asks him, deftly tugging off his gloves and lifting his bare hands into the air.

They are discoloured, like tea-stained maps, brown continents floating in a milky sea.

He is flawed.

Torrent rubs his skin as if he can erase the marks. "To save us…" he mutters.

Reade steps forward, eyes wide. His voice rings out.

"Citizens of Calde Valley, we have let you down. But put your faith in the council and we will give you a Virtue Season for *all*. It is what many of us have wanted for so long, what we have worked towards … and what we have been prevented in bringing you. We will eradicate the corrupt; we will build a *new* council."

The councillors are torn between a collective look of panic and awe. They look first at Torrent and then at Reade, pinning their gaze on him as if clinging to a raft.

"*All* will be invited to participate, and all will unite with freedom of choice, all preferences honoured. We will begin again. All decoms who have ascended will be repatriated. They will come home."

I wait for Reade to promise the end to the decommissionings too, but he does not. A heartbeat stalls in my chest. The crowd is whooping and cheering, the debs too, so his last words fall unheard. Except by me. I hear: "*They will come home. Once they have been processed at Castle Hill.*"

☽

On the street outside the Annulus, there is a fever of celebration. Wick has gone to find his family, and Agatha and Alsis have been lost inside a throng of debs who are taking turns to congratulate them, swallowing them up.

Through the crowd, I see a flash of red hair draped over a body. A shiver turns my heart cold. Father is lying on the ground, his chest heaving, gasping for breath. He breathes in, but it doesn't seem to soothe his need, as if the air hasn't found his lungs.

"Father," I call, running to them. "What happened?"

Mother has her palm pressed hard against his neck.

"It all went to plan," Mother says through gritted teeth. "He delivered the grain to Torrent's house and Agatha was waiting. She got your message. He hid her on the cart as planned. But they were spotted by a watcher," Mother tells me as she mops his forehead with cloth torn from her sleeve, the water brought by Cayte, from where I don't know.

The cloth darkens with sweat, and Mother folds it over, wipes his brow again. "He took a blade to the neck. Agatha drove him here; he was nearly unconscious when they arrived. She didn't want to leave him, but…"

Father is drifting in and out of consciousness, his eyes

varnished in pain. But he sees me and reaches for my hand, which I take and hold to my lips.

"But what?"

"He sent her inside."

"Of course he did," I say, looking into his eyes with a smile.

His gaze fixes on me, and he tries to speak but no sound comes, only blood-stained froth that sticks to the corner of his mouth. A thin slick of sweat has soaked his face, which has turned a sickening green.

"I realized when he didn't join us—" Mother says.

"It's only a flesh wound," I promise, kneeling at his side, grasping his arm.

It's only a flesh wound.

His breathing is so shallow it rattles, clicks in the back of his throat.

"I'm tired," he rasps between gulps, the effort draining his face. I clasp both my hands around his, hold on as tight as I can.

Stay with me, Father. My only father.

"Sleep then. Sleep now."

His eyes widen. He looks directly at me, unable to speak but his face full of love. His eyelids close slowly. And then I feel it go, the way his soul lifts from him. The wind swirls and takes him away from the land he loves – and the hot fury crouches deep and low and dreadful.

Agatha, Eighteen

The new hospital leers at Agatha as she steps off the boat with a backwards glance at Wick, who has rowed her out on this fresh, cold morning. He watches her make her way on to the shore as if waiting for the command to take her home instead. Her breath fogs the air as she thanks him, tells him to go.

"Good luck," he tells her as she stands looking at the grotesque building, its two front legs seeming to reach out for her either side of the entrance.

It feels like the first day of school, when everything seems possible, but nothing feels safe.

"For the favour," she tells Wick, offering a hessian sack of the Clines' cheese, but he shakes his head. Alsis had woken her with a kiss this morning, and told her Wick was waiting to take her to Castle Hill.

"Not hungry. Give it to the inmates," Wick jokes, but the word sticks in his throat and in her ears too. "I'll be back to get you before supper," he yells as he slowly cranks his oars, going back towards the rocky outline of Penn, a mere line drawing on the other side of the water.

She can see why Manon loves Wick. They are a good match, and it fills her with fresh sadness that Manon and Wick cannot have what she has, that the two of them are still trapped by the laws of Calde Valley whilst she and Alsis have been allowed to be together. The sole token of the council's promises. How backwards the world seems since the day of the pledges.

That word Wick used echoes in her ears. *Inmates*. It is like an insect burrowing, voicing fear she is trying to bury.

☾

"Agatha! You're here. I'm so glad," the grey woman says, opening her arms to greet Agatha, more quick and agile than she should be at her age. "We haven't been properly introduced – my name is Cathy. Did you bring your journals?"

"They're here," Agatha tells her, holding up the heavy satchel that bulges at the seams. The woman takes one out and turns the pages with fervour as she takes Agatha inside, barely looking where she's going.

As they enter the building, cold trails down Agatha's spine, knowing it is where every other decom in the valley is being held until they are processed. Knowing that it is what she has escaped.

"When will they start to come home?" Agatha asks, revulsion coiling in her stomach.

"The council has ordered more research. Each decom needs to be processed before being repatriated, and that means understanding the risk they pose."

It all sounds too familiar. An echo.

"The academics need to prove it is safe to end the decommissionings before the council allow them home, but we are working towards it, I assure you."

"But…"

Cathy shuts Agatha's journal and they stand in the dark corridor of the hospital, lined with doors, none of which open or close as they pause. There is a strange silence for a building so full of people.

"It is a compromise. We have to work with them. Some of the councillors prefer tradition. They are reluctant to welcome change."

"They have vowed to do so. Before the next season begins."

Cathy snorts. "Reade promised," she says. "And he knows he must deliver *something*. But—"

"What?"

"He is stalling for time. We all fear—"

"He will not allow them home?"

"That this is where he wanted them. Didn't he tell us that, at the Annulus, that the hospital was always meant as a prison? Did you really believe it was just Torrent's plan? It takes more than one man! Reade has promised the world but—"

"He will not deliver."

Cathy rubs her forehead with her finger and thumb as if it throbs. "We all hope we can prove—"

She cannot finish the sentence and puts her hands on

her hips as if she is in danger of falling over and needs to hold herself up, and Agatha knows she is keeping something back. She looks sad and guilty at the same time.

"But there is the almanac! That will mean the children, at least, will have medicine," and though she says it quietly, almost to herself, Agatha hears the sour threat that follows: "Still, that also means the population grows."

Cathy opens a door that leads into a laboratory, so bright and clean it almost sparkles. There are no windows, only a huge oblong skylight, like a pool in the sky. And there are specimens under glass cloches everywhere. Agatha busies her mind with naming them to quell the sinister feeling in her stomach. *Valerian, pafflower, opema.*

"We can work here," Cathy says, leading Agatha to a long, smooth table at one end of the room.

Agatha sets down her journals, unpacking them one at a time from her satchel, and Cathy snatches at them hungrily, running her finger over the ingredients and nodding, as if she has suddenly found the cures herself.

"You have great knowledge," she crows, pausing at the page Agatha added most recently, the liquorice root tea and marshmallow tincture that she uses to ease the symptoms of scarlet throat. "Who taught you?"

"My mother."

Agatha remembers then the sound of her mother's voice listing the ingredients, a song of its own, and is wounded anew by the loss of her. The memory of her is more vivid and true here.

"I think she must be here," Agatha tells Cathy, and the woman's eyes lift, something hard inside them.

"We *are* trying to bring them home," she says, but Agatha can hear the doubt that quivers in every syllable.

She spends the morning transcribing her notes, adding instructions, making pages for the almanac. The pages glisten when the clouds part, the wet ink made marvellous. She is transported back to the Dell, to her own kitchen table, to Wren and her father and Alsis and Manon. But it is her mother she needs. There are passages they wrote together that she can no longer make out, that have bled or faded over time.

"I need my mother to explain these," she says, watching the uncertainty flood Cathy's eyes. The blood thumps in her ears as she waits but at long last, Cathy yields and trudges away to fetch her. As easy as that after all this time.

Agatha waits for what seems like a long time, hopeful and scared, until she is too restless to sit still. She wanders back in the direction she thinks Cathy brought her in, searching for her, but the corridors all look the same and she finds herself lost in a hallway of doors, each with a name affixed to it, and a small hatch. They make her skin stand on end. She listens at the doors but there is an eerie silence behind each one. Is this how her mother is being kept?

His name, when she finds it, seems more indelible than the rest, though it is written in charcoal just the same.

Chief Councillor Torrent.

It chills her bones. Even in this place, with the world crumbling around them, they have given him his title. At first, she is not brave enough to open the hatch and almost walks away, back to the laboratory, hoping she can retrace her steps, but the need is too great. She wants to see what has become of him, though there is an agony in it she cannot bear. No one should be in this place, kept this way. There is a metallic click as she opens the catch and pulls the hatch open.

It is dark inside. He is sitting on the floor in the only shaft of light, which shines from a window in the ceiling, similar to the one in the laboratory, only smaller. He looks up when he hears the hatch open, and Agatha thinks she sees his lip tremble before he catches it in his teeth.

"Such beauty," he says.

"Why did you lie?" she asks him, feeling compelled to unlock the door and let him out. He is hugging his knees to his chest, his marked hands exposed, and she has the odd desire to hold them in her own.

"Because it was the only way."

"This place—"

"It is necessary," he says, his mouth twisted into a strange grimace. "We cannot feed them all—"

"But Reade promised—"

"And you believed him?"

When she returns to the laboratory her cheeks are stained with hot tears and her eyes sting. Torrent's laugh – both mocking and sorry – beats against the white walls.

The new world is worse than the old. Nothing has changed.

It is as she is thinking this that her mother appears in the doorway. Agatha stands up in a rush to hug her, to squeeze the flesh from her bones. Though she does not. For she is too late. The flesh is already gone and only bones remain. Agatha barely recognizes her from the sturdy, robust woman that nursed her as a child, held her hand on the first day of school, embraced her after her seizures. Her legs are like spindles and her arms bony. Her eyes are sunken and her skin is grey-green. So she does not hug her, does not let the ferocity of need catapult her across the room as she wishes but watches her mother come, slowly, like a woman twice her age. It is only the smile that is still hers, still quick at the sight of her daughter. It is she who takes Agatha, squeezes her with an energy she surely does not feel and says, "It's you… It's you…" in desperate gasps.

"It is," Agatha says, holding back fresh tears her mother would not want to see. She catches Cathy's eyes before they drop to the floor.

The council does not want them to come home, she knows now. They do not want the research to succeed.

It is simply a waiting game. Placate the valley, let them think they have won, and slowly let the decoms starve.

"You're going to come home," Agatha promises, holding her mother as best she can. "I'm going to bring you home."

CHAPTER NINETEEN

A Wave That Never Breaks

At midnight, we are ready to send Father out to sea, into eternity. He lies on a raft made from wood pulled from one side of the storehouse and tied together with reeds. Mother and I did it ourselves. Then dressed him in his union doublet. But it was me who carried him to the raft. Wick and Gillam. And Agatha too.

Now he lies near the water, ready for his final journey. Not in his cart, but across the sea. I put a scythe in his hands, and he holds it across his still chest.

"You lived a farmer. You will go to your rest as one," I whisper.

The grief has not come yet. But it threatens.

Everyone is here. The Curlews, the Flints, the Clines – my family. A slew of farmers, traders from the Summit. And watchers. Always on the periphery. Witnesses to life and death and everything in between.

People kneel to say their last goodbyes – weeping and whispering, or staunch and steadfast – until it is my turn. When it comes, I am torn. I want to tell him goodbye, and to honour him with all the words he deserves, but I feel as though keeping them from my lips might keep him here with me. Still, I kneel, feel the soft, wet grass chill my knees. There are no words for the raw pain, for the anger that answers his peacefulness with fury. I take his cold hand in my warm one, try to figure out how to let it go.

"Working hands," I tell him, memorizing them, the size of his knuckles, the shape of his nails, broad and unbreakable like mine, not flimsy and delicate like Mother's. I lift his hand to my mouth, a last kiss to send him on his way. "It is not for nothing," I promise as I lay his hand on his chest and take the scythe. The long handle touches the floor. With the neck in my hands, I break the wood with my foot. It snaps and splinters, a thunderclap in the silence.

"Your work is done. You've done enough," I tell him, laying the broken pieces back on his chest, almost believing he might clasp his hands around them, tell me I'm wrong. He is not done with this world. Not yet.

"It's time," Wick tells me, and I want him to hold me, to let the grief come and fall in his arms, but it is forbidden. We are to be debs again, to make our pledges anew. We do not know yet what that will mean, what it will look like.

"It is," I answer. It is time.

I help Wick and Gillam push the raft into the water where it bobs a while near the shore, as if clinging to us all. But, with the certainty of time, the current takes it. We all stand, watching from the edge of Wild Fell, as the raft becomes smaller and smaller until it is the size of a candle flame in the distant darkness.

The stars pierce the blanket of violet–black sky and are reflected and stretched in the mirror of water. I know he is one of them now. The brightest.

"I think he's almost at the Pull," I whisper, holding my breath as if I could stop time, waiting for the moment his body is taken and the grief expands.

The raft tips, the first lick of water tasting its edge. I want him to be at peace, but I do not want to lose sight of that raft and begin my life without him in it, so I barely blink as I watch him go. When it happens, when the last froth of water covers him, it is almost beautiful, the way the waves fold their arms over him, and take him to his rest.

It does not break me, though something inside shatters. There are no violent sobs or streams of tears. But my heart heaves, fills up with something bleak and angry. It is not Wick but Mother who holds me, her own grief shaking her. I hold her too, in a way I never have before.

☽

The world is on the cusp, caught between the last drear dregs of the hibernal moon and the coming of spring

322

when it will flush with pink, and the world will begin again with the start of the new season.

I am almost at the top of Wolfhole Crag, the sheerest scarp in the valley, which rears up and climbs towards the sky like a wave that never crashes. Sometimes I think I was not born of woman at all but grew out of the velvet folds of these moors.

The rules of this season were announced this morning in Miss Warne's sweet and sour lullaby, reading the words composed by the newly promoted Chief Councillor Reade, with help from Brack no doubt.

I dig in my boots, lean into the climb. Mud sucks at my feet, but the relief is visceral. Pain dissolving pain. And at the top, the valley unfurls. Penn, Foxfields, Waddow and Stone. And at the centre of it all, Castle Hill.

I reach for the thing that has been tucked in my boot since Penance Day, drive it into the earth, shocked when it does not fissure with the strength of my anger. I could soar down on them, Reade and Brack, a hawk beating its vast wings, a fearsome shriek ripping through their walls.

"Your Virtue Season is coming. Decoms will not participate, at least not for now. Preferences will be monitored, at least for now. The academics need more time. More research is required."

Stalemate.

Author's Note

We live in a world that *pretends* to be liberal. I would like to live in a world that actually *is*.

I didn't always know why I was writing this book, but I think that sums it up. Often, I felt more like it was writing itself through me, that I was just the vehicle. It was only after it was finished that I truly understood where it had come from, when I could look and listen to its beating heart … which had always been my own.

My dad was registered disabled. Not always. When my brother and I were kids, we thought he was a real-life Robinson Crusoe. A more physically capable man you could not have imagined. He was a cliff-diver, a sea-swimmer, and could build anything with his bare hands. But fate conspired against him. He was ill. He was left partially deaf and with mobility issues. He was not defeated, by no means, but he found himself at the whim and will of the government agencies that should have protected him. Instead of catching him as they should have, they treated him with suspicion and contempt. Time after time, he and my mum were forced to fight for the rights that should have been guaranteed. It was a long, arduous battle. And I was angry. And helpless. So I wrote.

And if the decoms' story is his, then Manon and Drewis's is mine. I've looked down the long lens of depression and anxiety, watched as the fog gathered on the road ahead, fought when it engulfed me, never let go. There is so much strength inside that squall. Manon doesn't always see it. Until she does. I came to that truth through writing her.

More than anything else, when I began writing this story, I knew *who* I was writing for. It was a crystal-clear thought, way back in 2015 when I was standing at the top of Clitheroe Castle, staring out towards Pendle Hill. It was for every student who had ever come through my classroom. All valid and capable and fierce and brave in different ways. And yet so many visibly struggling because … well, you were different, weren't you? You didn't fit in. The world had told you so. And you had believed it.

But it was also for all the students who *did not* come through my classroom, because my classroom was not accessible to you, because mainstream schools have so much to do on that front. I wondered about you often – every time "*inclusivity*" and "*diversity*" were bandied about the staffroom, in all those meetings when those were the words of the moment, through all the years I did not get to meet you because we were neither *inclusive* nor *diverse*. Not by a long stretch.

This is for all of you. And for me. And for Dad. A warrior call for everyone who has ever been made to feel wrong in a world full of "rights".

Acknowledgements

I have dedicated this book to my mum and dad, and rightly so. My first memories of storytelling came from you, Dad, from the way you could spellbind a room with your tall tales of the Duchess Street Kids. Your stories live on, though we don't tell them half as well as you did. To my fearless mum: one day I might be as courageous as you, but never as selfless, and never as kind. I am enormously proud of you. You are the embodiment of what this story stands for. In so many ways, you are where it began.

There are those who believed when I did not. Christine Montgomery and Louise Wright, the cauldron still bubbles. My Year 11 English class, who always cheered me on from the sides. Write wild, boys. And Elizabeth Sparrow: you always had a whoop on hand and it meant so much. Thank you all for sharing the journey, back when the destination seemed so far off.

To my yard family, who tended my daughter's dreams while I tended mine. Lorna Johnson, Virginia Rajski and Edith Perrin. Thank you for the endless favours.

I would never have finished this book if not for the people I met on my Curtis Brown Creative course. Jennifer Kerslake and Danni Georgiou, how many writers' careers have begun in your hands? Certainly mine. Cathi Unsworth, you sent me to Janet's Foss and gifted Manon a place to leap. Simon Wroe, Drewis lived because of you. Lisa Babalis, your words of praise were enormous. I held tight to them. I still do. And to my CBC alumni: Julia Boggio, Cathryn Campbell, Heidi Gallacher, Jen Hyatt, Paula Jones, Samantha Quinn, Stacey Thomas, Pip Townley, Hannah Sutherland, Alice Sutton, Barbara Whitfield, Dan Allen, Edward Crocker and Abhi Para, this story owes something to each of you – even you, dearest Henrietta, our faithful mascot. My go-to question will always be: *But where do they buy their socks?*

To my inimitable agent, Ciara Finan: I was gunning for you from the start. You know it. And my instincts were good. Agatha thanks you. I thank you. For all the things that are not seen, know that I know. May we always be on the same page. Send deadlines…

To my editor, Tierney Holm, thank you for *slaying* in the acquisitions meeting; for your vision, your faith, your tenacity… You are bringing dystopia back, baby! The world will be grateful. As am I. Eternally.

Everyone at Scholastic, including – but certainly not limited to – Lauren Fortune, Polly Lyall Grant, Sarah Dutton, Wendy Shakespeare, Genevieve Herr, Isabella Haigh, Olivia Towers, Hannah Griffiths, Tina Mories,

Holly Clarke, Harriet Dunlea, Penelope Daukes, Alice Duggan and Jamie Gregory. Louisa May Alcott said it takes two flints to make a fire. How little she knew. It took all of you.

My children keep asking when I'm going to write a book for them. I'm sorry, dears, but it probably isn't this one. Except that it is. Because all my words are for you, Georgiana and Benedict. All my efforts are for you. So that you will think I'm a little bit cool. Which you never will. But thank you for pretending to be impressed by this archaic thing called a book. And for suffering my 90s playlists without complaint.

And to Paul, who never so much as blinked when I quit my proper job. Thank you.

© Jo Bishop

L. M. Nathan grew up in the East Midlands, moving from there to Bristol, where she studied English and drama, and then to Malta where she completed an MA in literature. She also has an MA in journalism, which she studied for in Manchester. She now lives in rural Lancashire in the shadow of Pendle Hill, a landscape which has directly inspired her debut novel.